THE WORLD'S CLASSICS
# PRESTER JOHN

JOHN BUCHAN was born in Perth, Scotland, in 1875, the son of a Free Kirk minister. He was educated at Hutchesons' Grammar School, Glasgow, and Glasgow University, before winning a scholarship to Brasenose College, Oxford, where he took a First in Greats. He was called to the Bar in 1901, and combined journalism and work as a barrister until October of that year, when he became one of 'Milner's Young Men' in South Africa, resettling the country after the Boer War. Back in London he continued work in law and for the *Spectator*, and maintained his steady output of books, reviews, articles, and leaders. In 1907 he married Susan Grosvenor and became literary adviser to, and then partner in, the publishers Thomas Nelson & Sons.

In the First World War he worked as the Western Front correspondent for *The Times*, and in intelligence and propaganda for the Foreign Office and War Office, before being appointed director of the new Department (later Ministry) of Information. By the end of the war he had published some forty books, eleven of them novels, including the Richard Hannay stories which made him famous: *The Thirty-Nine Steps* and *Greenmantle*.

He settled near Oxford, and became Deputy Chairman of Reuters though continuing to work for Nelson's. His literary output increased, and included important biographies of Montrose, Walter Scott, Cromwell, and others. He also undertook a complete revision of his single-handed and massive history of the First World War. He became MP for the Scottish Universities in 1927, and was twice High Commissioner to the General Assembly of the Church of Scotland. Created Baron Tweedsmuir of Elsfield, he ended his life as an adventurous and pioneering Governor-General of Canada. He died in Montreal in February 1940.

His fiction is still widely loved, and his importance as a biographer and historian is being increasingly recognized.

DAVID DANIELL is General Editor of Buchan in World's Classics. He is Professor of English at University College, London.

THE WORLD'S CLASSICS

JOHN BUCHAN

# *Prester John*

*Edited with an Introduction by*
DAVID DANIELL

Oxford   New York
OXFORD UNIVERSITY PRESS
1994

Oxford University Press, Walton Street, Oxford OX2 6DP
Oxford  New York  Toronto
Delhi  Bombay  Calcutta  Madras  Karachi
Kuala Lumpur  Singapore  Hong Kong  Tokyo
Nairobi  Dar es Salaam  Cape Town
Melbourne  Auckland  Madrid
and associated companies in
Berlin  Ibadan

Oxford is a trade mark of Oxford University Press

Editorial material © David Daniell 1994
First published as a World's Classics paperback 1994

British Library Cataloguing in Publication Data
Data available

Library of Congress Cataloging in Publication Data
Buchan, John, 1875–1940.
Prester John / John Buchan; edited with an introduction by David
Daniell.
p.    cm.—(The World's classics)
1. Zulu (African people)—Fiction.  2. Clergy—South Africa—
Fiction.  3. Scots—South Africa—Fiction.  I. Daniell, David.
II. Title.  III. Series.
823'.912—dc20    PR6003.U13P74  1994  93-30482
ISBN 0–19–282936–X

1  3  5  7  9  10  8  6  4  2

Typeset by Cambridge Composing (UK) Ltd.
Printed in Great Britain by
BPC Paperbacks Ltd
Aylesbury, Bucks

# CONTENTS

# ACKNOWLEDGEMENTS

I am glad to acknowledge help from James C. G. Greig, Susan Irvine, Kate Love, and John Spiers. My greatest debt is to John Oxley, of Brooklyn, Pretoria, who answered all my questions about South African life promptly, fully, and with undiminished enthusiasm. I dedicate this edition to him.

D.J.D.

# INTRODUCTION

JOHN BUCHAN reached a new, wide, audience with his first successful adventure-story, *Prester John*. It was his nineteenth book, and his sixth novel. He wrote it during the latter half of 1909, when he was 34, six years after his return from Africa to London. It was published in August 1910 by his own firm, Thomas Nelson and Sons, and in America in October under the title *The Great Diamond Pipe*. Both editions sold well. London reviews noted indebtedness to R. L. Stevenson, the alluring map, and the absence of girls. Nelson's issued a French translation. The boys' magazine *The Captain* serialized a much-edited version from April to September 1910 as 'The Black General'.

When the book was written, Buchan was busy establishing himself. He was a working barrister and publisher, a London man who had made a very good marriage and had a 1-year-old daughter. Presently a son would be born, and Buchan would be adopted as parliamentary candidate for a Scottish lowland seat. Now, with wife and new family, shuttling between London and Edinburgh on Nelson's business, nursing his putative constituency, writing non-stop for the quality press, he might be thought to have had little time for anything else. Yet clearly something spoke to him as remaining undone, something about his time in Africa.

He had gone there in 1901. His brilliant Oxford career had led to London journalism and the Bar, and for a while he had been content with that. Among the many unsigned articles and leaders he wrote at the time for the *Spectator* were a number on the South African situation as the Boer War dragged on. One of these caught the eye of the High Commissioner for South Africa, Lord Milner, during a visit to London. He made enquiries about the author. The result was an invitation to John Buchan at 27 to join him in South Africa for two years as his Private Secretary, with particular responsibility for resettlement after the war. So in September 1901 Buchan sailed, to become one of 'Milner's Young Men', a group of hand-picked clever and energetic young Englishmen known, not always admiringly, as 'The Kindergarten'.

Africa made a tremendous impact on him, not least because so much of it seemed Scotland writ large. His first duties were with the problems of the refugee camps, which had been badly mismanaged by the army. When the appalling death-rate had been brought down, Buchan was able to turn to his other task, that of resettling on the farms that had been ruined in the war both Boers and suitable immigrants, for which work he was mainly responsible. He did this from January 1902 to March 1903, travelling widely, often on horseback and sometimes alone, and into remote and unpopulated regions. His final tasks, in the spring and summer of 1903, until he left for England in August, concerned problems in the Transvaal and Orange River Colony—in the former of which *Prester John* is located (west of the present-day Kruger National Park).

Outside *Prester John*, Buchan wrote notably about southern Africa. Articles, while he was there, appeared in the London *Times* and elsewhere, some of which were gathered into a book of long essays published by Blackwoods in 1903 as *The African Colony*, on the history and topography of the region, and its political and economic problems. Three of his short stories had African settings: 'The Kings of Orion' (1906), 'The Grove of Ashtaroth' (1910), and the much later 'The Green Wildebeest' of 1927. Four years after *Prester John*, as the Great War broke out, Buchan invented his most famous hero, Richard Hannay, for *The Thirty-Nine Steps*: Hannay is from South Africa, and chapter 3 of the second Hannay novel, *Greenmantle* (1916), suggests that the book is going to be about South Africa. Chapter 4 of the last Hannay book, *The Island of Sheep* (1936), is set in Rhodesia. Buchan's curious novel-cum-symposium, *A Lodge in the Wilderness* (1906), an elevated discussion of empire on a loose narrative framework, was published in 1906 and again in 1917.

Whatever it was that he felt remained to be done about Africa in the summer of 1910, it brought together forces in him, and the use of literary models, which produced a great step forward in his skill as a novelist. He discovered the clear pace, that splendid forward drive however complex and strange the material, which we value as a Buchan characteristic. In the two dozen novels which followed, he never lost it again.

Before he could let his experience go, it seems, he had to work something out about being a boy again. There is a telling phrase in *The African Colony*, in the essay called 'The Wood Bush'. He is writing about

the heavy tropical scents which the rain brought out of the ground, the intense silence of the drooping mists and water-laden forests, the clusters of beehive Kaffir huts in the hollows, all made up a world strange and new to the sight and yet familiar to the imagination. This was the old Africa of a boy's dream. . . . (*The African Colony*, 122)

Buchan, never before out of Britain, felt keenly the adventure of sailing to southern Africa and knew his youth returning. He met, it is clear, 'the old Africa of a boy's dream'. He wrote to his mother before he accepted Milner's invitation to say that if his absence across the world distressed her, he would not go. His sentence is underlined: '*I am not going if it is to hurt you deeply.*' But go he did, and he made a great personal success of the venture, his first great statement of his departure from the parental orbit (for even at Oxford he had kept his family wholly in the picture). This African success appears all the greater, however, when one realizes that his family followed him out. He landed at Cape Town in October 1901. About six weeks later, his mother, father, and young brother landed at Port Elizabeth for a nine-month stay. Absolutely exasperated, John never mentioned this in his public writing, though his letters, for example to his sister Anna in Peebles, are free with expressions of what he felt. He tends to couch his feelings in terms of what a bad idea it is for them, rather than how angry he must have been, and how he must have felt himself attacked at the very point of his claim to his detached selfhood.

It seems likely that something of this gets into the making of *Prester John*. There David Crawfurd, the 19-year-old minister's son from the Fife shore, who follows in Africa so many of Buchan's own trails, successfully triumphs over the compelling, multi-faceted, hugely powerful dark father, in successive acts of heroism, while fully aware of his own weakness. The Rev. John Laputa, in the great incident at the heart of the book in the cave of the Rooirand in Chapter XI, had as he prayed 'some of the tones of my father's voice'. The Rev. John Buchan, in the pews of whose kirk JB had spent his boyhood, though he appeared to some a gentle and in some ways even an inept man, was a powerfully effectual and sought-after preacher. So fresh boyhood, and 'the old Africa of a boy's dream', must have seemed a fine setting in which he could place a fictional confrontation with the dark inner figure of a tremendous father, undisturbed by the infuriating reality of being followed into the adventure by mother, father, and brother. The feelings produced by that following must have been still accessible. In the novel, David Crawfurd's own father dies early in Chapter II, and that death is the cause of the boy's adventure. When he wrote *Prester John*, John Buchan's father was 62, with only five more years to live. It could be that JB wanted, before it was too late, to work out what had not been fully completed in his own African adventure.

The legends surrounding Prester John had long been in Buchan's mind. One of his earliest stories, written in the spring of his second year at Oxford, 1897, is called 'Prester John'. First printed in *Chambers's Journal* for 5 June of that year, and collected in the 1899 *Grey Weather* volume of short stories (his second), where it is the opening story, it tells of a stormy fishing adventure at the head of the Tweed. The narrator loses his way, becomes mist-bound on the tops and in real danger, and finds a remote shepherd with whom he shelters. The atmosphere is of wild mountain topography, weather, sky, distant views, flocks of sheep, and navigation, at which the shepherd is an expert. He is 'a man bent and thin, with a beard ragged and torn with all weathers, and a great scarred face roughly brown with the hill air and the reek of peat' (*Great Weather*, 13). The mixture of physical extremity, of wild life, of extreme of climate, and of sharp self-awareness and observation, all look forward to the African tale. The key passage, however, is:

He was full of odd tales of the place, learned from a thousand old sources, of queer things that happened in these eternal deserts, and queer sights which he and others than himself had seen at dawning and at sunset. Some day I will put them all down in a book, but then I will inscribe it to children and label it fantasy, for no one would believe them if told with the circumstance of truth. (ibid. 18)

The words 'Prester John' appear only in the title. Eight years later, Buchan's poem 'The Song of the Sea Captain' tells of the Portuguese mariner who wooed Prester John's daughter. And the next year, in *A Lodge in the Wilderness*, the Cecil Rhodes figure, Francis Carey, begins to close the first night's discussion with the words:

Here we are in Prester John's country. . . . He may have had a daughter called Melissinde, and she may have been the Far-away Princess to some Portuguese adventurer who left his ship at Mombasa and wandered up into the hills. (*A Lodge in the Wilderness* (1917), 31)

The legend of Prester John, the remote Christian priest-king, is very ancient. The earliest reference in Western literature is dated 1145, but there is evidence that the story was old even then, and widespread in the East before it reached Europe, where in the Middle Ages it is found in every country. About 1165 there began to circulate the famous Letter of Prester John, which was translated into almost every European language. It relates in extravagant terms his vast territory and wealth and miraculous powers. The existence of such a virtuous Christian prince on the other side of the alarmingly increasing Muslim world, someone who would muster forces to help the Crusades, fitted exactly the hopes of medieval Europeans. He was located in various places, as far east as China, as far south as southern India, and principally in Central Asia and Africa. The supposed existence of Prester John first reached a wider British public when in the 1360s John Mandeville gave an account of thirty years of travelling, and included an account of Prester John taken from the famous Letter. His big book, *The Travels of Sir John Mandeville* (contemporary with the first works of Geoffrey Chaucer) was taken as gospel for several centuries. It dawned only slowly on his readers that many of his travels were fantasy. Prester John's name appears frequently after Mandeville. In Shakespeare's

*Much Ado About Nothing*, for example, Benedick asks to be sent on impossible journeys, to avoid meeting Beatrice: 'I will . . . bring you the length of Prester John's foot' (II. i. 240). As successive travellers failed to meet him where Mandeville said he was, in Asia, he was transferred to Africa, to Ethiopia, or further south, allowing speculation about whether he was black or white or mulatto, the subject of a remark in 1646 at the end of Book VI, chapter x, 'Of the blackness of *Negroes*' in Sir Thomas Browne's *Pseudodoxia Epidemica* or 'Vulgar Errors', about 'the Emperor of *Aethiopia*, or Prester John, who derived from *Solomon*'. Browne says he 'is not yet descended into the hue of his Country, but remains a *Mulatto* . . . unto this day'.

Buchan uses the legend in two striking ways. He makes Laputa the holder of the long-vanished talisman of Prester John, a figure thought of as being in the African north, and associated with biblical times and people: and he suggests the Zulu leader himself as priest-king, a 'Christian' warrior against the 'infidel', a latter-day Prester John who assumes tremendous power.

John Buchan, who ended his life as Governor-General of the largest British Dominion, taking Canada into the Second World War, was keenly interested in ideas of empire all his life. *Prester John* is his empire novel, and it can reveal a good deal of his thinking in 1910—as long as it is understood that Buchan's narrator and mouthpiece is an incompletely educated and very young man, and not a 35-year-old London barrister and publisher with a brilliant Oxford career behind him, whose current philosophies reflected or opposed those of the highest statesmen in the empire itself, many of them known to him personally.

The creation of David Crawfurd, who is 13 when the novel opens and only 19 when it ends, is significant for several reasons, one of them being what he wants to say about empire. Buchan's novel *The Half-Hearted* of 1900, written long before he had set foot out of Britain, begins in Scotland and ends in the remotest region of the North-West Frontier of India, where the previously unmasculine, rather chinless and 'half-hearted' hero finds his consummation in giving his life to prevent, with his mutilated body, the Russian invasion of India. It is not a very good novel, and it is as much about the hero's problems in failing to be a successful lover as it is about rather simple notions of empire. The symposium of empire talk which makes *A Lodge in the Wilderness* of 1906, though exhilarating and even breathless in its heights, which are intellectual and social as well as topographical, is scarcely a novel: and the young people who give the love-interest are very well connected and knowing; their world-leading and aristocratic elders and betters are a generation above, and the whole thing is set up by a version of Cecil Rhodes himself. It is heady stuff.

For the hero of his one true empire novel, Buchan chose an observant boy from the Fife coast, as he himself had been. Buchan's own ideas of empire grew organically, and by 1910 he had had to come to terms with the failure of some of them: but they all began in his childhood on that shore, and the summer afternoons which 'opened up the world for me'. Early in his autobiography, *Memory Hold-the-Door*, he tells how in his father's congregation were retired sea-captains with curios from outlandish spots who taught him about ships.

But my interest was less in seamanship than in the unknown lands which could be reached by ships. I became aware of the largeness of the globe. . . . All the things which fascinated me in books—tropic islands, forests of strange fruits, snow mountains, ports thronged with queer shipping and foreign faces—lay somewhere beyond the waters in which I swam with indifferent skill. (pp. 18–19)

The very bookish small boy, who had spent a year in bed reading and being read to after an accident to his head at the age of 5, whose father enchanted him with fairy-stories and the songs of Scotland (and that is not the common view of a Calvinist minister), who very early developed a sharp sense of history in the Borders landscape, found his already active imagination opened wide by the notion of foreign lands. As the presence of the Reverend John Laputa in Fife at the opening of Buchan's novel shows, Scottish kirks were alert to missionary work (a black minister once preached in his father's pulpit at Pathhead), and in those circles the popular accounts of, for example, Mary Slessor of Calabar or David Livingstone (whose *Travels* of 1857 and 1865 are still in print and selling well), would make central and southern Africa especially vivid. David Crawfurd is the product of that lively, open world. He is not, we must notice, an older public-school boy with military connections. This is important in the proper placing of the novel.

British popular literature of empire goes back at least four hundred years. (It is, as far as I can make out, unique. The post-Renaissance empires of Spain, Russia, Germany, and Japan produced nothing comparable, though the literature of the American frontier has some resemblance, and some science-fiction and space-adventures can be seen as part of a literature of a modern American empire.) The excitement of a remote frontier, of British possessions overseas, engagement in small, distant wars, the paramount importance of a navy, pressing problems of peace-keeping, and union, both overseas and at home, can all be found in Elizabethan writers and fairly continuously afterwards. The vast field of over four hundred years of British Protestant literature can show the British empire as something as attractive as simply the extension of the family overseas. Empire could, even in the mid-nineteenth century, mean exploration (or what was understood to be so— we now know that early African 'explorers' were often guided along ancient highways), map-making, engineering, medicine, and special interests in literatures, languages, and the problems of translation. Much of the writing about all this was inspired by, and often a part of, the growth of literature for children, without distinction of gender, from early in the nineteenth century, and it can be charted through a study of the founding and success of children's magazines after 1830. A great deal of it is now unreadable, being both tedious and pious: some of it is neither. Much of it was written for the Sunday School movement, which before universal education alone provided the poor (that is, almost the whole nation) with cheap reading matter, for which the Sunday Schools themselves had provided a readership.

Then, in the latter part of the century, a change quite clearly comes over the popular literature of all kinds: much of it moves towards being aggressively, and defensively, imperialist.

A large segment of it leaves behind Christian family ambience and becomes all-male and public-school: military values invade and take over the stories; religion is subordinated to fighting; weakness is at best discounted and at worst punished. In almost all such tales, white dominates black with cool superiority and, usually, brutal force, in the name of something called civilization. This quite sudden sideways shift, distressing to watch, dominates songs as well as novels, encyclopaedias as well as newspapers. It can be seen most clearly in the children's magazines. Even from about 1860 they had begun to focus on boys and 'manly' adventure: but the most famous, and the most 'manly', the *Boys' Own Paper*, was founded in 1897. Between 1880 and 1900 no fewer than a hundred children's journals were founded, over half of them devoted to 'manliness'. The boys in them are with little exception privileged, at public school and preparing to be officers in the armed forces. (The rather upper-crust boys' paper in which the mutilated version of Buchan's *Prester John* appeared was significantly called *The Captain* (see Appendix, pp. 204–7). The Sunday School movement continued, such schools sometimes having surprisingly large lending libraries, but the emphasis shifted over only a few decades from the spiritual one of being 'holy' to the physical one of being 'manly'. That meant being a public-school prefect, and going on, as often as not, to be a midshipman and a hero. The old Sunday School element, two hundred years after Bunyan still recognizably close to *The Pilgrim's Progress* of 1678, in that characters and events all had spiritual significance, changed to a new emphasis on deeds and actions, backed by a crude philosophy, and invariably in text and pictures focusing attention on a gun. The force of gunpowder in subduing both natives and wild animals had long been recognized, in the earliest American settlements, for example, or in seminal novels like Defoe's *Robinson Crusoe* (1719): but suddenly the gun is allowed to be central, in accounts of adventures, in novels and in the illustrations, almost as the single imperialist constant, openly declared. All this imperialist literature is oddly selective in location, as if history were generating sets of repeating myths. The Indian Mutiny, the Zulu wars, and of course the Boer War were all such establishing experiences. So much followed Kipling's India, Rider Haggard's Africa, and to a lesser extent Gilbert Parker's Canada: there is a notable lack of stories about the rest of the globe coloured red—few great popular stories about New Zealand, for example. The myths of personal testing seemed to cluster in northern India, southern Africa, and arctic Canada.

On the boat to Africa in 1901, Buchan tells us in *Memory Hold-the-Door*, 'at the age of twenty-five, youth came back to me like a spring tide, and every day on the voyage to the Cape saw me growing younger' (p. 99). He worked for Milner in a colony of an empire in which everything was already largely in place, though he had the experience of covering tracts of country as the first white man, and there were still large blank spaces on maps of Africa marking areas unknown to 'civilization'. Everything was largely in place—but it was not fixed. Much of the absorption Buchan found in the work he did came from knowing that so much was to be made afresh, and the potential was so huge, for making a successful nation in southern Africa, or for producing disaster. This is important. He saw that landscape first of all as not standing for mineral, pastoral, or agricultural wealth, but as making a nation. Whatever emerged, it would be, as in his own Scottish Borders, of mixed population, but even so, of identifiable, consciously felt nationhood, coming out of conflicts and settlements which had, on that territory, an ancient history. The boy in him that he recovered as he got off the boat at Cape Town was prepared for adventure, but had been made in consciousness of national Scottish selfhood on the Fife shore and on the banks of the Tweed. Both regions spoke to him of history, and he was unfashionable in 1903 in opening his book on *The African Colony* with an insistence that southern Africa had several very ancient histories indeed. One popular argument for empire was thus denied him, that the land had never belonged to anyone anyway and was there waiting to be occupied. (His African fiction presents the contrary view strongly, in the short stories 'The Grove of Ashtaroth' and 'The Kings of Orion' for example, as well as in *Prester John*.)

His immediate task, as we noted above, was in helping to resettle the farms that had been abandoned or ruined, putting back the original Boer farmers or putting in immigrants from other countries. It may be found reprehensible today by some, but it is not surprising that Buchan's philosophy of empire, as formulated in his South African life, expressed itself mainly in terms of settlement. Empire was Opportunity: the Boers, though having some admirable characteristics as farmers, in their Bible-bound conservatism lacked vision of what really could be done in that enchanting topography. So he, under Milner, thought that large numbers of energetic young people from other parts of the British Empire, and particularly from the unhealthy cities of Britain, should settle in 'the fairest country under the stars', as he described southern Africa in the dedicatory poem, and prosper in that healthy air. Such an influx would also keep the new nation properly connected with the motherland.

In this philosophy, Buchan approached the matter of what he called 'the subject races' with some care. That he was paternalistic is undeniable. His recommendation that only the most limited franchise was suitable for 'the Kaffir' (not at all as pejorative a term as it has become since) on the grounds of limited capacity must stick in modern gullets, especially when he writes of 'the native' as being mentally 'as crude and naive as a child'. 'With all his merits', he wrote in *The African Colony*, 'this instability of character and intellectual childishness make him politically far more impossible than even the lowest class of Europeans' (p. 290). Incapable of intellectual or spiritual growth, the native, if a boy, was to be trained in 'carpentry and ironwork and the rudiments of trade', and if a girl in 'sewing and basket-making and domestic employments . . . a far more potent influence than the Latin grammar or the primer of history'. The truths of a spiritual religion must be communicated in small crumbs: Buchan praises a missionary who says 'as to dogma, I think we must be content for the present with a few stories and hymns' (pp. 309–10).

Yet that book was praised in the *Times Literary Supplement* for its moderation, and at the end of the twentieth century we have to labour to understand the context of such writing at its beginning. We wince, rightly, at the scorn of Kipling's sarcastic 'White Man's Burden' of 1899, written in response to the American annexation of the Philippines:

> Take up the White Man's burden—
> Send forth the best ye breed—
> Go, bind your sons to exile
> To serve your captives' need;
> To wait in heavy harness
> On fluttered folk and wild—
> Your new-caught, sullen peoples,
> Half-devil and half-child.

Even when Kipling is sympathetic to the subject peoples, and acute about them, his concern is usually for what the service of them will do to improve the moral status of the imperial soldiers and administrators as rulers. We have to recognize that when Buchan writes of working positively to educate 'the native', even in such crudely limited ways as we have seen, he is a long way ahead of much popular thought, of which, as always, Kipling is an indicator. So the passage at the end of the penultimate chapter, XXII, of *Prester John*, where, some time after all those maturing experiences, David Crawfurd expounds the meaning of 'the white man's duty' as 'of being in a little way a king' and so on is in fact the reverse of what we take from it. Horribly paternalistic as it is (as befits a newly wealthy young laird, of course) it states that the white man 'has to take all risks, recking nothing of his life or his fortunes, and well content to find his reward in the fulfilment of his task'. That, as well as being the voice of the limited hero, is that of the maturer John Buchan (with echoes of Milner), and to anyone who knows the standard European reactions of the time at which *Prester John* is set, it is startling. Crawfurd does not write that 'the white man' is there to increase his own wealth mightily, by ravaging the country and exploiting, enslaving and, if necessary, slaughtering its people, as was one accepted belief: or even as a form of character-improvement, as some finer spirits understood. He is there to serve, at the cost of his life and fortunes. It must have seemed rather peculiar in 1910. John Buchan came away from South Africa 'more than a convert, a fanatic': but to something 'humanitarian and international . . . an ethical standard, serious and surely not ignoble' (*Memory Hold-the-Door*, 130).

Moreover, it is characteristic of Buchan that his true border is not between territories, and certainly not between races, but between savagery and civilization wherever they are found. A well-known remark in his 'shocker' *The Power-House* (written 1913, published 1916) catches this: the villainous Mr Andrew Lumley counteracts Sir Edward Leithen's self-assured lawyer's view; 'You think that a wall as solid as earth separates civilisation from barbarism. I tell you the division is a thread, a pane of glass. A touch here, a push there, and you bring back the reign of Saturn' (*The Thirty-Nine Steps and The Power House* (1922), 211–12). Throughout his fiction, his villains are not racial (and talk about 'Buchan's Jewish villains', which is still heard even now, shows ignorance of Buchan's writing), but out to destroy civilization from within: they are most potent when they are most 'civilized', like Dominick Medina in *The Three Hostages*. The worst enemies are always those within. *Prester John*, far from showing a them-and-us polarity, has a central Zulu figure very greatly to be admired who brings together the oldest tribal histories and Old Testament stories (about the Queen of Sheba, for example), Western classical civilization (Laputa quotes Virgil appositely), Christian theology (Laputa is acceptable in Free Kirk pulpits, where anything less than lengthy exposition of the toughest New Testament doctrine wold be scorned), large-scale military skill, and tribal magic. Yet he is an enemy because, within all that, he is out to destroy: Arcoll, the secret-service agent who had tracked him for years, wanted to shoot him like a dog. Instead, David Crawfurd privately watches Laputa go out very grandly indeed, in a way that is appropriate to his towering stature and high pride. In the penultimate Richard Hannay novel, *The Three Hostages* of 1924, Dominick Medina comes to a similar end: like Laputa he falls, literally, as a result of pride, betrayed by false judgement; Laputa of his weasely accomplice, Medina of Hannay's intentions.

It is uncharacteristic of all the imperial fiction of the time that Laputa's going-out is a matter of sorrow. It is hard to escape the judgement that Buchan is careful to show that it was not ignorant savage tribalism, and being one of a 'lesser breed' in Kipling's words, that brought about Laputa's downfall, but 'civilization'. In Buchan's African short story 'The Grove of Ashtaroth', the reasonable narrator, in order to save his apparently-possessed part-Jewish friend, destroys an ancient symbolic grove and tower. He ends the tale haunted by having murdered 'innocent gentleness . . . I knew that I had driven something lovely and adorable from its last refuge on earth.' Buchan is unmistakably suggesting that 'civilization' might destroy good and beautiful things.

Also uncharacteristic for the time is the lack of violence. Though imperialist writers stressed the presence of the British in Africa as bringers of law to Africans who were conveniently thought of as incapable of controlling themselves, their heroes were usually equally conveniently outside the law, and free to butcher 'the subject races' at whim. Rider Haggard is a case in point. His awe at certain native figures did not stand in the way of his obvious enthusiasm for rivers of (usually native) blood. The young heroes of the shelf-full of G. A. Henty's stories for boys, so seductively produced around the turn of the century in pictorial bindings by Blackie's, are often cold-blooded mass-murderers of natives, wiping out whole groups with little motive except that they are in some way offensive, or as a form of outrageously disproportionate revenge.

Buchan in *Prester John* has a story of a massive, impressively led Zulu rising against all whites, which in other hands would be made for big scenes of tremendous slaughter. They do not occur: not even little scenes of trivial slaughter. There are casualties when the uprising begins and Laputa's forces advance, but they are incidental and in no way dwelt on. The shot that Henriques, the disreputable villain, is found to have fired, at the novel's climax, is effective because of its singularity. In place of the mass of such expected carnage there is in Buchan's book a different tone, an altogether unexpected quality, which is that not of murderous confrontation but of quest.

This is in fact the key to Buchan's philosophy of empire. It explains the sense of movement in his thinking—empire always was for him an organic system, capable of growth unless prevented by neglect or malice. It explains the unusual qualities we have noticed. Like the hero of *Pilgrim's Progress*, Britain's African colony should move forward from one enriching experience to another, helped out of the Slough of Despond (produced by the Boer War), illuminated by well-timed encounters, and losing its burden of guilt. The end of the quest, as in Bunyan, is rarely visible, but its nature is increasingly understood. In the case of southern Africa, it is the creation of a colony which is a healthy, empire-settled land using its fabulous resources to restore jaded British blood and slowly, by British service, bringing the native to limited franchise. That Bunyan's book is continually in Buchan's mind in this book, as in so many others, is easily demonstrable. That some of the enthusiastic hopes that Buchan expressed in 1903 in *The African Colony* and in 1906 in *A Lodge in the Wilderness* had already faded by 1910 is also demonstrable: yet more than enough remains to make *Prester John* buoyant. At the close of the book, the wealthy David Crawfurd is proud of his contribution to South Africa and hopeful for the future.

He is a most untypical hero of the 'manly' kind of boys' imperialist fiction. David Crawfurd's literary forebears belong to an ancient strain of heroic romance: he is immediately descended from R. L. Stevenson's David Balfour in *Kidnapped* and *Catriona*, and before that in a line that goes back through Scott, Fielding, Defoe, and long before, to Spenser and Malory and the earlier medieval romance: figures combining chivalric or epic exploits with something almost commonplace, and familiarly human in their weaknesses. Buchan's hero has an unusual range of sensibilities. He is knowledgeable about, and responsive to, the countryside he passes through. Most paragraphs are illuminated by a touch of detailed observation. The landscape, as always with Buchan, comes clean off the page, as the narrator registers it. More than that, David Crawfurd is more frequently weak, defeated, collapsed, cowardly, in pain and need, desperate for relief from pain or bonds, than is permitted in all the other popular imperialist fiction that I have read. At the fall of Laputa, David says 'I remember that I looked over the brink into the yeasty abyss with a mind hovering between perplexity and tears. I wanted to sit down and cry—why, I did not know, except that some great thing had happened.' He tells us elsewhere that 'there were tears of weakness running down my cheeks' or 'I was in a torment of impotence' or 'I could only lie limply on the horse's back, clutching at his mane with trembling fingers'. Such things make his heroism all the greater, of course: he deserves his triumph not because he is British and therefore obviously superior (he isn't: except for the drunken Japp and the shifty Henriques, almost everyone, white or black, outclasses him in important ways, and Laputa toweringly). He deserves his triumph because from impossible weakness he wins through. This is what makes his climb out of the cave in Chapter XXI a rite of passage: in that dawn he achieves 'my own country'; and this significance is possible because David's whole narrative has the steady beat of a larger, particularly biblical, reference. The opening pages of the novel are set in, or just away from, a Scottish kirk on the sabbath of the spring Communion, in the town where the Rev. John Laputa is the visiting minister, so the Christian and biblical references throughout the novel, like those to *Pilgrim's Progress*, have an acceptable context. Such reference and imagery rise to control the action in the great scenes of ritual at the heart of the book in Chapter XI when Laputa, standing by a fire next to a wall of descending water in a cave shut in the mountainside, is dedicated to the leadership, and passes as it were from priest to king. It reminds David of 'Samuel anointing Saul king of Israel'. Spoken texts from Isaiah and Psalms and the Gospels and Revelation dominate the action in a way which is, to say the least, not at all common in the boys' literature of the period, though it had been more so fifty years before. (Such direct use of the Bible is very different from the strange pseudo-biblical, pseudo-blank-verse rhythms normal to Rider Haggard, for example, particularly at moments of slaughter.) In *Prester John* a mind steeped in the Bible is presenting a great enemy and an action, and himself as narrator, all steeped in the Bible: it is in fact a profoundly religious book, and in one aspect especially, as will appear presently.

Most unusual of all for the 'manly' genre is the hero's great respect for the black leader. At the lowest level, it is for his physical power.

The pace at which he moved must have been amazing. He had a great physique, hard as nails from long travelling, and in his own eyes he had an empire at stake. When I look at the map and see the journey which with vast fatigue I completed from Dupree's Drift to Machudi's, and then look at the huge spaces of country over which Laputa's legs took him on that night, I am lost in admiration of the man. (pp. 167–8)

Though we do not see it in any detail, his military strategy is grand (and owes something to John Buchan's interest in the Marquis of Montrose and Oliver Cromwell, Julius Caesar and Augustus, not to mention the Great War, as will appear in later books). Laputa has stature, and he is set in a kaleidoscopic context of lightly touched interests, historical, social, literary, geographic, and religious. His literary antecedents are Bunyan, Milton, Shakespeare; he quotes Virgil as well as the Bible. The dedication scene in the middle of the book can easily bear the rich freight of reference it is made to carry.

Yet of course, like Milton's Satan, he is an archangel fatally and dangerously flawed. That flaw is not his blackness but his pride—a theological and not a racial concept. The man is not dangerous because he is crazy, powerful, and black, but because he is human, and proud. At the height of the dedication, Laputa prays. David Crawfurd says

I listened spellbound as he prayed. . . . But there was in the prayer more than supplications of the quondam preacher. There was a tone of arrogant pride, the pride of the man to whom the Almighty is only another and greater Lord of Hosts. He prayed less as a suppliant than as an ally. (p. 104)

That passage begins, 'He had some of the tones of my father's voice.' With that phrase, and the reiteration of that point of David's childhood experience in Kirkcaple, we come to one of the central ideas of the novel. David Crawfurd's father's preaching, and his own Sunday School and church life, have given him a kind of work-a-day Calvinism. It has not much theological depth, but it does very well for the purposes of the book. He knows that he can rely on Divine Providence, which (or who) is mentioned fairly frequently in the story as the source both of special care for his welfare and of particular chances that he has to make the most of. So he can see small events, like the 'miracle' of the breaking of the horse's halter at the end of Chapter XVII, as indicators of the special interest of God. This concern has been foreordained: God's will has mapped everything out, in great detail. It is not bizarre for David to feel, early in Chapter X, that it was significant that he had been given special information.

Perhaps the Calvinism of my father's preaching had unconsciously taken grip of my soul. . . . Not for nothing had I been given a clue to the strange events which were coming. It was foreordained that I should go alone to Umvelos', and in the promptings of my own fallible heart I believed I saw the workings of Omnipotence. (p. 95)

He admits to being 'a fatalist in creed', and that seeing the 'workings of Omnipotence' in that way is 'our mortal arrogance', yet adds, 'without such a belief I think that mankind would have been content to lie sluggishly at home'. (That is a good basis for telling adventure-stories.) Similarly, as he finds in Chapter XI, God has ordained some to be kings and some to be servants. This can lead to a belief which is at root racist. It is characteristic that David Crawfurd, son of the manse and Sunday School scholar, knows his Bible very well, but quotes mainly from the Old Testament, with its God who is in special relation with his chosen people.

The dangerous Rev. John Laputa does not have to slant David Crawfurd's basic beliefs very much to make his own creed believable. He has also found his own specialness under God, but with himself aggrandized as cleansing prophet as well as priest and king, as is made explicit early in Chapter XVII. What disturbs David is not only seeing his own elementary and local Sunday School ideas taken over and enlarged on to a vast scale—theological, geographic (the whole of southern Africa), and historic (reaching back to the time of Prester John and even the Queen of Sheba): Calvinism always did stress omnipotence. It is especially that to make them evil they are given so apparently slight a twist. Not for nothing does Buchan in the first chapter of *Prester John* show us the aceptable, even lionized, visiting black minister with 'terror and devilish fury and amazement' on his face, and Archie saying 'he's going to raise Satan'.

This side of Laputa is private, and given to few to see. The first half of the book sketches his great public success: as the sort of outstanding visitor to be invited to preach in a Scottish kirk on a special sabbath; as a roving African evangelist; at a missionary conference in Cape Town; at a meeting of the Royal Geographical Society in London. But after the sabbath service, David saw his private pagan rituals; after his superb preaching on board ship, he is overheard plotting furtively with the unsavoury Henriques. Like other Buchan villains, Moxon Ivery in *Mr Standfast* (and *The Thirty-Nine Steps*) or Dominick Medina in *The Three Hostages*, Laputa is publicly a successful man, but unwittingly reveals to the hero his secret potential for great evil.

Even with his private knowledge, David has difficulty understanding why Captain Arcoll regrets not having shot Laputa like an animal in the same way that the farmer Coetzee so casually shot the baboon. Laputa has a voice that can sway multitudes. In a hidden place he is given a talisman almost beyond belief in historical association, the jewel that had once burned in Sheba's hair. In that experience David receives the explanation of Laputa's power in a trance, only waking too late to the danger he is in. Laputa is like his father realistically—with the same manner of preaching—and symbolically. Some of the quality of the relation between David and Laputa comes out of myth, as is proper to high romance. Like the experience of a father, a mixture of conscious and unconscious experiences, David sees Laputa in several lights. Early in Chapter XVII, he says

I had seen Laputa as the Christian minister, as the priest and king in the cave, as the leader of an army at Dupree's Drift, and at the kraal we had left as the savage with all self-control flung to the winds. I was to see this amazing man in a further part. For he now became a friendly and rational companion. He kept his horse at an easy walk, and talked to me as if we were two friends out for a trip together. (p. 150)

At the exact centre of the novel, in the middle of Chapter XI, the exposition and prayer are a distortion of Christian preach-

ing. Both the Bible-rich style and the latent corruption were
familiar to Buchan from his boyhood. Though his father
preached a milder version, at the heart of the historic Calvinism of his Scottish kirk was something which could easily be
made closer to the spirit of the vengeful, exclusive Jehovah of
the bloodier parts of the Old Testament than of the universal
redemptiveness of Christ. Buchan was haunted by that potential in the historic kirk for deluded perversion of the gospel,
and returned to it a number of times. It is in *Salute to
Adventurers* four years later, and particularly *Witch Wood* of
1927. It underlies his writing on Montrose. It can be seen in a
secular version in his 'shockers', the Hannay and Leithen
stories, where great evil is only 'a thread, a sheet of glass' from
good.

Here in *Prester John* Laputa is defeated. That victory is a
personal thing, belonging not to vast armies but to the courage
of an all-too-weak boy. John Buchan's own Africa, with its
marvellous mythic power, has given the real minister's son
from Fife a region of Empire in which to face his own Calvinist
inheritance. It seems that something left undone had now been
accomplished.

# NOTE ON THE TEXT

THE basic text remains that of the first edition of August 1910, followed in all the twelve reprints to the end of 1921, and occasionally after, including the translation into French of 1922. In May 1922, however, Nelson's issued an edition with three small changes, presumably on Buchan's authority, and now generally followed. It is this text which is given here. The changes are: p. 14, 'my bonny lamb' for 'my bonny man'; p. 19, 'paralytic stroke' for 'paralytic shock'; and p. 48, 'fifteen' miles for 'twenty-five'.

The severely cut and rewritten version for serialization in *The Captain*, April to September 1910, has no authority. (See Appendix, pp. 204–7.)

# SELECT BIBLIOGRAPHY

Place of publication is London, unless otherwise stated.

## Editions

A number of Buchan's books remain in print in various forms, and most can be found second-hand. The standard bibliography is Robert G. Blanchard, *The First Editions of John Buchan: A Collector's Bibliography* (Hamden, Conn., 1981).

## Letters

Buchan was a massively prolific—though usually brief—writer of letters. There is no complete edition. Some are quoted in Janet Adam Smith's biography (see below). Important collections are held in the National Library of Scotland, Edinburgh University Library, and especially the Douglas Library, Queen's University, Kingston, Ontario, Canada, where can be found a full assembly of Buchan material, including manuscripts and his personal library.

## Autobiography and Biography

Buchan's autobiography, *Memory Hold-the-Door*, written in Canada and published posthumously, is finely written and illuminating, but also at times, it must be said, baffling in its omissions (there is little mention of his beloved wife and children, for one example, or of his own famous fictions, for another) because the gentlemanly principle on which it is written meant that he could only write about the dead, and had to eschew intimate matters. Happily we have Janet Adam Smith's *John Buchan: A Biography* (1965; repr. Oxford, 1985), and his son William Buchan's *John Buchan: A Memoir* (1982), both of which fill out the picture.

## Criticism and Background

The only full-length study of Buchan as a writer remains David Daniell, *The Interpreter's House: A Critical Assessment of John Buchan* (1975). Buchan is attracting increasing attention, and the following essays may be found useful:

Michael Denning, *Cover Stories: Narrative and Ideology in the British Spy Thriller* (1987).

Martin Green, *Dreams of Adventure, Deeds of Empire* (1980).

Juanita Kruse, *John Buchan (1875–1940) and the Idea of Empire: Popular Literature and Political Ideology* (Lewiston, NY, 1989).

Jonathan Parry, 'From the Thirty-Nine Articles to the Thirty-Nine Steps: Reflections on the Thought of John Buchan', in Michael Bentley (ed.), *Public and Private Doctrine: Essays Presented to Maurice Cowling* (Cambridge, 1993).

M. R. Ridley, 'A Misrated Author?', in *Second Thoughts: More Studies in Literature* (1965).

Janet Adam Smith, *John Buchan and his World* (1979).

Arthur C. Turner, *Mr Buchan, Writer* (1949)—a short biography, good on the writing.

Richard Usborne, *Clubland Heroes: A Nostalgic Study of Some Recurrent Characters in the Romantic Fiction of Dornford Yates, John Buchan and Sapper* (1953; rev. 1974).

Robin W. Winks, 'John Buchan: Stalking the Wilder Game', in *The Four Adventures of Richard Hannay* (Boston, Mass., 1988).


*On* Prester John

C. F. Beckingham, 'The Quest for Prester John', *Bulletin of the John Rylands University Library*, 62 (1979–80), 290–310.

Jean Bramford, *A Dictionary of South African English*, 4th edn. (Cape Town, 1991).

John Buchan, *The African Colony* (1903).

—— *A Lodge in the Wilderness* (1906).

—— 'The Kings of Orion' and 'The Grove of Ashtaroth', in *The Moon Endureth* (1912): the latter story is also in *The Best Short Stories of John Buchan*, ed. David Daniell (1980).

—— 'The Green Wildebeest', in *The Runagates Club* (1928).

T. J. Couzens, '"The old Africa of a boy's dream"—Towards Interpreting Buchan's "Prester John"', *English Studies in Africa*, 24 (1981), 1–24.

David Daniell, 'Buchan and "The Black General"', in *The Black Presence in English Literature*, ed. David Dabydeen (Manchester, 1980), 135–53.

Malcolm Letts, *Sir John Mandeville* (1949).

David Ogilvie, '*Prester John*: David Crawfurd's Journeys', *John Buchan Journal*, 12 (Autumn 1992), 17–19.

Edward Ullendorf and C. F. Beckingham, *The Hebrew Letters of Prester John* (1982).

# A CHRONOLOGY OF
# JOHN BUCHAN

*Note*: Buchan wrote 130 books, contributed significantly to another 150, and was a prolific writer of articles and reviews. Only the major books are noted here.

1875    Born at 20 York Place, Perth, Scotland, first son of the Rev. John Buchan, Free Church minister, and his wife, Helen.

1876    Moves to Pathhead, Fife, a small town on the Firth of Forth (his boyhood there is later recalled in the first chapter of *Prester John*). Family holidays—with three younger siblings—spent at his mother's parents' house at Broughton in Tweeddale, a powerful influence on the rest of his life.

1888    Moves to 34 Queen Mary Avenue, Glasgow, his father now minister of John Knox Church in the Gorbals. Attends Hutchesons' Grammar School.

1892    Student at Glasgow University. Distinguishes himself in classical studies, latterly under the young Gilbert Murray.

1894    Publishes his first book at the age of 17 while a second-year student: an edition, with introduction, of *Essays and Apothegms of Francis Lord Bacon*, for the London publisher, Walter Scott.

1895    Publishes *Sir Quixote of the Moors*. Begins undergraduate life on a scholarship at Brasenose College, Oxford.

1896    Publishes *Scholar Gipsies*, a collection of his own writings about Tweeddale, and two weeks later, *Musa Piscatrix*, his anthology of fishing poems.

1897    Wins Stanhope and Newdigate Prizes.

1898    Publishes *John Burnet of Barns*, and a history, *Brasenose College*. Publisher's reader for John Lane.

1899    President of the Oxford Union; First in Greats. Publishes collection of his own short stories, *Grey Weather*, and *A Lost Lady of Old Years*.

1900    At 4 Brick Court in the Temple, reading for the Bar. For long stretches running the *Spectator*. Publishes *The Half-Hearted*.

1901    June, called to the Bar. Writing much for *Blackwood's Magazine*. Sails to South Africa to join Milner, working on settlement in the aftermath of the Boer War.

1902    Second collection of short stories published, *The Watcher by the Threshold*. In charge of Land Settlement, treks widely over South Africa.

1903    Publishes *The African Colony*. Returns to England and takes up work as barrister again, writing for, and partly running, the *Spectator*. Specializes in taxation questions.

1905    Publishes *The Law Relating to the Taxation of Foreign Income*. Begins *The Mountain*, 'a big novel' set in South Africa, never finished.

1906    Publishes his novel-cum-symposium *A Lodge in the Wilderness*, set in an imaginary house 9,000 feet up on the East African plateau, to which come senior world figures to debate the future of Africa.

1907    15 July, marries Susan Grosvenor, the start of a lifetime's happy partnership. Becomes chief literary adviser to the publishers Thomas Nelson & Sons. Moves to 40 Hyde Park Square, but travels to Nelson's Edinburgh base frequently. Begins the Nelson Sevenpennies, and other series, reprinting literary classics, which successfully rivalled Dent's Everyman's Library and Oxford University Press's World's Classics. Re-launches the *Scottish Review* with strong international and intellectual flavour.

1908    Birth of first child, Alice. Publishes collection of his own essays, *Some Eighteenth Century Byways*. *Scottish Review* ceases.

1910    Moves to 13 Bryanston Street. Publishes *Prester John*.

1911    Publishes *Sir Walter Raleigh*. Beloved father dies, eldest son, John, born. Adopted as Unionist candidate for Peebles and Selkirk.

1912    Moves to 76 Portland Place. Publishes third collection of his own short stories, *The Moon Endureth*. Much occasional writing, and travel to Nelson's in Edinburgh and across his constituency. Brother William dies.

1913    Publishes biographies *The Marquis of Montrose* and *Andrew Jameson, Lord Ardwall*. Continues to divide time between London and Scotland. *The Power-House* published in *Blackwood's Magazine*.

1914      Starts first of the twenty-four numbers of *Nelson's History of the War*. (Each number, *c*.50,000 words, was entirely written by Buchan.) Drawn into secret intelligence work. Summer holiday at Broadstairs. Ordered to bed at start of duodenal illness, with him for the rest of his life. Begins to write *The Thirty-Nine Steps*, completed after much government work and travel when ordered to bed again in November.

1915      Special correspondent for *The Times* on the Western Front. Publishes *Salute to Adventures*. 19 October, *The Thirty-Nine Steps* published, selling 25,000 copies before the end of the year, and never out of print since. Buchan becomes famous as a novelist and war correspondent. Working in propaganda.

1916      Birth of second son, William. Publishes *The Power-House* in book form and the second Hannay story, *Greenmantle*. Working for Foreign Office and War Office and as Intelligence officer at GHQ in France.

1917      Director of new Department of Information, responsible directly to the Prime Minister. Brother Alastair and best friend Tommy Nelson killed. Publishes collection of his own poetry, *Poems, Scots and English*. Begins writing *Mr Standfast*.

1918      Appointed Director of Intelligence in newly formed Ministry of Information. Birth of third son, Alastair.

1919      Buys Elsfield Manor, four miles north-east of Oxford. Publishes *Mr Standfast*; privately, *These for Remembrance*, commemorating six close friends killed in the war; and, with his wife Susan, a second novel-cum-symposium, *The Island of Sheep*. Becomes a director of Reuters.

1920      Writes at Smuts's request and publishes *The History of the South African Forces in France*. Publishes a memoir, *Francis and Riversdale Grenfell*.

1921–2    Rewrites the *Nelson History* as a four-volume *History of the Great War*.

1922      *Huntingtower* published. Also *A Book of Escapes and Hurried Journeys*.

1923      Publishes *Midwinter* and *The Last Secrets*. Deputy Chairman of Reuters.

1924      Publishes fourth Hannay story, *The Three Hostages*; biog-

raphy of Lord Minto, one-time Governor-General of Canada
and subsequently Viceroy of India. Publishes influential
anthology of Scottish vernacular poetry *The Northern Muse*.
Buchan's first visit to America. Recommended for Governor-
Generalship of Canada.

1925    Publishes *John Macnab* and *The History of the Royal Scots
Fusiliers*.

1926    Publishes *The Dancing Floor* and an anthology of his own
writing, *Homilies and Recreations*.

1927    Enters Parliament as MP for Scottish Universities as a
moderate Tory. Publishes *Witch Wood*.

1928    Publishes collection of his short stories, *The Runagates Club*,
and a large and significant reworking of his biography
*Montrose*. Close adviser to Prime Minister, Stanley Baldwin.

1929    Publishes *The Courts of the Morning*, and his Cambridge
Rede Lecture, *The Causal and the Casual in History*.
Resigns from Nelson's.

1930    Begins work in support of Jews in Palestine. Publishes *The
Kirk in Scotland*, written with George Adam Smith, and
*Castle Gay*.

1931    Close adviser to Labour Prime Minister, Ramsay Mac-
Donald. *The Blanket of the Dark* published.

1932    Biographies of *Sir Walter Scott* and *Julius Caesar* published,
and novels *The Gap in the Curtain* and *The Magic Walking-
Stick*, the latter for children. Discussed for Viceroyship of
India.

1933    *The Massacre of Glencoe* published, and *A Prince of the
Captivity*. Lord High Commissioner to the General Assembly of the Church of Scotland.

1934    High Commissioner again. *Gordon at Khartoum* published;
the biography, *Oliver Cromwell*; and *The Free Fishers*.
Second visit to America.

1935    *The King's Grace* published, an official history celebrating
the reign of King George V for his Jubilee. *The House of the
Four Winds* and a collection of essays, *Men and Deeds*,
published. As Lord Tweedsmuir of Elsfield, sails to Canada
as Governor-General.

1936    *The Island of Sheep* published. Travels widely in Canada.

1937    Biography *Augustus* published. Journeys far 'Down North' into the Arctic (first Governor-General to do so).

1939    Takes Canada into the war. Begins *Sick Heart River*, and autobiography, *Memory Hold-the-Door*. Seriously ill.

1940    11 February, dies after an accident, and mourned across Canada. *Memory Hold-the-Door* published, and two collections, *Comments and Characters* and *Canadian Occasions*.

1941    *Sick Heart River* published, and *The Long Traverse*.

# PRESTER JOHN

The Various Journeys of
Mr DAVID CRAWFURD

*To*

## *LIONEL PHILLIPS**

Time, they say, must the best of us capture,
   And travel and battle and gems and gold
No more can kindle the ancient rapture,
   For even the youngest of hearts grows old.
But in you, I think, the boy is not over;
   So take this medley of ways and wars
As the gift of a friend and a fellow-lover
   Of the fairest country under the stars.

                          J.B.

# CONTENTS

# CONTENTS

# PRESTER JOHN

## CHAPTER I

### THE MAN ON THE KIRKCAPLE SHORE

I MIND as if it were yesterday my first sight of the man. Little
I knew at the time how big the moment was with destiny, or
how often that face seen in the fitful moonlight would haunt
my sleep and disturb my waking hours. But I mind yet the
cold grue* of terror I got from it, a terror which was surely
more than the due of a few truant lads breaking the Sabbath
with their play.

The town of Kirkcaple, of which and its adjacent parish of
Portincross my father was the minister, lies on a hillside above
the little bay of Caple,* and looks squarely out on the North
Sea. Round the horns of land which enclose the bay the coast
shows on either side a battlement of stark red cliffs through
which a burn or two makes a pass to the water's edge. The bay
itself is ringed with fine clean sands, where we lads of the
burgh* school loved to bathe in the warm weather. But on
long holidays the sport was to go farther afield among the
cliffs; for there there were many deep caves and pools, where
podleys* might be caught with the line, and hid treasures
sought for at the expense of the skin of the knees and the
buttons of the trousers. Many a long Saturday I have passed
in a crinkle of the cliffs, having lit a fire of driftwood, and
made believe that I was a smuggler or a Jacobite new landed
from France. There was a band of us in Kirkcaple, lads of my
own age, including Archie Leslie, the son of my father's
session-clerk,* and Tam Dyke, the provost's* nephew. We
were sealed to silence by the blood oath, and we bore each the
name of some historic pirate or sailorman. I was Paul Jones,
Tam was Captain Kidd, and Archie, need I say it, was Morgan
himself. Our tryst was a cave where a little water called the
Dyve Burn had cut its way through the cliffs to the sea. There

we forgathered in the summer evenings and of a Saturday afternoon in winter, and told mighty tales of our prowess and flattered our silly hearts. But the sober truth is that our deeds were of the humblest, and a dozen of fish or a handful of apples was all our booty, and our greatest exploit a fight with the roughs at the Dyve tan-work.*

My father's spring Communion fell on the last Sabbath of April, and on the particular Sabbath of which I speak the weather was mild and bright for the time of year. I had been surfeited with the Thursday's and Saturday's services, and the two long diets of worship on the Sabbath were hard for a lad of twelve to bear with the spring in his bones and the sun slanting through the gallery window. There still remained the service on the Sabbath evening—a doleful prospect, for the Rev. Mr Murdoch of Kilchristie, noted for the length of his discourses, had exchanged pulpits with my father. So my mind was ripe for the proposal of Archie Leslie, on our way home to tea, that by a little skill we might give the kirk the slip. At our Communion the pews were emptied of their regular occupants and the congregation seated itself as it pleased. The manse seat was full of the Kirkcaple relations of Mr Murdoch, who had been invited there by my mother to hear him, and it was not hard to obtain permission to sit with Archie and Tam Dyke in the cock-loft* in the gallery. Word was sent to Tam, and so it happened that three abandoned lads duly passed the plate* and took their seats in the cock-loft. But when the bell had done jowing,* and we heard by the sounds of their feet that the elders had gone in* to the kirk, we slipped down the stairs and out of the side door. We were through the churchyard in a twinkling, and hot-foot on the road to the Dyve Burn.

It was the fashion of the genteel in Kirkcaple to put their boys into what were known as Eton suits—long trousers, cut-away jackets, and chimney-pot hats. I had been one of the earliest victims, and well I remember how I fled home from the Sabbath school with the snowballs of the town roughs rattling off my chimney-pot. Archie had followed, his family being in all things imitators of mine. We were now clothed in this wearisome garb, so our first care was to secrete safely our hats in a marked spot under some whin bushes on the links.

Tam was free from the bondage of fashion, and wore his ordinary best knickerbockers. From inside his jacket he unfolded his special treasure, which was to light us on our expedition—an evil-smelling old tin lantern with a shutter.

Tam was of the Free Kirk* persuasion, and as his Communion fell on a different day from ours, he was spared the bondage of church attendance from which Archie and I had revolted. But notable events had happened that day in his church. A black man, the Rev. John Something-or-other, had been preaching. Tam was full of the portent. 'A nigger,' he said, 'a great black chap as big as your father, Archie.' He seemed to have banged the bookboard with some effect, and had kept Tam, for once in his life, awake. He had preached about the heathen in Africa, and how a black man was as good as a white man in the sight of God, and he had forecast a day when the negroes would have something to teach the British in the way of civilization. So at any rate ran the account of Tam Dyke, who did not share the preacher's views. 'It's all nonsense, Davie. The Bible says* that the children of Ham were to be our servants. If I were the minister I wouldn't let a nigger* into the pulpit. I wouldn't let him farther than the Sabbath school.'

Night fell as we came to the broomy spaces of the links, and ere we had breasted the slope of the neck which separates Kirkcaple Bay from the cliffs it was as dark as an April evening with a full moon can be. Tam would have had it darker. He got out his lantern, and after a prodigious waste of matches kindled the candle-end inside, turned the dark shutter, and trotted happily on. We had no need of his lighting till the Dyve Burn was reached and the path began to descend steeply through the rift in the crags.

It was here we found that some one had gone before us. Archie was great in those days at tracking, his ambition running in Indian paths. He would walk always with his head bent and his eyes on the ground, whereby he several times found lost coins and once a trinket dropped by the provost's wife. At the edge of the burn, where the path turns downward, there is a patch of shingle washed up by some spate. Archie was on his knees in a second. 'Lads,' he cried, 'there's spoor here;' and then after some nosing, 'it's a man's track, going downward, a big man with flat feet. It's fresh, too, for it crosses the damp bit of gravel, and the water has scarcely filled the holes yet.'

We did not dare to question Archie's woodcraft, but it puzzled us who the stranger could be. In summer weather you might find a party of picnickers here, attracted by the fine hard sands at the burn mouth. But at this time of night and season of the year there was no call for any one to be trespassing on our preserves. No fishermen came this way, the lobster-pots being all to the east, and the stark headland of the Red Neb made the road to them by the water's edge difficult. The tan-work lads used to come now and then for a swim, but you would not find a tan-work lad bathing on a chill April night. Yet there was no question where our precursor had gone. He was making for the shore. Tam unshuttered his lantern, and the steps went clearly down the corkscrew path. 'Maybe he is after our cave. We'd better go cannily.'

The glim was dowsed*—the words were Archie's—and in the best contraband manner we stole down the gully. The business had suddenly taken an eerie turn, and I think in our hearts we were all a little afraid. But Tam had a lantern, and it would never do to turn back from an adventure which had all the appearance of being the true sort. Half way down there is a scrog* of wood, dwarf alders and hawthorn, which makes an arch over the path. I, for one, was glad when we got through this with no worse mishap than a stumble from Tam which caused the lantern door to fly open and the candle to go out. We did not stop to relight it, but scrambled down the screes till we came to the long slabs of reddish rock which abutted on the beach. We could not see the track, so we gave up the business of scouts, and dropped quietly over the big boulder and into the crinkle of cliff which we called our cave.

There was nobody there, so we relit the lantern and examined our properties. Two or three fishing-rods for the burn, much damaged by weather; some sea-lines on a dry shelf of rock; a couple of wooden boxes; a pile of driftwood for fires, and a heap of quartz in which we thought we had found veins of gold—such was the modest furnishing of our den. To this I must add some broken clay pipes, with which we made believe to imitate our elders, smoking a foul mixture of coltsfoot leaves and brown paper. The band was in session, so following our ritual we sent out a picket. Tam was deputed to go round the edge of the cliff from which the shore was visible, and report if the coast was clear.

He returned in three minutes, his eyes round with amazement in the lantern light. 'There's a fire on the sands,' he repeated, 'and a man beside it.'

Here was news indeed. Without a word we made for the open, Archie first, and Tam, who had seized and shuttered his lantern, coming last. We crawled to the edge of the cliff and peered round, and there sure enough, on the hard bit of sand which the tide had left by the burn mouth, was a twinkle of light and a dark figure.

The moon was rising, and besides there was that curious sheen from the sea which you will often notice in spring. The glow was maybe a hundred yards distant, a little spark of fire I could have put in my cap, and, from its crackling and smoke, composed of dry seaweed and half-green branches from the burnside thickets. A man's figure stood near it, and as we looked it moved round and round the fire in circles which first of all widened and then contracted.*

The sight was so unexpected, so beyond the beat of our experience, that we were all a little scared. What could this strange being want with a fire at half-past eight of an April Sabbath night on the Dyve Burn sands? We discussed the thing in whispers behind a boulder, but none of us had any solution. 'Belike he's come ashore in a boat,' said Archie. 'He's maybe a foreigner.' But I pointed out that, from the tracks which Archie himself had found, the man must have come overland down the cliffs. Tam was clear he was a madman, and was for withdrawing promptly from the whole business.

But some spell kept our feet tied there in that silent world of sand and moon and sea. I remember looking back and seeing the solemn, frowning faces of the cliffs, and feeling somehow shut in with this unknown being in a strange union. What kind of errand had brought this interloper into our territory? For a wonder I was less afraid than curious. I wanted to get to the heart of the matter, and to discover what the man was up to with his fire and his circles.

The same thought must have been in Archie's head, for he dropped on his belly and began to crawl softly seawards. I followed, and Tam, with sundry complaints, crept after my heels. Between the cliffs and the fire lay some sixty yards of *débris* and boulders above the level of all but the high spring tides. Beyond lay a string of seaweedy pools and then the hard sands of the burnfoot. There was excellent cover among the big stones, and apart from the distance and the dim light, the man by the fire was too preoccupied in his task to keep much look-out towards the land. I remember thinking he had chosen his place well, for save from the sea he could not be seen. The cliffs are so undercut that unless a watcher on the coast were on their extreme edge he would not see the burnfoot sands.

Archie, the skilled tracker, was the one who all but betrayed us. His knee slipped on the seaweed, and he rolled off a boulder, bringing down with him a clatter of small stones. We lay as still as mice, in terror lest the man should have heard the noise and have come to look for the cause. By-and-by when I ventured to raise my head above a flat-topped stone I saw that he was undisturbed. The fire still burned, and he was pacing round it.

On the edge of the pools was an outcrop of red sandstone much fissured by the sea. Here was an excellent vantage-ground, and all three of us curled behind it, with our eyes just over the edge. The man was not twenty yards off, and I could see clearly what manner of fellow he was. For one thing he was huge of size, or so he seemed to me in the half-light. He wore nothing but a shirt and trousers, and I could hear by the flap of his feet on the sand that he was barefoot.

Suddenly Tam Dyke gave a gasp of astonishment. 'Gosh, it's the black minister!' he said.

It was indeed a black man, as we saw when the moon came out of a cloud. His head was on his breast, and he walked round the fire with measured, regular steps. At intervals he would stop and raise both hands to the sky, and bend his body in the direction of the moon. But he never uttered a word.

'It's magic,' said Archie. 'He's going to raise Satan. We must bide here and see what happens, for he'll grip us if we try to go back. The moon's ower high.'

The procession continued as if to some slow music. I had been in no fear of the adventure back there by our cave; but now that I saw the thing from close at hand, my courage began to ebb. There was something desperately uncanny about this great negro, who had shed his clerical garments, and was now practising some strange magic alone by the sea. I had no doubt it was the black art, for there was that in the air and the scene which spelled the unlawful. As we watched, the circles stopped, and the man threw something on the fire. A thick smoke rose of which we could feel the aromatic scent, and when it was gone the flame burned with a silvery blueness like moonlight. Still no sound came from the minister, but he took something from his belt, and began to make odd markings in the sand between the inner cricle and the fire. As he turned, the moon gleamed on the implement, and we saw it was a great knife.

We were now scared in real earnest. Here were we, three boys, at night in a lonely place a few yards from a savage with a knife. The adventure was far past my liking, and even the intrepid Archie was having qualms, if I could judge from his set face. As for Tam, his teeth were chattering like a threshing-mill.

Suddenly I felt something soft and warm on the rock at my right hand. I felt again, and, lo! it was the man's clothes. There were his boots and socks, his minister's coat and his minister's hat.*

This made the predicament worse, for if we waited till he finished his rites we should for certain be found by him. At the same time, to return over the boulders in the bright moonlight seemed an equally sure way to discovery. I whispered to Archie, who was for waiting a little longer. 'Something may turn up,' he said. It was always his way.

I do not know what would have turned up, for we had no chance of testing it. The situation had proved too much for the nerves of Tam Dyke. As the man turned towards us in his bowings and bendings, Tam suddenly sprang to his feet and shouted at him a piece of schoolboy rudeness then fashionable in Kirkcaple.

'Wha called ye partan-face, my bonny lamb?'* Then, clutching his lantern, he ran for dear life, while Archie and I raced at his heels. As I turned I had a glimpse of a huge figure, knife in hand, bounding towards us.

Though I only saw it in the turn of a head, the face stamped itself indelibly upon my mind. It was black, black as ebony, but it was different from the ordinary negro. There were no thick lips and flat nostrils; rather, if I could trust my eyes, the nose was high-bridged, and the lines of the mouth sharp and firm. But it was distorted into an expression of such a devilish fury and amazement that my heart became like water.

We had a start, as I have said, of some twenty or thirty yards. Among the boulders we were not at a great disadvantage, for a boy can flit quickly over them, while a grown man must pick his way. Archie, as ever, kept his wits the best of us. 'Make straight for the burn,' he shouted in a hoarse whisper; 'we'll beat him on the slope.'

We passed the boulders and slithered over the outcrop of red rock and the patches of sea-pink till we reached the channel of the Dyve water, which flows gently among pebbles after leaving the gully. Here for the first time I looked back and saw nothing. I stopped involuntarily, and that halt was nearly my undoing. For our pursuer had reached the burn before us, but lower down, and was coming up its bank to cut us off.

At most times I am a notable coward, and in these days I was still more of one, owing to a quick and easily-heated imagination. But now I think I did a brave thing, though more by instinct than resolution. Archie was running first, and had already splashed through the burn; Tam came next, just about to cross, and the black man was almost at his elbow. Another second and Tam would have been in his clutches had I not yelled out a warning and made straight up the bank of the burn. Tam fell into the pool—I could hear his spluttering cry—but he got across; for I heard Archie call to him, and the two vanished into the thicket which clothes all the left bank of the gully. The pursuer, seeing me on his own side of the water, followed straight on; and before I knew it had become a race between the two of us.

I was hideously frightened, but not without hope, for the screes and shelves of this right side of the gully were known to me from many a day's exploring. I was light on my feet and uncommonly sound in wind, being by far the best long-distance runner in Kirkcaple. If I could only keep my lead till I reached a certain corner I knew of, I could outwit my enemy; for it was possible from that place to make a detour behind a waterfall and get into a secret path of ours among the bushes. I flew up the steep screes, not daring to look round; but at the top, where the rocks begin, I had a glimpse of my pursuer. The man could run. Heavy in build though he was he was not six yards behind me, and I could see the white of his eyes and the red of his gums. I saw something else—a glint of white metal in his hand. He still had his knife.

Fear sent me up the rocks like a seagull, and I scrambled and leaped, making for the corner I knew of. Something told me that the pursuit was slackening, and for a moment I halted to look round. A second time a halt was nearly the end of me. A great stone flew through the air, and took the cliff an inch from my head, half-blinding me with splinters. And now I began to get angry. I pulled myself into cover, skirted a rock till I came to my corner, and looked back for the enemy. There he was scrambling by the way I had come, and making a prodigious clatter among the stones. I picked up a loose bit of rock and hurled it with all my force in his direction. It broke before it reached him, but a considerable lump, to my joy, took him full in the face. Then my terrors revived. I slipped behind the waterfall and was soon in the thicket, and toiling towards the top.

I think this last bit was the worst in the race, for my strength was failing, and I seemed to hear those horrid steps at my heels. My heart was in my mouth as, careless of my best clothes, I tore through the hawthorn bushes. Then I struck the path and, to my relief, came on Archie and Tam, who were running slowly in desperate anxiety about my fate. We then took hands and soon reached the top of the gully.

For a second we looked back. The pursuit had ceased, and

far down the burn we could hear the sounds as of some one going back to the sands.

'Your face is bleeding, Davie. Did he get near enough to hit you?' Archie asked.

'He hit me with a stone. But I gave him better. He's got a bleeding nose to remember this night by.'

We did not dare take the road by the links,* but made for the nearest human habitation. This was a farm about half a mile inland, and when we reached it we lay down by the stack-yard gate and panted.

'I've lost my lantern,' said Tam. 'The big black brute! See if I don't tell my father.'

'Ye'll do nothing of the kind,' said Archie fiercely. 'He knows nothing about us and can't do us any harm. But if the story got out and he found out who we were, he'd murder the lot of us.'

He made us swear secrecy, which we were willing enough to do, seeing very clearly the sense in his argument. Then we struck the highroad and trotted back at our best pace to Kirkcaple, fear of our families gradually ousting fear of pursuit. In our excitement Archie and I forgot about our Sabbath hats, reposing quietly below a whin bush on the links.

We were not destined to escape without detection. As ill luck would have it, Mr Murdoch had been taken ill with the stomach-ache after the second psalm, and the congregation had been abruptly dispersed. My mother had waited for me at the church door, and, seeing no signs of her son, had searched the gallery. Then the truth came out, and, had I been only for a mild walk on the links, retribution would have overtaken my truantry. But to add to this I arrived home with a scratched face, no hat, and several rents in my best trousers. I was well cuffed and sent to bed, with the promise of full-dress chastisement when my father should come home in the morning.

My father arrived before breakfast next day, and I was duly and soundly whipped. I set out for school with aching bones to add to the usual depression of Monday morning. At the corner of the Nethergate I fell in with Archie, who was staring at a trap carrying two men which was coming down the street. It was the Free Church minister—he had married a rich wife

and kept a horse—driving the preacher of yesterday to the
railway station. Archie and I were in behind a doorpost in a
twinkling, so that we could see in safety the last of our enemy.
He was dressed in minister's clothes, with a heavy fur-coat and
a brand new yellow-leather Gladstone bag. He was talking
loudly as he passed, and the Free Church minister seemed to
be listening attentively. I heard his deep voice saying something about the 'work of God in this place.' But what I noticed
specially—and the sight made me forget my aching hinder
parts—was that he had a swollen eye, and two strips of
sticking-plaster on his cheek.

# CHAPTER II

## FURTH! FORTUNE!*

IN this plain story of mine there will be so many wild doings ere the end is reached, that I beg my reader's assent to a prosaic digression. I will tell briefly the things which happened between my sight of the man on the Kirkcaple sands and my voyage to Africa.

I continued for three years at the burgh school, where my progress was less notable in my studies than in my sports. One by one I saw my companions pass out of idle boyhood and be set to professions. Tam Dyke on two occasions ran off to sea in the Dutch schooners which used to load with coal in our port; and finally his father gave him his will, and he was apprenticed to the merchant service. Archie Leslie, who was a year my elder, was destined for the law, so he left Kirkcaple for an Edinburgh office, where he was also to take out classes at the college. I remained on at school till I sat alone by myself in the highest class—a position of little dignity and deep loneliness. I had grown a tall, square-set lad, and my prowess at Rugby football was renowned beyond the parishes of Kirkcaple and Portincross. To my father I fear I was a disappointment. He had hoped for something in his son more bookish and sedentary, more like his gentle, studious self.

On one thing I was determined: I should follow a learned profession. The fear of being sent to an office, like so many of my schoolfellows, inspired me to the little progress I ever made in my studies. I chose the ministry, not, I fear, out of any reverence for the sacred calling, but because my father had followed it before me. Accordingly I was sent at the age of sixteen for a year's finishing at the High School of Edinburgh, and the following winter began my Arts course at the university.

If Fate had been kinder to me, I think I might have become a scholar.* At any rate I was just acquiring a taste for philosophy and the dead languages when my father died suddenly of a paralytic stroke, and I had to set about earning a living.

My mother was left badly off, for my poor father had never been able to save much from his modest stipend. When all things were settled, it turned out that she might reckon on an income of about fifty pounds a year. This was not enough to live on, however modest the household, and certainly not enough to pay for the colleging of a son. At this point an uncle of hers stepped forward with a proposal. He was a well-to-do bachelor, alone in the world, and he invited my mother to live with him and take care of his house. For myself he proposed a post in some mercantile concern, for he had much influence in the circles of commerce. There was nothing for it but to accept gratefully. We sold our few household goods, and moved to his gloomy house in Dundas Street. A few days later he announced at dinner that he had found for me a chance which might lead to better things.

'You see, Davie,' he explained, 'you don't know the rudiments of business life. There's no house in the country that would take you in except as a common clerk, and you would never earn much more than a hundred pounds a year all your days. If you want to better your future you must go abroad, where white men are at a premium. By the mercy of Providence I met yesterday an old friend, Thomas Mackenzie, who was seeing his lawyer about an estate he is bidding for. He is the head of one of the biggest trading and shipping concerns in the world—Mackenzie, Mure, and Oldmeadows—you may have heard the name. Among other things he has half the stores in South Africa, where they sell everything from Bibles to fish-hooks. Apparently they like men from home to manage the stores, and to make a long story short, when I put your case to him, he promised you a place. I had a wire from him this morning confirming the offer. You are to be assistant storekeeper at—' (my uncle fumbled in his pocket, and then read from the yellow slip) 'at Blaauwildebeestefontein. There's a mouthful for you.'

In this homely way I first heard of a place which was to be the theatre of so many strange doings.

'It's a fine chance for you,' my uncle continued. 'You'll only be assistant at first, but when you have learned your job you'll have a store of your own. Mackenzie's people will pay you three hundred pounds a year, and when you get a store you'll get a percentage on sales. It lies with you to open up new trade among the natives. I hear that Blaauw—something or other, is in the far north of the Transvaal, and I see from the map that it is in a wild, hilly country. You may find gold or diamonds up there, and come back and buy Portincross House.'* My uncle rubbed his hands and smiled cheerily.

Truth to tell I was both pleased and sad. If a learned profession was denied me I vastly preferred a veld store to an Edinburgh office stool. Had I not been still under the shadow of my father's death I might have welcomed the chance of new lands and new folk. As it was, I felt the loneliness of an exile. That afternoon I walked on the Braid Hills, and when I saw in the clear spring sunlight the coast of Fife, and remembered Kirkcaple and my boyish days, I could have found it in me to sit down and cry.

A fortnight later I sailed. My mother bade me a tearful farewell, and my uncle, besides buying me an outfit and paying my passage money, gave me a present of twenty sovereigns. 'You'll not be your mother's son, Davie,' were his last words, 'if you don't come home with it multiplied by a thousand.' I thought at the time that I would give more than twenty thousand pounds to be allowed to bide on the windy shores of Forth.

I sailed from Southampton by an intermediate steamer, and went steerage to save expense. Happily my acute homesickness was soon forgotten in another kind of malady. It blew half a gale before we were out of the Channel, and by the time we had rounded Ushant it was as dirty weather as ever I hope to see. I lay mortal sick in my bunk, unable to bear the thought of food, and too feeble to lift my head. I wished I had never left home, but so acute was my sickness that if some one had there and then offered me a passage back or an immediate landing on shore I should have chosen the latter.

It was not till we got into the fair-weather seas around Madeira that I recovered enough to sit on deck and observe my fellow-passengers. There were some fifty of us in the steerage, mostly wives and children going to join relations, with a few emigrant artisans and farmers. I early found a friend in a little man with a yellow beard and spectacles, who sat down beside me and remarked on the weather in a strong Scotch accent. He turned out to be a Mr Wardlaw from Aberdeen, who was going out to be a schoolmaster. He was a man of good education, who had taken a university degree, and had taught for some years as an under-master in a school in his native town. But the east winds had damaged his lungs, and he had been glad to take the chance of a poorly paid country school in the veld. When I asked him where he was going I was amazed to be told, 'Blaauwildebeestefontein.'

Mr Wardlaw was a pleasant little man, with a sharp tongue but a cheerful temper. He laboured all day at primers of the Dutch and Kaffir* languages, but in the evening after supper he would walk with me on the after-deck and discuss the future. Like me, he knew nothing of the land he was going to, but he was insatiably curious, and he affected me with his interest. 'This place, Blaauwildebeestefontein,' he used to say, 'is among the Zoutpansberg mountains,* and as far as I can see, not above ninety miles from the railroad. It looks from the map a well-watered country, and the Agent-General in London told me it was healthy or I wouldn't have taken the job. It seems we'll be in the heart of native reserves up there, for here's a list of chiefs—'Mpefu, Sikitola, Majinje, Magata;* and there are no white men living to the east of us because of the fever.* The name means the 'spring of the blue wildebeeste,' whatever fearsome animal that may be. It sounds like a place for adventure, Mr Crawfurd. You'll exploit the pockets of the black men and I'll see what I can do with their minds.'

There was another steerage passenger whom I could not help observing because of my dislike of his appearance. He, too, was a little man, by name Henriques, and in looks the most atrocious villain I have ever clapped eyes on. He had a face the colour of French mustard—a sort of dirty green—and bloodshot, beady eyes with the whites all yellowed with fever. He had waxed moustaches, and a curious, furtive way of walking and looking about him. We of the steerage were careless in our dress, but he was always clad in immaculate white linen, with pointed, yellow shoes to match his complexion. He spoke to no one, but smoked long cheroots all day in the stern of the ship, and studied a greasy pocket-book. Once I tripped over him in the dark, and he turned on me with a snarl and an oath. I was short enough with him in return, and he looked as if he could knife me.

'I'll wager that fellow has been a slave-driver in his time,' I told Mr Wardlaw, who said, 'God pity his slaves, then.'

And now I come to the incident which made the rest of the voyage pass all too soon for me, and foreshadowed the strange events which were to come. It was the day after we crossed the Line, and the first-class passengers were having deck sports. A tug-of-war had been arranged between the three classes, and a half-dozen of the heaviest fellows in the steerage, myself included, were invited to join. It was a blazing hot afternoon, but on the saloon deck there were awnings and a cool wind blowing from the bows. The first-class beat the second easily, and after a tremendous struggle beat the steerage also. Then they regaled us with iced-drinks and cigars to celebrate the victory.

I was standing at the edge of the crowd of spectators, when my eye caught a figure which seemed to have little interest in our games. A large man in clerical clothes was sitting on a deck-chair reading a book. There was nothing novel about the stranger, and I cannot explain the impulse which made me wish to see his face. I moved a few steps up the deck, and then I saw that his skin was black. I went a little farther, and suddenly he raised his eyes from his book and looked round. It was the face of the man who had terrified me years ago on the Kirkcaple shore.

I spent the rest of the day in a brown study. It was clear to me that some destiny had prearranged this meeting. Here was this man travelling prosperously as a first-class passenger with all the appurtenances of respectability. I alone had seen him invoking strange gods in the moonlight, I alone knew of the devilry in his heart, and I could not but believe that some day or other there might be virtue in that knowledge.

The second engineer and I had made friends, so I got him

to consult the purser's list for the name of my acquaintance. He was down as the Rev. John Laputa,* and his destination was Durban.

The next day being Sunday, who should appear to address us steerage passengers but the black minister. He was introduced by the captain himself, a notably pious man, who spoke of the labours of his brother in the dark places of heathendom. Some of us were hurt in our pride in being made the target of a black man's oratory. Especially Mr Henriques, whose skin spoke of the tar-brush, protested with oaths against the insult. Finally he sat down on a coil of rope, and spat scornfully in the vicinity of the preacher.

For myself I was intensely curious, and not a little impressed. The man's face was as commanding as his figure, and his voice was the most wonderful thing that ever came out of human mouth. It was full and rich, and gentle, with the tones of a great organ. He had none of the squat and preposterous negro lineaments, but a hawk nose like an Arab, dark flashing eyes, and a cruel and resolute mouth. He was black as my hat, but for the rest he might have sat for a figure of a Crusader. I do not know what the sermon was about, though others told me that it was excellent. All the time I watched him, and kept saying to myself, 'You hunted me up the Dyve Burn, but I bashed your face for you.' Indeed, I thought I could see faint scars on his cheek.

The following night I had toothache, and could not sleep. It was too hot to breathe under cover, so I got up, lit a pipe, and walked on the after-deck to ease the pain. The air was very still, save for the whish of water from the screws and the steady beat of the engines. Above, a great yellow moon looked down on me, and a host of pale stars.

The moonlight set me remembering the old affair of the Dyve Burn, and my mind began to run on the Rev. John Laputa. It pleased me to think that I was on the track of some mystery of which I alone had the clue. I promised myself to search out the antecedents of the minister when I got to Durban, for I had a married cousin there, who might know something of his doings. Then, as I passed by the companion-way to the lower deck, I heard voices, and peeping over the rail, I saw two men sitting in the shadow just beyond the hatch of the hold.

I thought they might be two of the sailors seeking coolness on the open deck, when something in the figure of one of them made me look again. The next second I had slipped back and stolen across the after-deck to a point just above them. For the two were the black minister and that ugly yellow villain, Henriques.

I had no scruples about eavesdropping, but I could make nothing of their talk. They spoke low, and in some tongue which may have been Kaffir or Portuguese, but was in any case unknown to me. I lay, cramped and eager, for many minutes, and was just getting sick of it when a familiar name caught my ear. Henriques said something in which I caught the word 'Blaauwildebeestefontein.' I listened intently, and there could be no mistake. The minister repeated the name, and for the next few minutes it recurred often in their talk. I went back stealthily to bed, having something to make me forget my aching tooth. First of all, Laputa and Henriques were allies. Second, the place I was bound for had something to do with their schemes.

I said nothing to Mr Wardlaw, but spent the next week in the assiduous toil of the amateur detective. I procured some maps and books from my friend, the second engineer, and read all I could about Blaauwildebeestefontein. Not that there was much to learn; but I remember I had quite a thrill when I discovered from the chart of the ship's run one day that we were in the same latitude as that uncouthly-named spot. I found out nothing, however, about Henriques or the Rev. John Laputa. The Portuguese still smoked in the stern, and thumbed his greasy notebook; the minister sat in his deck-chair, and read heavy volumes from the ship's library. Though I watched every night, I never found them again together.

At Cape Town Henriques went ashore and did not return. The minister did not budge from the ship the three days we lay in port, and, indeed, it seemed to me that he kept his cabin. At any rate I did not see his great figure on deck till we were tossing in the choppy seas round Cape Agulhas. Sea-

sickness again attacked me, and with short lulls during our
stoppages at Port Elizabeth and East London, I lay wretchedly
in my bunk till we sighted the bluffs of Durban harbour.

Here it was necessary for me to change my ship, for in the
interests of economy I was going by sea to Delagoa Bay, and
thence by the cheap railway journey into the Transvaal. I
sought out my cousin, who lived in a fine house on the Berea,
and found a comfortable lodging for the three days of my stay
there. I made inquiries about Mr Laputa, but could hear
nothing. There was no native minister of that name, said my
cousin, who was a great authority on all native questions. I
described the man, but got no further light. No one had seen
or heard of such a being, 'unless,' said my cousin, 'he is one of
those American Ethiopian* rascals.'

My second task was to see the Durban manager of the firm
which I had undertaken to serve. He was a certain Mr Colles,
a big fat man, who welcomed me in his shirt-sleeves, with a
cigar in his mouth. He received me pleasantly, and took me
home to dinner with him.

'Mr Mackenzie has written about you,' he said. 'I'll be quite
frank with you, Mr Crawfurd. The firm is not exactly satisfied
about the way business has been going lately at Blaauwildebeestefontein. There's a grand country up there, and a grand
opportunity for the man who can take it. Japp, who is in
charge, is an old man now and past his best, but he has been
long with the firm, and we don't want to hurt his feelings.
When he goes, which must be pretty soon, you'll have a good
chance of the place, if you show yourself an active young
fellow.'

He told me a great deal more about Blaauwildebeestefontein,
principally trading details. Incidentally he let drop that Mr
Japp had had several assistants in the last few years. I asked
him why they had left, and he hesitated.

'It's a lonely place, and they didn't like the life. You see,
there are few white men near, and young fellows want society.
They complained, and were moved on. But the firm didn't
think the more of them.'

I told him I had come out with the new schoolmaster.

'Yes,' he said reflectively, 'the school. That's been vacant pretty often lately. What sort of fellow is this Wardlaw? Will he stay, I wonder?'

'From all accounts,' I said, 'Blaauwildebeestefontein does not seem popular.'

'It isn't. That's why we've got you out from home. The colonial-born doesn't find it fit in with his idea of comfort. He wants society, and he doesn't like too many natives. There's nothing up there but natives and a few back-veld Dutchmen with native blood in them. You fellows from home are less set on an easy life, or you wouldn't be here.'

There was something in Mr Colles's tone which made me risk another question.

'What's the matter with the place? There must be more wrong with it than loneliness to make everybody clear out. I have taken on this job, and I mean to stick to it, so you needn't be afraid to tell me.'

The manager looked at me sharply. 'That's the way to talk, my lad. You look as if you had a stiff back, so I'll be frank with you. There *is* something about the place. It gives the ordinary man the jumps. What it is, I don't know, and the men who come back don't know themselves. I want you to find out for me. You'll be doing the firm an enormous service if you can get on the track of it. It may be the natives, or it may be the *takhaars*,* or it may be something else. Only old Japp can stick it out, and he's too old and doddering to care about moving. I want you to keep your eyes skinned, and write privately to me if you want any help. You're not out here for your health, I can see, and here's a chance for you to get your foot on the ladder.

'Remember, I'm your friend,' he said to me again at the garden gate. 'Take my advice and lie very low. Don't talk, don't meddle with drink, learn all you can of the native jabber, but don't let on you understand a word. You're sure to get on the track of something. Good-bye, my boy,' and he waved a fat hand to me.

That night I embarked on a cargo-boat which was going round the coast to Delagoa Bay. It is a small world—at least for us far-wandering Scots. For who should I find when I got

on board but my old friend Tam Dyke, who was second mate
on the vessel? We wrung each other's hands, and I answered,
as best I could, his questions about Kirkcaple. I had supper
with him in the cabin, and went on deck to see the moorings
cast.

Suddenly there was a bustle on the quay, and a big man
with a handbag forced his way up the gangway. The men who
were getting ready to cast off tried to stop him, but he elbowed
his way forward, declaring he must see the captain. Tam went
up to him and asked civilly if he had a passage taken. He
admitted he had not, but said he would make it right in two
minutes with the captain himself. The Rev. John Laputa, for
some reason of his own, was leaving Durban with more haste
than he had entered it.

I do not know what passed with the captain, but the minister
got his passage right enough, and Tam was even turned out of
his cabin to make room for him. This annoyed my friend
intensely.

'That black brute must be made of money, for he paid
through the nose for this, or I'm a Dutchman. My old man
doesn't take to his black brethren any more than I do. Hang it
all, what are we coming to, when we're turning into a blooming
cargo boat for niggers?'

I had all too little of Tam's good company, for on the
afternoon of the second day we reached the little town of
Lourenço Marques. This was my final landing in Africa, and I
mind how eagerly I looked at the low, green shores and the
bush-covered slopes of the mainland. We were landed from
boats while the ship lay out in the bay, and Tam came ashore
with me to spend the evening. By this time I had lost every
remnant of homesickness. I had got a job before me which
promised better things than colleging at Edinburgh, and I was
as keen to get up country now as I had been loth to leave
England. My mind being full of mysteries, I scanned every
Portuguese loafer on the quay as if he had been a spy, and
when Tam and I had had a bottle of Collares in a café I felt
that at last I had got to foreign parts and a new world.

Tam took me to supper with a friend of his, a Scot by the
name of Aitken, who was landing-agent for some big mining

house on the Rand. He hailed from Fife and gave me a hearty welcome, for he had heard my father preach in his young days. Aitken was a strong, broad-shouldered fellow who had been a sergeant in the Gordons, and during the war* he had done secret-service work in Delagoa. He had hunted, too, and traded up and down Mozambique, and knew every dialect of the Kaffirs. He asked me where I was bound for, and when I told him there was the same look in his eyes as I had seen with the Durban manager.

'You're going to a rum place, Mr Crawfurd,' he said.

'So I'm told. Do you know anything about it? You're not the first who has looked queer when I've spoken the name.'

'I've never been there,' he said, 'though I've been pretty near it from the Portuguese side. That's the funny thing about Blaauwildebeestefontein. Everybody has heard of it, and nobody knows it.'

'I wish you would tell me what you have heard.'

'Well, the natives are queer up thereaways. There's some kind of a holy place which every Kaffir from Algoa Bay to the Zambesi and away beyond knows about. When I've been hunting in the bush-veld I've often met strings of Kaffirs from hundreds of miles distant, and they've all been going or coming from Blaauwildebeestefontein. It's like Mecca to the Mohammedans, a place they go to on pilgrimage. I've heard of an old man up there who is believed to be two hundred years old. Anyway, there's some sort of great witch or wizard living in the mountains.'

Aitken smoked in silence for a time; then he said, 'I'll tell you another thing. I believe there's a diamond mine. I've often meant to go up and look for it.'

Tam and I pressed him to explain, which he did slowly after his fashion.

'Did you ever hear of I.D.B.—illict diamond broking?' he asked me. 'Well, it's notorious that the Kaffirs on the diamond fields get away with a fair number of stones, and they are bought by Jew and Portuguese traders. It's against the law to deal in them, and when I was in the intelligence here we used to have a lot of trouble with the vermin.* But I discovered that most of the stones came from natives in one part of the

country—more or less round Blaauwildebeestefontein—and I
see no reason to think that they had all been stolen from
Kimberley or the Premier. Indeed some of the stones I got
hold of were quite different from any I had seen in South
Africa before. I shouldn't wonder if the Kaffirs in the Zoutpansberg had struck some rich pipe, and had the sense to keep
quiet about it. Maybe some day I'll take a run up to see you
and look into the matter.'

After this the talk turned on other topics till Tam, still
nursing his grievance, asked a question on his own account.

'Did you ever come across a great big native parson called
Laputa? He came on board as we were leaving Durban, and I
had to turn out of my cabin for him.' Tam described him
accurately but vindictively, and added that 'he was sure he was
up to no good.'

Aitken shook his head. 'No, I don't know the man. You say
he landed here? Well, I'll keep a look-out for him. Big native
parsons are not so common.'

Then I asked about Henriques, of whom Tam knew nothing. I described his face, his clothes, and his habits. Aitken
laughed uproariously.

'Tut, my man, most of the subjects of his Majesty the King
of Portugal would answer to that description. If he's a rascal,
as you think, you may be certain he's in the I.D.B. business,
and if I'm right about Blaauwildebeestefontein you'll likely
have news of him there some time or other. Drop me a line if
he comes, and I'll get on to his record.'

I saw Tam off in the boat with a fairly satisfied mind. I was
going to a place with a secret, and I meant to find it out. The
natives round Blaauwildebeestefontein were queer, and diamonds were suspected somewhere in the neighbourhood.
Henriques had something to do with the place, and so had the
Rev. John Laputa, about whom I knew one strange thing. So
did Tam by the way, but he had not identified his former
pursuer, and I had told him nothing. I was leaving two men
behind me, Colles at Durban and Aitken at Lourenço Marques, who would help me if trouble came. Things were shaping
well for some kind of adventure.

The talk with Aitken had given Tam an inkling of my

thoughts. His last words to me were an appeal to let him know if there was any fun going.

'I can see you're in for a queer job. Promise to let me hear from you if there's going to be a row, and I'll come up country, though I should have to desert the service. Send us a letter to the agents at Durban in case we should be in port. You haven't forgotten the Dyve Burn, Davie?'

# CHAPTER III

## BLAAUWILDEBEESTEFONTEIN

THE *Pilgrim's Progress*\* had been the Sabbath reading of my boyood, and as I came in sight of Blaauwildebeestefontein a passage ran in my head. It was that which tells how Christian and Hopeful, after many perils of the way, came to the Delectable Mountains, from which they had a prospect of Canaan.\* After many dusty miles by rail, and a weariful journey in a Cape-cart through arid plains and dry and stony gorges, I had come suddenly into a haven of green. The Spring of the Blue Wildebeeste was a clear rushing mountain torrent, which swirled over blue rocks into deep fern-fringed pools. All around was a tableland of lush grass with marigolds and arum lilies instead of daisies and buttercups. Thickets of tall trees dotted the hill slopes and patched the meadows as if some landscape-gardener had been at work on them. Beyond, the glen fell steeply to the plains, which ran out in a faint haze to the horizon. To north and south I marked the sweep of the Berg, now rising high to a rocky peak and now stretching in a level rampart of blue. On the very edge of the plateau where the road dipped for the descent stood the shanties of Blaauwildebeestefontein. The fresh hill air had exhilarated my mind, and the aromatic scent of the evening gave the last touch of intoxication. Whatever serpent might lurk in it, it was a veritable Eden I had come to.

Blaauwildebeestefontein had no more than two buildings of civilized shape; the store, which stood on the left side of the river, and the schoolhouse opposite. For the rest, there were some twenty native huts, higher up the slope, of the type which the Dutch call *rondavels*. The schoolhouse had a pretty garden, but the store stood bare in a patch of dust with a few outhouses and sheds beside it. Round the door lay a few old ploughs and empty barrels, and beneath a solitary blue gum was a wooden bench with a rough table. Native children played in the dust, and an old Kaffir squatted by the wall.

My few belongings were soon lifted from the Cape-cart, and I entered the shop. It was the ordinary pattern of up-country store—a bar in one corner with an array of bottles, and all round the walls tins of canned food and the odds and ends of trade. The place was empty, and a cloud of flies buzzed over the sugar cask.

Two doors opened at the back, and I chose the one to the right. I found myself in a kind of kitchen with a bed in one corner, and a litter of dirty plates on the table. On the bed lay a man, snoring heavily. I went close to him, and found an old fellow with a bald head, clothed only in a shirt and trousers. His face was red and swollen, and his breath came in heavy grunts. A smell of bad whisky hung over everything. I had no doubt that this was Mr Peter Japp, my senior in the store. One reason for the indifferent trade at Blaauwildebeestefontein was very clear to me: the storekeeper was a sot.

I went back to the shop and tried the other door. It was a bedroom too, but clean and pleasant. A little native girl—Zeeta, I found they called her—was busy tidying it up, and when I entered she dropped me a curtsy. 'This is your room, Baas,' he said in very good English in reply to my question. The child had been well trained somewhere, for there was a cracked dish full of oleander blossom on the drawers'-head, and the pillow-slips on the bed were as clean as I could wish. She brought me water to wash, and a cup of strong tea, while I carried my baggage indoors and paid the driver of the cart. Then, having cleaned myself and lit a pipe, I walked across the road to see Mr Wardlaw.

I found the schoolmaster sitting under his own fig-tree reading one of his Kaffir primers. Having come direct by rail from Cape Town, he had been a week in the place, and ranked as the second oldest white resident.

'Yon's a bonny chief you've got, Davie,' were his first words. 'For three days he's been as fou* as the Baltic.'

I cannot pretend that the misdeeds of Mr Japp greatly annoyed me. I had the reversion of his job, and if he chose to play the fool it was all in my interest. But the schoolmaster was depressed at the prospect of such company. 'Besides you and me, he's the only white man in the place. It's a poor look-out on the social side.'

The school, it appeared, was the merest farce. There were only five white children, belonging to Dutch farmers in the mountains. The native side was more flourishing, but the mission schools at the locations got most of the native children in the neighbourhood. Mr Wardlaw's educational zeal ran high. He talked of establishing a workshop and teaching carpentry and blacksmith's work, of which he knew nothing. He rhapsodized over the intelligence of his pupils and bemoaned his inadequate gift of tongues. 'You and I, Davie,' he said, 'must sit down and grind at the business. It is to the interest of both of us. The Dutch is easy enough. It's a sort of kitchen dialect you can learn in a fortnight. But these native languages are a stiff job. Sesuto* is the chief hereabouts, and I'm told once you've got that it's easy to get the Zulu. Then there's the thing the Shangaans* speak—Baronga, I think they call it. I've got a Christian Kaffir living up in one of the huts who comes every morning to talk to me for an hour. You'd better join me.'

I promised, and in the sweet-smelling dust crossed the road to the store. Japp was still sleeping, so I got a bowl of mealie porridge from Zeeta and went to bed.

Japp was sober next morning and made me some kind of apology. He had chronic lumbago, he said, and 'to go on the bust' now and then was the best cure for it. Then he proceeded to initiate me into my duties in a tone of exaggerated friendli-ness. 'I took a fancy to you the first time I clapped eyes on you,' he said. 'You and me will be good friends, Crawfurd, I can see that. You're a spirited young fellow, and you'll stand no nonsense. The Dutch about here are a slim lot, and the Kaffirs are slimmer. Trust no man, that's my motto. The firm know that, and I've had their confidence for forty years.'

The first day or two things went well enough. There was no doubt that, properly handled, a fine trade could be done in Blaauwildebeestefontein. The countryside was crawling with natives, and great strings used to come through from Shangaan territory on the way to the Rand mines. Besides, there was business to be done with the Dutch farmers, especially with the tobacco, which I foresaw could be worked up into a profitable export. There was no lack of money either, and we had to give very little credit, though it was often asked for. I flung myself into the work, and in a few weeks had been all round the farms and locations. At first Japp praised my energy, for it left him plenty of leisure to sit indoors and drink. But soon he grew suspicious, for he must have seen that I was in a fair way to oust him altogether. He was very anxious to know if I had seen Colles in Durban, and what the manager had said. 'I have letters,' he told me a hundred times, 'from Mr Mackenzie himself praising me up to the skies. The firm couldn't get along without old Peter Japp, I can tell you.' I had no wish to quarrel with the old man, so I listened politely to all he said. But this did not propitiate him, and I soon found him so jealous as to be a nuisance. He was Colonial-born and was always airing the fact. He rejoiced in my rawness, and when I made a blunder would crow over it for hours. 'It's no good, Mr Crawfurd; you new chums from England may think yourselves mighty clever, but we men from the Old Colony can get ahead of you every time. In fifty years you'll maybe learn a little about the country, but we know all about it before we start.' He roared with laughter at my way of tying a *voorslag*,* and he made merry (no doubt with reason) on my management of a horse. I kept my temper pretty well, but I own there were moments when I came near to kicking Mr Japp.

The truth is he was a disgusting old ruffian. His character was shown by his treatment of Zeeta. The poor child slaved all day and did two men's work in keeping the household going. She was an orphan from a mission station, and in Japp's opinion a creature without rights. Hence he never spoke to her except with a curse, and used to cuff her thin shoulders till my blood boiled. One day things became too much for my temper. Zeeta had spilled half a glass of Japp's whisky while tidying up the room. He picked up a sjambok,* and proceeded to beat her unmercifully till her cries brought me on the scene. I tore the whip from his hands, seized him by the scruff and flung him on a heap of potato sacks, where he lay pouring out abuse and shaking with rage. Then I spoke my mind. I told him that if anything of the sort happened again I would report it at once to Mr Colles at Durban. I added that before making my report I would beat him within an inch of his degraded life. After a time he apologized, but I could see that thenceforth he regarded me with deadly hatred.

There was another thing I noticed about Mr Japp. He might brag about his knowledge of how to deal with natives, but to my mind his methods were a disgrace to a white man. Zeeta came in for oaths and blows, but there were other Kaffirs whom he treated with a sort of cringing friendliness. A big black fellow would swagger into the shop, and be received by Japp as if he were his long-lost brother. The two would collogue for hours; and though at first I did not understand the tongue, I could see that it was the white man who fawned and the black man who bullied. Once when Japp was away one of these fellows came into the store as if it belonged to him, but he went out quicker than he entered. Japp complained afterwards of my behaviour. "Mwanga is a good friend of mine,' he said, 'and brings us a lot of business. I'll thank you to be civil to him the next time.' I replied very shortly that 'Mwanga or anybody else who did not mend his manners would feel the weight of my boot.

The thing went on, and I am not sure that he did not give the Kaffirs drink on the sly. At any rate, I have seen some very drunk natives on the road between the locations and Blaauwil-debeestefontein, and some of them I recognized as Japp's friends. I discussed the matter with Mr Wardlaw, who said, 'I believe the old villain has got some sort of black secret, and the natives know it, and have got a pull on him.' And I was inclined to think he was right.

By-and-by I began to feel the lack of company, for Wardlaw was so full of his books that he was of little use as a companion. So I resolved to acquire a dog, and bought one from a prospector, who was stony-broke and would have sold his soul for a drink. It was an enormous Boer hunting-dog, a mongrel in whose blood ran mastiff and bulldog and foxhound, and

Heaven knows what beside. In colour it was a kind of brindled*
red, and the hair on its back grew against the lie of the rest of
its coat. Some one had told me, or I may have read it, that a
back like this meant that a dog would face anything mortal,
even to a charging lion, and it was this feature which first
caught my fancy. The price I paid was ten shillings and a pair
of boots, which I got at cost price from stock, and the owner
departed with injunctions to me to beware of the brute's
temper. Colin—for so I named him—began his career with
me by taking the seat out of my breeches and frightening Mr
Wardlaw into a tree. It took me a stubborn battle of a fortnight
to break his vice, and my left arm to-day bears witness to the
struggle. After that he became a second shadow, and woe
betide the man who had dared to raise his hand to Colin's
master. Japp declared that the dog was a devil, and Colin
repaid the compliment with a hearty dislike.

    With Colin, I now took to spending some of my ample
leisure in exploring the fastnesses of the Berg. I had brought
out a shot-gun of my own, and I borrowed a cheap Mauser
sporting rifle from the store. I had been born with a good eye
and a steady hand, and very soon I became a fair shot with a
gun and, I believe, a really fine shot with the rifle. The sides
of the Berg were full of quail and partridge and bush pheasant,
and on the grassy plateau there was abundance of a bird not
unlike our own blackcock, which the Dutch called *korhaan*.
But the great sport was to stalk bush-buck in the thickets,
which is a game in which the hunter is at small advantage. I
have been knocked down by a wounded bush-buck ram, and
but for Colin might have been badly damaged. Once, in a kloof
not far from the Letaba, I killed a fine leopard, bringing him
down with a single shot from a rocky shelf almost on the top
of Colin. His skin lies by my fireside as I write this tale. But it
was during the days I could spare for an expedition into the
plains that I proved the great qualities of my dog. There we
had nobler game to follow—wildebeest and hartebeest, impala,
and now and then a koodoo.* At first I was a complete duffer,
and shamed myself in Colin's eyes. But by-and-by I learned
something of veld-craft: I learned how to follow spoor, how to
allow for the wind, and stalk under cover. Then, when a shot

had crippled the beast, Colin was on its track like a flash to pull it down. The dog had the nose of a retriever, the speed of a greyhound, and the strength of a bull-terrier. I blessed the day when the wandering prospector had passed the store.

Colin slept at night at the foot of my bed, and it was he who led me to make an important discovery. For I now became aware that I was being subjected to constant espionage. It may have been going on from the start, but it was not till my third month at Blaauwildebeestefontein that I found it out. One night I was going to bed, when suddenly the bristles rose on the dog's back and he barked uneasily at the window. I had been standing in the shadow, and as I stepped to the window to look out I saw a black face disappear below the palisade of the backyard. The incident was trifling, but it put me on my guard. The next night I looked, but saw nothing. The third night I looked, and caught a glimpse of a face almost pressed to the pane. Thereafter I put up the shutters after dark, and shifted my bed to a part of the room out of line with the window.

It was the same out of doors. I would suddenly be conscious, as I walked on the road, that I was being watched. If I made as if to walk into the roadside bush there would be a faint rustling, which told that the watcher had retired. The stalking was brilliantly done, for I never caught a glimpse of one of the stalkers. Wherever I went—on the road, on the meadows of the plateau, or on the rugged sides of the Berg—it was the same. I had silent followers, who betrayed themselves now and then by the crackling of a branch, and eyes were always looking at me which I could not see. Only when I went down to the plains did the espionage cease. This thing annoyed Colin desperately, and his walks abroad were one continuous growl. Once, in spite of my efforts, he dashed into the thicket, and a squeal of pain followed. He had got somebody by the leg, and there was blood on the grass.

Since I came to Blaauwildebeestefontein I had forgotten the mystery I had set out to track in the excitement of a new life and my sordid contest with Japp. But now this espionage brought back my old preoccupation. I was being watched because some person or persons thought that I was dangerous.

My suspicions fastened on Japp, but I soon gave up that clue. It was my presence in the store that was a danger to him, not my wanderings about the countryside. It might be that he had engineered the espionage so as to drive me out of the place in sheer annoyance; but I flattered myself that Mr Japp knew me too well to imagine that such a game was likely to succeed.

The mischief was that I could not make out who the trackers were. I had visited all the surrounding locations, and was on good enough terms with all the chiefs. There was 'Mpefu, a dingy old fellow who had spent a good deal of his life in a Boer gaol before the war. There was a mission station at his place, and his people seemed to me to be well behaved and prosperous. Majinje was a chieftainess, a little girl whom nobody was allowed to see. Her location was a miserable affair, and her tribe was yearly shrinking in numbers. Then there was Magata farther north among the mountains. He had no quarrel with me, for he used to give me a meal when I went out hunting in that direction; and once he turned out a hundred of his young men, and I had a great battue of wild dogs. Sikitola, the biggest of all, lived some distance out in the flats. I knew less about him; but if his men were the trackers, they must have spent most of their days a weary way from their kraal. The Kaffirs in the huts at Blaauwildebeestefontein were mostly Christians, and quiet, decent fellows, who farmed their little gardens, and certainly preferred me to Japp. I thought at one time of riding into Pietersdorp* to consult the Native Commissioner. But I discovered that the old man, who knew the country, was gone, and that his successor was a young fellow from Rhodesia, who knew nothing about anything. Besides, the natives round Blaauwildebeestefontein were well conducted, and received few official visitations. Now and then a couple of Zulu policemen passed in pursuit of some minor malefactor, and the collector came for the hut-tax; but we gave the Government little work, and they did not trouble their heads about us.

As I have said, the clues I had brought out with me to Blaauwildebeestefontein began to occupy my mind again; and the more I thought of the business the keener I grew. I used to amuse myself with setting out my various bits of knowledge.

There was first of all the Rev. John Laputa, his doings on the Kirkcaple shore, his talk with Henriques about Blaauwilde-beestefontein, and his strange behaviour at Durban. Then there was what Colles had told me about the place being queer, how nobody would stay long either in the store or the schoolhouse. Then there was my talk with Aitken at Lourenço Marques, and his story of a great wizard in the neighbourhood to whom all Kaffirs made pilgrimages, and the suspicion of a diamond pipe. Last and most important, there was this perpetual spying on myself. It was as clear as daylight that the place held some secret, and I wondered if old Japp knew. I was fool enough one day to ask him about diamonds. He met me with contemptuous laughter. 'There's your ignorant Brit-isher,' he cried. 'If you had ever been to Kimberley you would know the look of a diamond country. You're as likely to find diamonds here as ocean pearls. But go out and scrape in the spruit* if you like; you'll maybe find some garnets.'

I made cautious inquiries, too, chiefly through Mr Wardlaw, who was becoming a great expert at Kaffir, about the existence of Aitken's wizard, but he could get no news. The most he found out was that there was a good cure for fever among Sikitola's men, and that Majinje, if she pleased, could bring rain.

The upshot of it all was that, after much brooding, I wrote a letter to Mr Colles, and, to make sure of its going, gave it to a missionary to post in Pietersdorp. I told him frankly what Aitken had said, and I also told him about the espionage. I said nothing about old Japp, for, beast as he was, I did not want him at his age to be without a livelihood.

# CHAPTER IV

## MY JOURNEY TO THE WINTER-VELD

A REPLY came from Colles, addressed not to me but to Japp. It seemed that the old fellow had once suggested the establishment of a branch store at a place out in the plains called Umvelos', and the firm was now prepared to take up the scheme. Japp was in high good humour, and showed me the letter. Not a word was said of what I had written about, only the bare details about starting the branch. I was to get a couple of masons, load up two wagons with bricks and timber, and go down to Umvelos' and see the store built. The stocking of it and the appointment of a storekeeper would be matter for further correspondence. Japp was delighted, for, besides getting rid of me for several weeks, it showed that his advice was respected by his superiors. He went about bragging that the firm could not get on without him, and was inclined to be more insolent to me than usual in his new self-esteem. He also got royally drunk over the head of it.

I confess I was hurt by the manager's silence on what seemed to me more vital matters. But I soon reflected that if he wrote at all he would write direct to me, and I eagerly watched for the post-runner. No letter came, however, and I was soon too busy with preparations to look for one. I got the bricks and timber from Pietersdorp, and hired two Dutch masons to run the job. The place was not very far from Sikitola's kraal, so there would be no difficulty about native helpers. Having my eyes open for trade, I resolved to kill two birds with one stone. It was the fashion among the old-fashioned farmers on the high-veld to drive the cattle down into the bush-veld—which they call the winter-veld—for winter pasture. There is no fear of red-water* about that season, and the grass of the plains is rich and thick compared with the uplands. I discovered that some big droves were passing on a certain day, and that the owners and their families were travelling with them in wagons. Accordingly I had a light *naachtmaal** fitted up as a sort of travelling store, and with my two wagons full of building material joined the caravan. I hoped to do good trade in selling little luxuries to the farmers on the road and at Umvelos'.

It was a clear cold morning when we started down the Berg. At first my hands were full with the job of getting my heavy wagons down the awesome precipice which did duty as a highway. We locked the wheels with chains, and tied great logs of wood behind to act as brakes. Happily my drivers knew their business, but one of the Boer wagons got a wheel over the edge, and it was all that ten men could do to get it back again.

After that the road was easier, winding down the side of a slowly opening glen. I rode beside the wagons, and so heavenly was the weather that I was content with my own thoughts. The sky was clear blue, the air warm, yet with a wintry tonic in it, and a thousand aromatic scents came out of the thickets. The pied birds called 'Kaffir queens'* fluttered across the path. Below, the Klein Labongo churned and foamed in a hundred cascades. Its waters were no more the clear grey of the 'Blue Wildebeeste's Spring,' but growing muddy with its approach to the richer soil of the plains.

Oxen travel slow, and we outspanned that night half a day's march short of Umvelos'. I spent the hour before sunset lounging and smoking with the Dutch farmers. At first they had been silent and suspicious of a newcomer, but by this time I talked their *taal** fluently, and we were soon on good terms. I recall a discussion arising about a black thing in a tree about five hundred yards away. I thought it was an aasvogel,* but another thought it was a baboon. Whereupon the oldest of the party, a farmer called Coetzee, whipped up his rifle and, apparently without sighting, fired. A dark object fell out of the branch, and when we reached it we found it a *baviaan*[1] sure enough, shot through the head. 'Which side are you on in the next war?' the old man asked me, and, laughing, I told him 'Yours.'

After supper, the ingredients of which came largely from my

---

[1] Baboon.

*naachtmaal*, we sat smoking and talking round the fire, the women and children being snug in the covered wagons. The Boers were honest companionable fellows, and when I had made a bowl of toddy in the Scotch fashion* to keep out the evening chill, we all became excellent friends. They asked me how I got on with Japp. Old Coetzee saved me the trouble of answering, for he broke in with *Skellum! Skellum!*[1] I asked him his objection to the storekeeper, but he would say nothing beyond that he was too thick with the natives. I fancy at some time Mr Japp had sold him a bad plough.

We spoke of hunting, and I heard long tales of exploits—away on the Limpopo, in Mashonaland, on the Sabi and in the Lebombo. Then we verged on politics, and I listened to violent denunciations of the new land tax. These were old residenters, I reflected, and I might learn perhaps something of value. So very carefully I repeated a tale I said I had heard at Durban of a great wizard somewhere in the Berg, and asked if any one knew of it. They shook their heads. The natives had given up witchcraft and big medicine, they said, and were more afraid of a parson or a policeman than any witch-doctor. Then they were starting on reminiscences, when old Coetzee, who was deaf, broke in and asked to have my question repeated.

'Yes,' he said, 'I know. It is in the Rooirand. There is a devil dwells there.'

I could get no more out of him beyond the fact that there was certainly a great devil there. His grandfather and father had seen it, and he himself had heard it roaring when he had gone there as a boy to hunt. He would explain no further, and went to bed.

Next morning, close to Sikitola's kraal, I bade the farmers good-bye, after telling them that there would be a store in my wagon for three weeks at Umvelos' if they wanted supplies. We then struck more to the north towards our destination. As soon as they had gone I had out my map and searched it for the name old Coetzee had mentioned. It was a very bad map, for there had been no surveying east of the Berg, and most of

---

[1] *Schelm* = Rascal.

the names were mere guesses. But I found the word 'Rooirand'
marking an eastern continuation of the northern wall, and
probably set down from some hunter's report. I had better
explain here the chief features of the country, for they bulk
largely in my story. The Berg runs north and south, and from
it run the chief streams which water the plain. They are,
beginning from the south, the Olifants, the Groot Letaba, the
Letsitela, the Klein Letaba, and the Klein Labongo, on which
stands Blaauwildebeestefontein. But the greatest river of the
plain, into which the others ultimately flow, is the Groot
Labongo, which appears full-born from some subterranean
source close to the place called Umvelos'. North from Blaauwildebeestefontein the Berg runs for some twenty miles, and
then makes a sharp turn eastward, becoming, according to my
map, the Rooirand.

I pored over these details, and was particularly curious about
the Great Labongo. It seemed to me unlikely that a spring in
the bush could produce so great a river, and I decided that its
source must lie in the mountains to the north. As well as I
could guess, the Rooirand, the nearest part of the Berg, was
about thirty miles distant. Old Coetzee had said that there was
a devil in the place, but I thought that if it were explored the
first thing found would be a fine stream of water.

We got to Umvelos' after midday, and outspanned for our
three weeks' work. I set the Dutchmen to unload and clear the
ground for foundations, while I went off to Sikitola to ask for
labourers. I got a dozen lusty blacks, and soon we had a
business-like encampment, and the work went on merrily. It
was rough architecture and rougher masonry. All we aimed at
was a two-roomed shop with a kind of outhouse for stores. I
was architect, and watched the marking out of the foundations
and the first few feet of the walls. Sikitola's people proved
themselves good helpers, and most of the building was left to
them, while the Dutchmen worked at the carpentry. Bricks
ran short before we got very far, and we had to set to brick-
making on the bank of the Labongo, and finish off the walls
with green bricks, which gave the place a queer piebald look.

I was not much of a carpenter, and there were plenty of
builders without me, so I found a considerable amount of time

on my hands. At first I acted as shopkeeper in the *naachtmaal*, but I soon cleared out my stores to the Dutch farmers and the natives. I had thought of going back for more, and then it occurred to me that I might profitably give some of my leisure to the Rooirand. I could see the wall of the mountains quite clear to the north, within an easy day's ride. So one morning I packed enough food for a day or two, tied my sleeping-bag on my saddle, and set off to explore, after appointing the elder of the Dutchmen foreman of the job in my absence.

It was very hot jogging along the native path with the eternal olive-green bush around me. Happily there was no fear of losing the way, for the Rooirand stood very clear in front, and slowly, as I advanced, I began to make out the details of the cliffs. At luncheon-time, when I was about half-way, I sat down with my Zeiss glass—my mother's farewell gift—to look for the valley. But valley I saw none. The wall—reddish purple it looked, and, I thought, of porphyry—was continuous and unbroken. There were chimneys and fissures, but none great enough to hold a river. The top was sheer cliff; then came loose kranzes* in tiers, like the seats in a gallery, and, below, a dense thicket of trees. I raked the whole line for a break, but there seemed none. 'It's a bad job for me,' I thought, 'if there is no water, for I must pass the night there.'

The night was spent in a sheltered nook at the foot of the rocks, but my horse and I went to bed without a drink. My supper was some raisins and biscuits, for I did not dare to run the risk of increasing my thirst. I had found a great bank of *débris* sloping up to the kranzes, and thick wood clothing all the slope. The grass seemed wonderfully fresh, but of water there was no sign. There was not even the sandy channel of a stream to dig in.

In the morning I had a difficult problem to face. Water I must find at all costs, or I must go home. There was time enough for me to get back without suffering much, but if so I must give up my explorations. This I was determined not to do. The more I looked at these red cliffs the more eager I was to find out their secret. There must be water somewhere; otherwise how account for the lushness of the vegetation?

My horse was a veld pony, so I set him loose to see what he

would do. He strayed back on the path to Umvelos'. This looked bad, for it meant that he did not smell water along the cliff front. If I was to find a stream it must be on the top, and I must try a little mountaineering.*

Then, taking my courage in both my hands, I decided. I gave my pony a cut, and set him off on the homeward road. I knew he was safe to get back in four or five hours, and in broad day there was little fear of wild beasts attacking him. I had tied my sleeping bag on to the saddle, and had with me but two pocketfuls of food. I had also fastened on the saddle a letter to my Dutch foreman, bidding him send a native with a spare horse to fetch me by the evening. Then I started off to look for a chimney.

A boyhood spent on the cliffs at Kirkcaple had made me a bold cragsman, and the porphyry of the Rooirand clearly gave excellent holds. But I walked many weary miles along the cliff-foot before I found a feasible road. To begin with, it was no light task to fight one's way through the dense undergrowth of the lower slopes. Every kind of thorn-bush lay in wait for my skin, creepers tripped me up, high trees shut out the light, and I was in constant fear lest a black *mamba** might appear out of the tangle. It grew very hot, and the screes above the thicket were blistering to the touch. My tongue, too, stuck to the roof of my mouth with thirst.

The first chimney I tried ran out on the face into nothing-ness, and I had to make a dangerous descent. The second was a deep gully, but so choked with rubble that after nearly braining myself I desisted. Still going eastwards, I found a sloping ledge which took me to a platform from which ran a crack with a little tree growing in it. My glass showed me that beyond this tree the crack broadened into a clearly defined chimney which led to the top. If I can once reach that tree, I thought, the battle is won.

The crack was only a few inches wide, large enough to let in an arm and a foot, and it ran slantwise up a perpendicular rock. I do not think I realized how bad it was till I had gone too far to return. Then my foot jammed, and I paused for breath with my legs and arms cramping rapidly. I remember that I looked to the west, and saw through the sweat which kept dropping into my eyes that about half a mile off a piece of cliff which looked unbroken from the foot had a fold in it to the right. The darkness of the fold showed me that it was a deep, narrow gully. However, I had no time to think of this, for I was fast in the middle of my confounded crack. With immense labour I found a chockstone above my head, and managed to force my foot free. The next few yards were not so difficult, and then I stuck once more.

For the crack suddenly grew shallow as the cliff bulged out above me. I had almost given up hope, when I saw that about three feet above my head grew the tree. If I could reach it and swing out I might hope to pull myself up to the ledge on which it grew. I confess it needed all my courage, for I did not know but that the tree might be loose, and that it and I might go rattling down four hundred feet. It was my only hope, however, so I set my teeth, and wriggling up a few inches, made a grab at it. Thank God it held, and with a great effort I pulled my shoulder over the ledge, and breathed freely.

My difficulties were not ended, but the worst was past. The rest of the gully gave me good and safe climbing, and presently a very limp and weary figure lay on the cliff-top. It took me many minutes to get back my breath and to conquer the faintness which seized me as soon as the need for exertion was over.

When I scrambled to my feet and looked round, I saw a wonderful prospect. It was a plateau like the high-veld, only covered with bracken and little bushes like hazels. Three or four miles off the ground rose, and a shallow vale opened. But in the foreground, half a mile or so distant, a lake lay gleaming in the sun.

I could scarcely believe my eyes as I ran towards it, and doubts of a mirage haunted me. But it was no mirage, but a real lake, perhaps three miles in circumference, with bracken-fringed banks, a shore of white pebbles, and clear deep blue water. I drank my fill, and then stripped and swam in the blessed coolness. After that I ate some luncheon, and sunned myself on a flat rock. 'I have discovered the source of the Labongo,' I said to myself. 'I will write to the Royal Geographical Society, and they will give me a medal.'

I walked round the lake to look for an outlet. A fine mountain stream came in at the north end, and at the south end, sure enough, a considerable river debouched.* My exploring zeal redoubled, and I followed its course in a delirium of expectation. It was a noble stream, clear as crystal, and very unlike the muddy tropical Labongo at Umvelos'. Suddenly, about a quarter of a mile from the lake, the land seemed to grow over it, and with a swirl and a hollow roar, it disappeared into a mighty pot-hole. I walked a few steps on, and from below my feet came the most uncanny rumbling and groaning. Then I knew what old Coetzee's devil was that howled in the Rooirand.

Had I continued my walk to the edge of the cliff, I might have learned a secret which would have stood me in good stead later. But the descent began to make me anxious, and I retraced my steps to the top of the chimney whence I had come. I was resolved that nothing would make me descend by that awesome crack, so I kept on eastward along the top to look for a better way. I found one about a mile farther on, which, though far from easy, had no special risks save from the appalling looseness of the *débris*. When I got down at length, I found that it was near sunset. I went to the place I had bidden my native look for me at, but, as I had feared, there was no sign of him. So, making the best of a bad job, I had supper and a pipe, and spent a very chilly night in a hole among the boulders.

I got up at dawn stiff and cold, and ate a few raisins for breakfast. There was no sign of horses, so I resolved to fill up the time in looking for the fold of the cliff which, as I had seen from the horrible crack of yesterday, contained a gully. It was a difficult job, for to get the sidelong view of the cliff I had to scramble through the undergrowth of the slopes again, and even a certain way up the kranzes. At length I got my bearings, and fixed the place by some tall trees in the bush. Then I descended and walked westwards.

Suddenly, as I neared the place, I heard the strangest sound coming from the rocks. It was a deep muffled groaning, so eerie and unearthly that for the moment I stood and shivered. Then I remembered my river of yesterday. It must be above this place that it descended into the earth, and in the hush of dawn the sound was naturally louder. No wonder old Coetzee had been afraid of devils. It reminded me of the lines in *Marmion*—

> 'Diving as if condemned to lave
> Some demon's subterranean cave,
> Who, prisoned by enchanter's spell,
> Shakes the dark rock with groan and yell.'*

While I was standing awestruck at the sound, I observed a figure moving towards the cliffs. I was well in cover, so I could not have been noticed. It was a very old man, very tall, but bowed in the shoulders, who was walking slowly with bent head. He could not have been thirty yards from me, so I had a clear view of his face. He was a native, but of a type I had never seen before. A long white beard fell on his breast, and a magnificent kaross* of leopard skin covered his shoulders. His face was seamed and lined and shrunken, so that he seemed as old as Time itself.

Very carefully I crept after him, and found myself opposite the fold where the gully was. There was a clear path through the jungle, a path worn smooth by many feet. I followed it through the undergrowth and over the screes till it turned inside the fold of the gully. And then it stopped short. I was in a deep cleft, but in front was a slab of sheer rock. Above, the gully looked darker and deeper, but there was this great slab to pass. I examined the sides, but they were sheer rock with no openings.

Had I had my wits about me, I would have gone back and followed the spoor, noting where it stopped. But the whole thing looked black magic to me; my stomach was empty and my enterprise small. Besides, there was the terrible moaning of the imprisoned river in my ears. I am ashamed to confess it, but I ran from that gully as if the devil and all his angels had been following me. Indeed, I did not slacken till I had put a good mile between me and those uncanny cliffs. After that I set out to foot it back. If the horses would not come to me I must go to them.

I walked fifteen* miles in a vile temper, enraged at my

Dutchmen, my natives, and everybody. The truth is, I had been frightened, and my pride was sore about it. It grew very hot, the sand rose and choked me, the mopani* trees with their dull green wearied me, the 'Kaffir queens' and jays and rollers* which flew about the path seemed to be there to mock me. About half-way home I found a boy and two horses, and roundly I cursed him. It seemed that my pony had returned right enough, and the boy had been sent to fetch me. He had got half-way before sunset the night before, and there he had stayed. I discovered from him that he was scared to death, and did not dare go any nearer the Rooirand. It was accursed, he said, for it was an abode of devils, and only wizards went near it. I was bound to admit to myself that I could not blame him. At last I had got on the track of something certain about this mysterious country, and all the way back I wondered if I should have the courage to follow it up.

# CHAPTER V

## MR WARDLAW HAS A PREMONITION

A WEEK later the building job was finished, I locked the door of the new store, pocketed the key, and we set out for home. Sikitola was entrusted with the general care of it, and I knew him well enough to be sure that he would keep his people from doing mischief. I left my empty wagons to follow at their leisure and rode on, with the result that I arrived at Blaauwildebeestefontein two days before I was looked for.

I stabled my horse, and went round to the back to see Colin. (I had left him at home in case of fights with native dogs, for he was an ill beast in a crowd.) I found him well and hearty, for Zeeta had been looking after him. Then some whim seized me to enter the store through my bedroom window. It was open, and I crawled softly in to find the room fresh and clean from Zeeta's care. The door was ajar, and, hearing voices, I peeped into the shop.

Japp was sittng on the counter talking in a low voice to a big native—the same 'Mwanga whom I had bundled out unceremoniously. I noticed that the outer door giving on the road was shut, a most unusual thing in the afternoon. Japp had some small objects in his hand, and the two were evidently arguing about a price. I had no intention at first of eavesdropping, and was just about to push the door open, when something in Japp's face arrested me. He was up to no good, and I thought it my business to wait.

The low tones went on for a little, both men talking in Kaffir, and then Japp lifted up one of the little objects between finger and thumb. It was a small roundish stone about the size of a bean, but even in that half light there was a dull lustre in it.

At that I shoved the door open and went in. Both men started as if they had been shot. Japp went as white as his mottled face permitted. 'What the—' he gasped, and he dropped the thing he was holding.

I picked it up, and laid it on the counter. 'So,' I said, 'diamonds, Mr Japp. You have found the pipe* I was looking for. I congratulate you.'

My words gave the old ruffian his cue. 'Yes, yes,' he said, 'I have, or rather my friend 'Mwanga has. He has just been telling me about it.'

The Kaffir looked miserably uncomfortable. He shifted from one leg to the other, casting longing glances at the closed door. 'I tink I go,' he said. 'Afterwards we will speak more.'

I told him I thought he had better go, and opened the door for him. Then I bolted it again, and turned to Mr Japp.

'So that's your game,' I said. 'I thought there was something funny about you, but I didn't know it was I.D.B. you were up to.'

He looked as if he could kill me. For five minutes he cursed me with a perfection of phrase which I had thought beyond him. It was no I.D.B., he declared, but a pipe which 'Mwanga had discovered.

'In this kind of country?' I said, quoting his own words. 'Why, you might as well expect to find ocean pearls as diamonds. But scrape in the spruit if you like; you'll maybe find some garnets.'

He choked down his wrath, and tried a new tack. 'What will you take to hold your tongue? I'll make you a rich man if you'll come in with me.' And then he started with offers which showed that he had been making a good thing out of the traffic.

I stalked over to him, and took him by the shoulder. 'You old reprobate,' I roared, 'if you breathe such a proposal to me again, I'll tie you up like a sack and carry you to Pietersdorp.'

At this he broke down and wept maudlin tears, disgusting to witness. He said he was an old man who had always lived honestly, and it would break his heart if his grey hairs were to be disgraced. As he sat rocking himself with his hands over his face, I saw his wicked little eyes peering through the slits of his fingers to see what my next move would be.

'See here, Mr Japp,' I said, 'I'm not a police spy, and it's no business of mine to inform against you. I'm willing to keep you out of gaol, but it must be on my own conditions. The first if that you resign this job and clear out. You will write to

Mr Colles a letter at my dictation, saying that you find the work too much for you. The second is that for the time you remain here the diamond business must utterly cease. If 'Mwanga or anybody like him comes inside the store, and if I get the slightest hint that you're back at the trade, in you go to Pietersdorp. I'm not going to have my name disgraced by being associated with you. The third condition is that when you leave this place you go clear away. If you come within twenty miles of Blaauwildebeestefontein and I find you, I will give you up.'

He groaned and writhed at my terms, but in the end accepted them. He wrote the letter, and I posted it. I had no pity for the old scamp, who had feathered his nest well. Small wonder that the firm's business was not as good as it might be, when Japp was giving most of his time to buying diamonds from native thieves. The secret put him in the power of any Kaffir who traded him a stone. No wonder he cringed to ruffians like 'Mwanga.

The second thing I did was to shift my quarters. Mr Wardlaw had a spare room which he had offered me before, and now I accepted it. I wanted to be no more mixed up with Japp than I could help, for I did not know what villainy he might let me in for. Moreover, I carried Zeeta with me, being ashamed to leave her at the mercy of the old bully. Japp went up to the huts and hired a slattern to mind his house, and then drank heavily for three days to console himself.

That night I sat smoking with Mr Wardlaw in his sitting-room, where a welcome fire burned, for the nights on the Berg were chilly. I remember the occasion well for the queer turn the conversation took. Wardlaw, as I have said, had been working like a slave at the Kaffir tongues. I talked a kind of Zulu well enough to make myself understood, and I could follow it when spoken; but he had real scholarship in the thing, and knew all about the grammar and the different dialects. Further, he had read a lot about native history, and was full of the doings of Tchaka and Mosilikatse and Moshesh, and the kings of old. Having little to do in the way of teaching, he had made up for it by reading omnivorously. He used to borrow books from the missionaries, and he must have spent half his salary in buying new ones.

To-night as he sat and puffed in his armchair, he was full of stories about a fellow called Monomotapa.* It seems he was a great black emperor whom the Portuguese discovered about the sixteenth century. He lived to the north in Mashonaland, and had a mountain full of gold. The Portuguese did not make much of him, but they got his son and turned him into a priest.

I told Wardlaw that he was most likely only a petty chief, whose exploits were magnified by distance, the same as the caciques* in Mexico. But the schoolmaster would not accept this.

'He must have been a big man, Davie. You know that the old ruins in Rhodesia, called Zimbabwe,* were long believed to be Phoenician in origin. I have a book here which tells all about them. But now it is believed that they were built by natives. I maintain that the men who could erect piles like that'—and he showed me a picture—'were something more than petty chiefs.'

Presently the object of this conversation appeared. Mr Wardlaw thought that we were underrating the capacity of the native. This opinion was natural enough in a schoolmaster, but not in the precise form Wardlaw put it. It was not his intelligence which he thought we underrated, but his danger-ousness. His reasons, shortly, were these: There were five or six of them to every white man; they were all, roughly speaking, of the same stock, with the same tribal beliefs; they had only just ceased being a warrior race, with a powerful military discipline; and, most important, they lived round the rim of the high-veld plateau, and if they combined could cut off the white man from the sea. I pointed out to him that it would only be a matter of time before we opened the road again. 'Ay,' he said, 'but think of what would happen before then. Think of the lonely farms and the little dorps* wiped out of the map. It would be a second and bloodier Indian mutiny.*

'I'm not saying it's likely,' he went on, 'but I maintain it's possible. Supposing a second Tchaka* turned up, who could get the different tribes to work together. It wouldn't be so very hard to smuggle in arms. Think of the long, unwatched coast in Gazaland and Tongaland. If they got a leader with prestige enough to organize a crusade against the white man, I don't see what could prevent a rising.'

'We should get wind of it in time to crush it at the start,' I said.

'I'm not so sure. They are cunning fellows, and have arts that we know nothing about. You have heard of native telepathy. They can send news over a thousand miles as quick as the telegraph, and we have no means of tapping the wires. If they ever combined they could keep it as secret as the grave. My houseboy might be in the rising, and I would never suspect it till one fine morning he cut my throat.'

'But they would never find a leader. If there was some exiled prince of Tchaka's blood, who came back like Prince Charlie to free his people, there might be danger; but their royalties are fat men with top hats and old frock-coats, who live in dirty locations.'

Wardlaw admitted this, but said that there might be other kinds of leaders. He had been reading a lot about Ethiopianism, which educated American negroes had been trying to preach in South Africa. He did not see why a kind of bastard Christianity should not be the motive of a rising. 'The Kaffir finds it an easy job to mix up Christian emotion and pagan practice. Look at Hayti and some of the performances in the Southern States.'

Then he shook the ashes out of his pipe and leaned forward with a solemn face. 'I'll admit the truth to you, Davie. I'm black afraid.'

He looked so earnest and serious sitting there with his short-sighted eyes peering at me that I could not help being impressed.

'Whatever is the matter?' I asked. 'Has anything happened?'

He shook his head. 'Nothing I can put a name to. But I have a presentiment that some mischief is afoot in these hills. I feel it in my bones.'

I confess I was startled by these words. You must remember that I had never given a hint of my suspicions to Mr Wardlaw beyond asking him if a wizard lived in the neighbourhood—a question anybody might have put. But here was the schoolmaster discovering for himself some mystery in Blaauwildebeestefontein.

I tried to get at his evidence, but it was very little. He thought there were an awful lot of blacks about. 'The woods are full of them,' he said. I gathered he did not imagine he was being spied on, but merely felt that there were more natives about than could be explained.

'There's another thing,' he said. 'The native bairns have all left the school. I've only three scholars left, and they are from Dutch farms. I went to Majinje to find out what was up, and an old crone told me the place was full of bad men. I tell you, Davie, there's something brewing, and that something is not good for us.'

There was nothing new to me in what Wardlaw had to tell, and yet that talk late at night by a dying fire made me feel afraid for the second time since I had come to Blaauwildebeestefontein. I had a clue and had been on the look-out for mysteries, but that another should feel the strangeness for himself made it seem desperately real to me. Of course I scoffed at Mr Wardlaw's fears. I could not have him spoiling all my plans by crying up a native rising for which he had not a scrap of evidence.

'Have you been writing to anybody?' I asked him.

He said that he had told no one, but he meant to, unless things got better. 'I haven't the nerve for this job, Davie,' he said; 'I'll have to resign. And it's a pity, for the place suits my health fine. You see I know too much, and I haven't your whinstone* nerve and total lack of imagination.'

I told him that it was simply fancy, and came from reading too many books and taking too little exercise. But I made him promise to say nothing to anybody either by word of mouth or letter, without telling me first. Then I made him a rummer* of toddy and sent him to bed a trifle comforted.

The first thing I did in my new room was to shift the bed into the corner out of line with the window. There were no shutters, so I put up an old table-top and jammed it between the window frames. Also, I loaded my shot-gun and kept it by my bedside. Had Wardlaw seen these preparations he might have thought more of my imagination and less of my nerve. It was a real comfort to me to put out a hand in the darkness and feel Colin's shaggy coat.

# CHAPTER VI

### THE DRUMS BEAT AT SUNSET

JAPP was drunk for the next day or two, and I had the business of the store to myself. I was glad of this, for it gave me leisure to reflect upon the various perplexities of my situation. As I have said, I was really scared, more out of a sense of impotence than from dread of actual danger. I was in a fog of uncertainty. Things were happening around me which I could only dimly guess at, and I had no power to take one step in defence. That Wardlaw should have felt the same without any hint from me was the final proof that the mystery was no figment of my nerves. I had written to Colles and got no answer. Now the letter with Japp's resignation in it had gone to Durban. Surely some notice would be taken of that. If I was given the post, Colles was bound to consider what I had said in my earlier letter and give me some directions. Meanwhile it was my business to stick to my job till I was relieved.

A change had come over the place during my absence. The natives had almost disappeared from sight. Except the few families living round Blaauwildebeestefontein one never saw a native on the roads, and none came into the store. They were sticking close to their locations, or else they had gone after some distant business. Except a batch of three Shangaans returning from the Rand, I had nobody in the store for the whole of one day. So about four o'clock I shut it up, whistled on Colin, and went for a walk along the Berg.

If there were no natives on the road, there were plenty in the bush. I had the impression, of which Wardlaw had spoken, that the native population of the countryside had suddenly been hugely increased. The woods were simply *hotching** with them. I was being spied on as before, but now there were so many at the business that they could not all conceal their tracks. Every now and then I had a glimpse of a black shoulder or leg, and Colin, whom I kept on the leash, was half-mad with excitement. I had seen all I wanted, and went home with a preoccupied mind. I sat long on Wardlaw's garden-seat, trying to puzzle out the truth of this spying.

What perplexed me was that I had been left unmolested when I had gone to Umvelos'. Now, as I conjectured, the secret of the neighbourhood, whatever it was, was probably connected with the Rooirand. But when I had ridden in that direction and had spent two days in exploring, no one had troubled to watch me. I was quite certain about this, for my eye had grown quick to note espionage, and it is harder for a spy to hide in the spare bush of the flats than in the dense thickets on these uplands.

The watchers, then, did not mind my fossicking* round their sacred place. Why, then, was I so closely watched in the harmless neighbourhood of the store? I thought for a long time before an answer occurred to me. The reason must be that going to the plains I was going into native country and away from civilization. But Blaauwildebeestefontein was near the frontier. There must be some dark business brewing of which they may have feared that I had an inkling. They wanted to see if I proposed to go to Pietersdorp or Wesselsburg and tell what I knew, and they clearly were resolved that I should not. I laughed, I remember, thinking that they had forgotten the post-bag. But then I reflected that I knew nothing of what might be happening daily to the post-bag.

When I had reached this conclusion, my first impulse was to test it by riding straight west on the main road. If I was right, I should certainly be stopped. On second thoughts, however, this seemed to me to be flinging up the game prematurely, and I resolved to wait a day or two before acting.

Next day nothing happened, save that my sense of loneliness increased. I felt that I was being hemmed in by barbarism, and cut off in a ghoulish land from the succour of my own kind. I only kept my courage up by the necessity of presenting a brave face to Mr Wardlaw, who was by this time in a very broken condition of nerves. I had often thought that it was my duty to advise him to leave, and to see him safely off, but I shrank from severing myself from my only friend. I thought, too, of the few Dutch farmers within riding distance, and had half a mind to visit them, but they were far off over the plateau and could know little of my anxieties.

The third day events moved faster. Japp was sober and wonderfully quiet. He gave me good-morning quite in a friendly tone, and set to posting up the books as if he had never misbehaved in his days. I was so busy with my thoughts that I, too, must have been gentler than usual, and the morning passed like a honeymoon, till I went across to dinner.

I was just sitting down when I remembered that I had left my watch in my waistcoat behind the counter, and started to go back for it. But at the door I stopped short. For two horsemen had drawn up before the store.

One was a native with what I took to be saddle-bags; the other was a small slim man with a sun helmet, who was slowly dismounting. Something in the cut of his jib struck me as familiar. I slipped into the empty schoolroom and stared hard. Then, as he half-turned in handing his bridle to the Kaffir, I got a sight of his face. It was my former shipmate, Henriques. He said something to his companion, and entered the store.

You may imagine that my curiosity ran to fever-heat. My first impulse was to march over for my waistcoat, and make a third with Japp at the interview. Happily I reflected in time that Henriques knew my face, for I had grown no beard, having a great dislike to needless hair. If he was one of the villains in the drama, he would mark me down for his vengeance once he knew I was here, whereas at present he had probably forgotten all about me. Besides, if I walked in boldly I would get no news. If Japp and he had a secret, they would not blab it in my presence.

My next idea was to slip in by the back to the room I had once lived in. But how was I to cross the road? It ran white and dry some distance each way in full view of the Kaffir with the horses. Further, the store stood on a bare patch, and it would be a hard job to get in by the back, assuming, as I believed, that the neighbourhood was thick with spies.

The upshot was that I got my glasses and turned them on the store. The door was open, and so was the window. In the gloom of the interior I made out Henriques' legs. He was standing by the counter, and apparently talking to Japp. He moved to shut the door, and came back inside my focus opposite the window. There he stayed for maybe ten minutes, while I hugged my impatience. I would have given a hundred pounds to be snug in my old room with Japp thinking me out of the store.

Suddenly the legs twitched up, and his boots appeared above the counter. Japp had invited him to his bedroom, and the game was now to be played beyond my ken. This was more than I could stand, so I stole out at the back door and took to the thickest bush on the hillside. My notion was to cross the road half a mile down, when it had dropped into the defile of the stream, and then to come swiftly up the edge of the water so as to effect a back entrance into the store.

As fast as I dared I tore through the bush, and in about a quarter of an hour had reached the point I was making for. Then I bore down to the road, and was in the scrub about ten yards off it, when the clatter of horses pulled me up again. Peeping out I saw that it was my friend and his Kaffir follower, who were riding at a very good pace for the plains. Toilfully and crossly I returned on my tracks to my long-delayed dinner. Whatever the purport of their talk, Japp and the Portuguese had not taken long over it.

In the store that afternoon I said casually to Japp that I had noticed visitors at the door during my dinner hour. The old man looked me frankly enough in the face. 'Yes, it was Mr Hendricks,' he said, and explained that the man was a Portuguese trader from Delagoa way, who had a lot of Kaffir stores east of the Lebombo Hills. I asked his business, and was told that he always gave Japp a call in when he was passing.

'Do you take every man that calls into your bedroom, and shut the door?' I asked.

Japp lost colour and his lip trembled. 'I swear to God, Mr Crawfurd, I've been doing nothing wrong. I've kept the promise I gave you like an oath to my mother. I see you suspect me, and maybe you've cause, but I'll be quite honest with you. I have dealt in diamonds before this with Hendricks. But to-day, when he asked me, I told him that that business was off. I only took him to my room to give him a drink. He likes brandy, and there's no supply in the shop.'

I distrusted Japp whole-heartedly enough, but I was convinced that in this case he spoke the truth.

'Had the man any news?' I asked.

'He had and he hadn't,' said Japp. 'He was always a sullen beggar, and never spoke much. But he said one queer thing. He asked me if I was going to retire, and when I told him "yes," he said I had put it off rather long. I told him I was as healthy as I ever was, and he laughed in his dirty Portugoose way. "Yes, Mr Japp," he says, "but the country is not so healthy." I wonder what the chap meant. He'll be dead of blackwater* before many months, to judge by his eyes.'

This talk satisfied me about Japp, who was clearly in desperate fear of offending me, and disinclined to return for the present to his old ways. But I think the rest of the afternoon was the most wretched time in my existence. It was as plain as daylight that we were in for some grave trouble, trouble to which I believed that I alone held any kind of clue. I had a pile of evidence—the visit of Henriques was the last bit— which pointed to some great secret approaching its disclosure. I thought that that disclosure meant blood and ruin. But I knew nothing definite. If the commander of a British army had come to me then and there and offered help, I could have done nothing, only asked him to wait like me. The peril, whatever it was, did not threaten me only, though I and Wardlaw and Japp might be the first to suffer; but I had a terrible feeling that I alone could do something to ward it off, and just what that something was I could not tell. I was horribly afraid, not only of unknown death, but of my impotence to play any manly part. I was alone, knowing too much and yet too little, and there was no chance of help under the broad sky. I cursed myself for not writing to Aitken at Lourenço Marques weeks before. He had promised to come up, and he was the kind of man who kept his word.

In the late afternoon I dragged Wardlaw out for a walk. In his presence I had to keep up a forced cheerfulness, and I believe the pretence did me good. We took a path up the Berg among groves of stinkwood and essenwood,* where a falling stream made an easy route. It may have been fancy, but it seemed to me that the wood was emptier and that we were followed less closely. I remember it was a lovely evening, and in the clear fragrant gloaming every foreland of the Berg stood out like a great ship above the dark green sea of the bush. When we reached the edge of the plateau we saw the sun sinking between two far blue peaks in Makapan's country, and away to the south the great roll of the high veld. I longed miserably for the places where white men were thronged together in dorps and cities.

As we gazed a curious sound struck our ears. It seemed to begin far up in the north—a low roll like the combing of breakers on the sand. Then it grew louder and travelled nearer—a roll, with sudden spasms of harsher sound in it; reminding me of the churning in one of the pot-holes of Kirkcaple cliffs.* Presently it grew softer again as the sound passed south, but new notes were always emerging. The echo came sometimes, as it were, from stark rock, and sometimes from the deep gloom of the forests. I have never heard an eerier sound. Neither natural nor human it seemed, but the voice of that world between which is hid from man's sight and hearing.

Mr Wardlaw clutched my arm, and in that moment I guessed the explanation. The native drums were beating, passing some message from the far north down the line of the Berg, where the locations were thickest, to the great black population of the south.

'But that means war,' Mr Wardlaw cried.

'It means nothing of the kind,' I said shortly. 'It's their way of sending news. It's as likely to be some change in the weather or an outbreak of cattle disease.'

When we got home I found Japp with a face like grey paper. 'Did you hear the drums?' he asked.

'Yes,' I said shortly. 'What about them?'

'God forgive you for an ignorant Britisher,' he almost shouted. 'You may hear drums any night, but a drumming like that I only once heard before. It was in '79 in the 'Zeti valley. Do you know what happened next day? Cetewayo's impis* came over the hills, and in an hour there wasn't a living white soul in the glen. Two men escaped, and one of them was called Peter Japp.'

'We are in God's hands then, and must wait on His will,' I said solemnly.

There was no more sleep for Wardlaw and myself that night. We made the best barricade we could of the windows, loaded all our weapons, and trusted to Colin to give us early news. Before supper I went over to get Japp to join us, but found that that worthy had sought help from his old protector, the bottle, and was already sound asleep with both door and window open.

I had made up my mind that death was certain, and yet my heart belied my conviction, and I could not feel the appropriate mood. If anything I was more cheerful since I had heard the drums. It was clearly now beyond the power of me or any man to stop the march of events. My thoughts ran on a native rising, and I kept telling myself how little that was probable. Where were the arms, the leader, the discipline? At any rate such arguments put me to sleep before dawn, and I wakened at eight to find that nothing had happened. The clear morning sunlight, as of old, made Blaauwildebeestefontein the place of a dream. Zeeta brought in my cup of coffee as if this day were just like all others, my pipe tasted as sweet, the fresh air from the Berg blew as fragantly on my brow. I went over to the store in reasonably good spirits, leaving Wardlaw busy on the penitential Psalms.*

The post-runner had brought the mail as usual, and there was one private letter for me. I opened it with great excitement, for the envelope bore the stamp of the firm. At last Colles had deigned to answer.

Inside was a sheet of the firm's notepaper, with the signature of Colles across the top. Below some one had pencilled these five words:

'*The Blesbok*[1] *are changing ground.*'

[1] A species of buck.

I looked to see that Japp had not suffocated himself, then shut up the store, and went back to my room to think out this new mystification.

The thing had come from Colles, for it was the private notepaper of the Durban office, and there was Colles' signature. But the pencilling was in a different hand. My deduction from this was that some one wished to send me a message, and that Colles had given that some one a sheet of signed paper to serve as a kind of introduction. I might take it, therefore, that the scribble was Colles' reply to my letter.

Now, my argument continued, if the unknown person saw fit to send me a message, it could not be merely one of warning. Colles must have told him that I was awake to some danger, and as I was in Blaauwildebeestefontein, I must be nearer the heart of things than any one else. The message must therefore be in the nature of some password, which I was to remember when I heard it again.

I reasoned the whole thing out very clearly, and I saw no gap in my logic. I cannot describe how that scribble had heartened me. I felt no more the crushing isolation of yesterday. There were others beside me in the secret. Help must be on the way, and the letter was the first tidings.

But how near?—that was the question; and it occurred to me for the first time to look at the postmark. I went back to the store and got the envelope out of the waste-paper basket. The postmark was certainly not Durban. The stamp was a Cape Colony one, and of the mark I could only read three letters, T.R.S. This was no sort of clue, and I turned the thing over, completely baffled. Then I noticed that there was no mark of the post town of delivery. Our letters to Blaauwildebeestefontein came through Pietersdorp and bore that mark. I compared the envelope with others. They all had a circle, and 'Pietersdorp' in broad black letters. But this envelope had nothing except the stamp.

I was still slow at detective work, and it was some minutes before the explanation flashed on me. The letter had never been posted at all. The stamp was a fake, and had been borrowed from an old envelope. There was only one way in which it could have come. It must have been put in the letter-bag while the postman was on his way from Pietersdorp. My unknown friend must therefore be somewhere within eighty miles of me. I hurried off to look for the post-runner, but he had started back an hour before. There was nothing for it but to wait on the coming of the unknown.

That afternoon I again took Mr Wardlaw for a walk. It is an ingrained habit of mine that I never tell anyone more of a business than is practically necessary. For months I had kept all my knowledge to myself, and breathed not a word to a soul. But I thought it my duty to tell Wardlaw about the letter, to let him see that we were not forgotten. I am afraid it did not encourage his mind. Occult messages seemed to him only the last proof of a deadly danger encompassing us, and I could not shake his opinion.

We took the same road to the crown of the Berg, and I was confirmed in my suspicion that the woods were empty and the watchers gone. The place was as deserted as the bush at Umvelos'. When we reached the summit about sunset we waited anxiously for the sound of drums. It came, as we expected, louder and more menacing than before. Wardlaw stood pinching my arm as the great tattoo swept down the escarpment, and died away in the far mountains beyond the Olifants. Yet it no longer seemed to be a wall of sound, shutting us out from our kindred in the West. A message had pierced the wall. If the blesbok were changing ground, I believed that the hunters were calling out their hounds and getting ready for the chase.

# CHAPTER VII

## CAPTAIN ARCOLL TELLS A TALE

It froze in the night, harder than was common on the Berg even in winter, and as I crossed the road next morning it was covered with rime. All my fears had gone, and my mind was strung high with expectation. Five pencilled words* may seem a small thing to build hope on, but it was enough for me, and I went about my work in the store with a reasonably light heart. One of the first things I did was to take stock of our armoury.* There were five sporting Mausers of a cheap make, one Mauser pistol, a Lee-Speed carbine, and a little nickel-plated revolver. There was also Japp's shot-gun, an old hammered breech-loader, as well as the gun I had brought out with me. There was a good supply of cartridges, including a stock for a .400 express which could not be found. I pocketed the revolver, and searched till I discovered a good sheath-knife. If fighting was in prospect I might as well look to my arms.

All the morning I sat among flour and sugar possessing my soul in as much patience as I could command. Nothing came down the white road from the west. The sun melted the rime; the flies came out and buzzed in the window; Japp got himself out of bed, brewed strong coffee, and went back to his slumbers. Presently it was dinner-time, and I went over to a silent meal with Wardlaw. When I returned I must have fallen asleep over a pipe, for the next thing I knew I was blinking drowsily at the patch of sun in the door, and listening for footsteps. In the dead stillness of the afternoon I thought I could discern a shuffling in the dust. I got up and looked out, and there, sure enough, was some one coming down the road.

But it was only a Kaffir, and a miserable-looking object at that. I had never seen such an anatomy. It was a very old man, bent almost double, and clad in a ragged shirt and a pair of foul khaki trousers. He carried an iron pot, and a few belongings were tied up in a dirty handkerchief. He must have been a *dacha*[1] smoker, for he coughed hideously, twisting his body with the paroxysms. I had seen the type before—the old broken-down native who had no kin to support him, and no tribe to shelter him. They wander about the roads, cooking their wretched meals by their little fires, till one morning they are found stiff under a bush.

The native gave me a good-day in Kaffir, then begged for tobacco or a handful of mealie-meal.

I asked him where he came from.

'From the west, Inkoos,' he said, 'and before that from the south. It is a sore road for old bones.'

I went into the store to fetch some meal, and when I came out he had shuffled close to the door. He had kept his eyes on the ground, but now he looked up at me, and I thought he had very bright eyes for such an old wreck.

'The nights are cold, Inkoos,' he wailed, 'and my folk are scattered, and I have no kraal.* The aasvogels* follow me, and I can hear the blesbok.'

'What about the blesbok?' I asked with a start.

'The blesbok are changing ground,' he said, and looked me straight in the face.

'And where are the hunters?' I asked.

'They are here and behind me,' he said in English, holding out his pot for my meal, while he began to edge into the middle of the road.

I followed, and, speaking English, asked him if he knew of a man named Colles.

'I come from him, young Baas. Where is your house? Ah, the school. There will be a way in by the back window? See that it is open, for I'll be there shortly.' Then lifting up his voice he called down in Sesuto all manner of blessings on me for my kindness, and went shuffling down the sunlit road, coughing like a volcano.

In high excitement I locked up the store and went over to Mr Wardlaw. No children had come to school that day, and he

[1] Hemp.

was sitting idle, playing patience. 'Lock the door,' I said, 'and come into my room. We're on the brink of explanations.'

In about twenty minutes the bush below the back-window parted and the Kaffir slipped out. He grinned at me, and after a glance round, hopped very nimbly over the sill. Then he examined the window and pulled the curtains.

'Is the outer door shut?' he asked in excellent English. 'Well, get me some hot water, and any spare clothes you may possess, Mr Crawfurd. I must get comfortable before we begin our *indaba*.[1] We've the night before us, so there's plenty of time. But get the house clear, and see that nobody disturbs me at my toilet. I am a modest man, and sensitive about my looks.'

I brought him what he wanted, and looked on at an amazing transformation.* Taking a phial from his bundle, he rubbed some liquid on his face and neck and hands, and got rid of the black colouring. His body and legs he left untouched, save that he covered them with shirt and trousers from my wardrobe. Then he pulled off a scaly wig, and showed beneath it a head of close-cropped grizzled hair. In ten minutes the old Kaffir had been transformed into an active soldierly-looking man of maybe fifty years. Mr Wardlaw stared as if he had seen a resurrection.

'I had better introduce myself,' he said, when he had taken the edge off his thirst and hunger. 'My name is Arcoll, Captain James Arcoll. I am speaking to Mr Crawfurd, the storekeeper, and Mr Wardlaw, the schoolmaster, of Blaauwildebeestefontein. Where, by the way, is Mr Peter Japp? Drunk? Ah, yes, it was always his failing. The quorum, however, is complete without him.'

By this time it was about sunset, and I remember I cocked my ear to hear the drums beat. Captain Arcoll noticed the movement as he noticed all else.

'You're listening for the drums, but you won't hear them. That business is over here. To-night they beat in Swaziland and down into the Tonga border. Three days more, unless you and I, Mr Crawfurd, are extra smart, and they'll be hearing them in Durban.'

[1] Council.

It was not till the lamp was lit, the fire burning well, and the house locked and shuttered, that Captain Arcoll began his tale.

'First,' he said, 'let me hear what you know. Colles told me that you were a keen fellow, and had wind of some mystery here. You wrote him about the way you were spied on, but I told him to take no notice. Your affair, Mr Crawfurd, had to wait on more urgent matters. Now, what do you think is happening?'

I spoke very shortly, weighing my words, for I felt I was on trial before these bright eyes. 'I think that some kind of native rising is about to commence.'

'Ay,' he said dryly, 'you would, and your evidence would be the spying and drumming. Anything more?'

'I have come on the tracks of a lot of I.D.B. work in the neighbourhood. The natives have some supply of diamonds, which they sell bit by bit, and I don't doubt but they have been getting guns with the proceeds.'

He nodded. 'Have you any notion who has been engaged in the job?'

I had it on my tongue to mention Japp, but forbore, remembering my promise. 'I can name one,' I said, 'a little yellow Portugoose, who calls himself Henriques or Hendricks. He passed by here the day before yesterday.'

Captain Arcoll suddenly was consumed with quiet laughter. 'Did you notice the Kaffir who rode with him and carried his saddlebags? Well, he's one of my men. Henriques would have a fit if he knew what was in those saddlebags. They contain my change of clothes, and other odds and ends. Henriques' own stuff is in a hole in the spruit. A handy way of getting one's luggage sent on, eh? The bags are waiting for me at a place I appointed.' And again Captain Arcoll indulged his sense of humour. Then he became grave, and returned to his examination.

'A rising, with diamonds as the sinews of war, and Henriques as the chief agent. Well and good! But who is to lead, and what are the natives going to rise about?'

'I know nothing further, but I have made some guesses.'

'Let's hear your guesses,' he said, blowing smoke rings from his pipe.

'I think the main mover is a great black minister who calls himself John Laputa.'

Captain Arcoll nearly sprang out of his chair. 'Now, how on earth did you find that out? Quick, Mr Crawfurd, tell me all you know, for this is desperately important.'

I began at the beginning, and told him the story of what happened on the Kirkcaple shore. Then I spoke of my sight of him on board ship, his talk with Henriques about Blaauwilde-beestefontein, and his hurried departure from Durban.

Captain Arcoll listened intently, and at the mention of Durban he laughed. 'You and I seem to have been running on lines which nearly touched. I thought I had grabbed my friend Laputa that night in Durban, but I was too cocksure and he slipped off. Do you know, Mr Crawfurd, you have been on the right trail long before me? When did you say you saw him at his devil-worship? Seven years ago? Then you were the first man alive to know the Reverend John in his true colours. You knew seven years ago what I only found out last year.'

'Well, that's my story,' I said. 'I don't know what the rising is about, but there's one other thing I can tell you. There's some kind of sacred place for the Kaffirs, and I've found out where it is.' I gave him a short account of my adventures in the Rooirand.

He smoked silently for a bit after I had finished. 'You've got the skeleton of the whole thing right, and you only want the filling up. And you found out everything for yourself? Colles was right; you're not wanting in intelligence, Mr Crawfurd.'

It was not much of a compliment, but I have never been more pleased in my life. This slim, grizzled man, with his wrinkled face and bright eyes, was clearly not lavish in his praise. I felt it was no small thing to have earned a word of commendation.

'And now I will tell you my story,' said Captain Arcoll. 'It is a long story, and I must begin far back. It has taken me years to decipher it,* and, remember, I've been all my life at this native business. I can talk every dialect, and I have the customs of every tribe by heart. I've travelled over every mile of South Africa, and Central and East Africa too. I was in both the Matabele wars,* and I've seen a heap of other fighting which never got into the papers. So what I tell you you can take as gospel, for it is knowledge that was not learned in a day.'

He puffed away, and then asked suddenly, 'Did you ever hear of Prester John?'*

'The man that lived in Central Asia?' I asked, with a reminiscence of a story-book I had as a boy.

'No, no,' said Mr Wardlaw, 'he means the King of Abyssinia in the fifteenth century. I've been reading all about him. He was a Christian, and the Portuguese sent expedition after expedition to find him, but they never got there. Albuquerque wanted to make an alliance with him and capture the Holy Sepulchre.'

Arcoll nodded. 'That's the one I mean. There's not very much known about him, except Portuguese legends. He was a sort of Christian, but I expect that his practices were as pagan as his neighbours'. There is no doubt that he was a great conqueror. Under him and his successors, the empire of Ethiopia extended far south of Abyssinia away down to the Great Lakes.'

'How long did this power last?' I asked wondering to what tale this was prologue.

'That's a mystery no scholar has ever been able to fathom. Anyhow, the centre of authority began to shift southward, and the warrior tribes moved in that direction. At the end of the sixteenth century the chief native power was round about the Zambesi. The Mazimba and the Makaranga had come down from the Lake Nyassa quarter, and there was a strong kingdom in Manicaland. That was the Monomotapa that the Portuguese thought so much of.'

Wardlaw nodded eagerly. The story was getting into ground that he knew about.

'The thing to remember is that all these little empires thought themselves the successors of Prester John. It took me a long time to find this out, and I have spent days in the best libraries in Europe over it. They all looked back to a great king in the north, whom they called by about twenty different names. They had forgotten about his Christianity, but they remembered that he was a conqueror.

'Well, to make a long story short, Monomotapa disappeared

in time, and fresh tribes came down from the north, and pushed right down to Natal and the Cape. That is how the Zulus first appeared. They brought with them the story of Prester John, but by this time it had ceased to be a historical memory, and had become a religious cult. They worshipped a great Power who had been their ancestor, and the favourite Zulu word for him was Umkulunkulu. The belief was perverted into fifty different forms, but this was the central creed—that Umkulunkulu had been the father of the tribe, and was alive as a spirit to watch over them.

'They brought more than a creed with them. Somehow or other, some fetich had descended from Prester John by way of the Mazimba and Angoni and Makaranga. What it is I do not know, but it was always in the hands of the tribe which for the moment held the leadership. The great native wars of the sixteenth century, which you can read about in the Portuguese historians, were not for territory but for leadership, and mainly for the possession of this fetich. Anyhow, we know that the Zulus brought it down with them. They called it *Ndhlondhlo*,\* which means the Great Snake, but I don't suppose that it was any kind of snake. The snake was their totem, and they would naturally call their most sacred possession after it.

'Now I will tell you a thing that few know. You have heard of Tchaka. He was a sort of black Napoleon early in the last century, and he made the Zulus the paramount power in South Africa, slaughtering about two million souls to accomplish it. Well, he had the fetich, whatever it was, and it was believed that he owed his conquests to it. Mosilikatse tried to steal it, and that was why he had to fly to Matabeleland. But with Tchaka it disappeared. Dingaan did not have it, nor Panda, and Cetewayo never got it, though he searched the length and breadth of the country for it. It had gone out of existence, and with it the chance of a Kaffir empire.'

Captain Arcoll got up to light his pipe, and I noticed that his face was grave. He was not telling us this yarn for our amusement.

'So much for Prester John and his charm,' he said. 'Now I have to take up the history at a different point. In spite of risings here and there, and occasional rows, the Kaffirs have been quiet for the better part of half a century. It is no credit to us. They have had plenty of grievances, and we are no nearer understanding them than our fathers were. But they are scattered and divided. We have driven great wedges of white settlement into their territory, and we have taken away their arms. Still, they are six times as many as we are, and they have long memories, and a thoughtful man may wonder how long the peace will last. I have often asked myself that question, and till lately I used to reply, "For ever because they cannot find a leader with the proper authority, and they have no common cause to fight for." But a year or two ago I began to change my mind.

'It is my business to act as chief Intelligence officer among the natives. Well, one day, I came on the tracks of a curious person. He was a Christian minister called Laputa, and he was going among the tribes from Durban to the Zambesi as a roving evangelist. I found that he made an enormous impression, and yet the people I spoke to were chary of saying much about him. Presently I found that he preached more than the gospel. His word was "Africa for the Africans," and his chief point was that the natives had had a great empire in the past, and might have a great empire again. He used to tell the story of Prester John, with all kinds of embroidery of his own. You see, Prester John was a good argument for him, for he had been a Christian as well as a great potentate.

'For years there has been plenty of this talk in South Africa, chiefly among Christian Kaffirs. It is what they call "Ethiopianism," and American negroes are the chief apostles. For myself, I always thought the thing perfectly harmless. I don't care a fig whether the native missions break away from the parent churches in England and call themselves by fancy names. The more freedom they have in their religious life, the less they are likely to think about politics. But I soon found out that Laputa was none of your flabby educated negroes from America, and I began to watch him.

'I first came across him at a revival meeting in London, where he was a great success. He came and spoke to me about my soul, but he gave up when I dropped into Zulu. The next time I met him was on the lower Limpopo, when I had the pleasure of trying to shoot him from a boat.'

Captain Arcoll took his pipe from his mouth and laughed at the recollection.

'I had got on to an I.D.B. gang, and to my amazement found the evangelist among them. But the Reverend John was too much for me. He went overboard in spite of the crocodiles, and managed to swim below water to the reed bed at the side. However, that was a valuable experience for me, for it gave me a clue.

'I next saw him at a Missionary Conference in Cape Town, and after that at a meeting of the Geographical Society in London, where I had a long talk with him. My reputation does not follow me home, and he thought I was an English publisher with an interest in missions. You see I had no evidence to connect him with I.D.B., and besides I fancied that his real game was something bigger than that; so I just bided my time and watched.

'I did my best to get on to his *dossier*, but it was no easy job. However, I found out a few things. He had been educated in the States, and well educated too, for the man is a good scholar and a great reader, besides the finest natural orator I have ever heard. There was no doubt that he was of Zulu blood, but I could get no traces of his family. He must come of high stock, for he is a fine figure of a man.

'Very soon I found it was no good following him in his excursions into civilization. There he was merely the educated Kaffir; a great pet of missionary societies, and a favourite speaker at Church meetings. You will find evidence given by him in Blue-Books on native affairs, and he counted many members of Parliament at home among his correspondents. I let that side go, and resolved to dog him when on his evangelizing tours in the back-veld.

'For six months I stuck to him like a leech. I am pretty good at disguises, and he never knew who was the broken-down old Kaffir who squatted in the dirt at the edge of the crowd when he spoke, or the half-caste who called him "Sir" and drove his Cape-cart. I had some queer adventures, but these can wait.

The gist of the thing is, that after six months which turned my hair grey I got a glimmering of what he was after. He talked Christianity to the mobs in the kraals, but to the indunas[1] he told a different story.'

Captain Arcoll helped himself to a drink. 'You can guess what that story was, Mr Crawfurd. At full moon when the black cock was blooded, the Reverend John forgot his Christianity. He was back four centuries among the Mazimba sweeping down on the Zambesi. He told them, and they believed him, that he was the Umkulunkulu, the incarnated spirit of Prester John. He told them that he was there to lead the African race to conquest and empire. Ay, and he told them more: for he has, or says he has, the Great Snake itself, the necklet of Prester John.'

Neither of us spoke; we were too occupied with fitting this news into our chain of knowledge.

Captain Arcoll went on. 'Now that I knew his purpose, I set myself to find out his preparations. It was not long before I found a mighty organization at work from the Zambesi to the Cape. The great tribes were up to their necks in the conspiracy, and all manner of little sects had been taken in. I have sat at tribal councils and been sworn a blood brother, and I have used the secret password to get knowledge in odd places. It was a dangerous game, and, as I have said, I had my adventures, but I came safe out of it—with my knowledge.

'The first thing I found out was that there was a great deal of wealth somewhere among the tribes. Much of it was in diamonds, which the labourers stole from the mines and the chiefs impounded. Nearly every tribe had its secret chest, and our friend Laputa had the use of them all. Of course the difficulty was changing the diamonds into coin, and he had to start I.D.B. on a big scale. Your pal, Henriques, was the chief agent for this, but he had others at Mozambique and Johannesburg, ay, and in London, whom I have on my list. With the money, guns and ammunition were bought, and it seems that a pretty flourishing trade has been going on for some time. They came in mostly overland through Portuguese territory,

[1] Lesser chiefs.

though there have been cases of consignments to Johannesburg houses, the contents of which did not correspond with the invoice. You ask what the Governments were doing to let this go on. Yes, and you may well ask. They were all asleep. They never dreamed of danger from the natives, and in any case it was difficult to police the Portuguese side. Laputa knew our weakness, and he staked everything on it.

'My first scheme was to lay Laputa by the heels; but no Government would act on my information. The man was strongly buttressed by public support at home, and South Africa has burned her fingers before this with arbitrary arrests. Then I tried to fasten I.D.B. on him, but I could not get my proofs till too late. I nearly had him in Durban, but he got away; and he never gave me a second chance. For five months he and Henriques have been lying low, because their scheme was getting very ripe. I have been following them through Zululand and Gazaland, and I have discovered that the train is ready, and only wants the match. For a month I have never been more than five hours behind him on the trail; and if he has laid his train, I have laid mine also.'

Arcoll's whimsical, humorous face had hardened into grimness, and in his eyes there was the light of a fierce purpose. The sight of him comforted me, in spite of his tale.

'But what can he hope to do?' I asked. 'Though he roused every Kaffir in South Africa he would be beaten. You say he is an educated man. He must know he has no chance in the long run.'

'I said he was an educated man, but he is also a Kaffir. He can see the first stage of a thing, and maybe the second, but no more. That is the native mind. If it was not like that our chance would be the worse.'

'You say the scheme is ripe,' I said; 'how ripe?'

Arcoll looked at the clock. 'In half an hour's time Laputa will be with 'Mpefu. There he will stay the night. To-morrow morning he goes to Umvelos' to meet Henriques. To-morrow evening the gathering begins.'

'One question,' I said. 'How big a man is Laputa?'

'The biggest thing that the Kaffirs have ever produced. I

tell you, in my opinion he is a great genius. If he had been white he might have been a second Napoleon. He is a born leader of men, and as brave as a lion. There is no villainy he would not do if necessary, and yet I should hesitate to call him a blackguard. Ay, you may look surprised at me, you two pragmatical Scotsmen; but I have, so to speak, lived with the man for months, and there's fineness and nobility in him. He would be a terrible enemy, but a just one. He has the heart of a poet and a king, and it is God's curse that he has been born among the children of Ham.* I hope to shoot him like a dog in a day or two, but I am glad to bear testimony to his greatness.'

'If the rising starts to-morrow,' I asked, 'have you any of his plans?'

He picked up a map from the table and opened it. 'The first rendezvous is somewhere near Sikitola's. Then they move south, picking up contingents; and the final concentration is to be on the high veld near Amsterdam, which is convenient for the Swazis and the Zulus. After that I know nothing, but of course there are local concentrations along the whole line of the Berg from Mashonaland to Basutoland. Now, look here. To get to Amsterdam they must cross the Delagoa Bay Railway. Well, they won't be allowed to. If they get as far, they will be scattered there. As I told you, I too have laid my train. We have the police ready all along the scarp of the Berg. Every exit from native territory is watched, and the frontier farmers are out on commando.* We have regulars on the Delagoa Bay and Natal lines, and a system of field telegraphs laid which can summon further troops to any point. It has all been kept secret, because we are still in the dark ourselves. The newspaper public knows nothing about any rising, but in two days every white household in South Africa will be in a panic. Make no mistake, Mr Crawfurd; this is a grim business. We shall smash Laputa and his men, but it will be a fierce fight, and there will be much good blood shed. Besides, it will throw the country back another half-century. Would to God I had been man enough to put a bullet through his head in cold blood. But I could not do it—it was too like murder; and maybe I shall never have the chance now.'

'There's one thing puzzles me,' I said. 'What makes Laputa come up here to start with? Why doesn't he begin with Zululand?'

'God knows! There's sure to be sense in it, for he does nothing without reason. We may know to-morrow.'

But as Captain Arcoll spoke, the real reason suddenly flashed into my mind: Laputa had to get the Great Snake, the necklet of Prester John, to give his leadership prestige. Apparently he had not yet got it, or Arcoll would have known. He started from this neighbourhood because the fetich was somewhere hereabouts. I was convinced that my guess was right, but I kept my own counsel.

'To-morrow Laputa and Henriques meet at Umvelos', probably at your new store, Mr Crawfurd. And so the ball commences.'

My resolution was suddenly taken.

'I think,' I said, 'I had better be present at the meeting, as representing the firm.'

Captain Arcoll stared at me and laughed. 'I had thought of going myself,' he said.

'Then you go to certain death, disguise yourself as you please. You cannot meet them in the store as I can. I'm there on my ordinary business, and they will never suspect. If you're to get any news, I'm the man to go.'

He looked at me steadily for a minute or so. 'I'm not sure that's such a bad idea of yours. I would be better employed myself on the Berg, and, as you say, I would have little chance of hearing anything. You're a plucky fellow, Mr Crawfurd. I suppose you understand that the risk is pretty considerable.'

'I suppose I do; but since I'm in this thing, I may as well see it out. Besides, I've an old quarrel with our friend Laputa.'

'Good and well,' said Captain Arcoll. 'Draw in your chair to the table, then, and I'll explain to you the disposition of my men. I should tell you that I have loyal natives in my pay in most tribes, and can count on early intelligence. We can't match their telepathy; but the new type of field telegraph is not so bad, and may be a trifle more reliable.'

Till midnight we pored over maps, and certain details were

burned in on my memory. Then we went to bed and slept soundly, even Mr Wardlaw. It was strange how fear had gone from the establishment, now that we knew the worst and had a fighting man by our side.

# CHAPTER VIII

## I FALL IN AGAIN WITH THE REVEREND JOHN LAPUTA

ONCE, as a boy, I had earnestly desired to go into the army, and had hopes of rising to be a great general. Now that I know myself better, I do not think I would have been much good at a general's work. I would have shirked the loneliness of it, the isolation of responsibility. But I think I would have done well in a subaltern command, for I had a great notion of carrying out orders, and a certain zest in the mere act of obedience. Three days before I had been as nervous as a kitten because I was alone and it was 'up to me,' as Americans say, to decide on the next step. But now that I was only one wheel in a great machine of defence my nervousness seemed to have fled. I was well aware that the mission I was bound on was full of risk; but, to my surprise, I felt no fear. Indeed, I had much the same feeling as a boy on a Saturday's holiday who has planned a big expedition. One thing only I regretted—that Tam Dyke was not with me to see the fun. The thought of that faithful soul, now beating somewhere on the seas, made me long for his comradeship. As I shaved, I remember wondering if I would ever shave again, and the thought gave me no tremors. For once in my sober life I was strung up to the gambler's pitch of adventure.

My job was to go to Umvelos' as if on my ordinary business, and if possible find out something of the evening's plan of march. The question was how to send back a message to Arcoll, assuming I had any difficulty in getting away. At first this puzzled us both, and then I thought of Colin. I had trained the dog to go home at my bidding, for often when I used to go hunting I would have occasion to visit a kraal where he would have been a nuisance. Accordingly, I resolved to take Colin with me, and, if I got into trouble, to send word by him.

I asked about Laputa's knowledge of our preparations. Arcoll was inclined to think that he suspected little. The police and the commandos had been kept very secret, and, besides, they were moving on the high veld and out of the ken of the tribes. Natives, he told me, were not good scouts so far as white man's work was concerned, for they did not understand the meaning of what we did. On the other hand, his own native scouts brought him pretty accurate tidings of any Kaffir movements. He thought that all the bush country of the plain would be closely watched, and that no one would get through without some kind of pass. But he thought also that the storekeeper might be an exception, for his presence would give rise to no suspicions. Almost his last words to me were to come back hell-for-leather if I saw the game was hopeless, and in any case to leave as soon as I got any news. 'If you're there when the march begins,' he said, 'they'll cut your throat for a certainty.' I had all the various police posts on the Berg clear in my mind, so that I would know where to make for if the road to Blaauwildebeestefontein should be closed.

I said good-bye to Arcoll and Wardlaw with a light heart, though the schoolmaster broke down and implored me to think better of it. As I turned down into the gorge I heard the sound of horses' feet far behind, and, turning back, saw white riders dismounting at the dorp. At any rate I was leaving the country well guarded in my rear.

It was a fine morning in mid-winter, and I was in very good spirits as I jogged on my pony down the steep hill-road, with Colin running beside me. A month before I had taken the same journey, with no suspicion in my head of what the future was to bring. I thought about my Dutch companions, now with their cattle far out on the plains. Did they know of the great danger, I wondered. All the way down the glen I saw no sign of human presence. The game-birds mocked me from the thicket; a brace of white *berghaan* circled far up in the blue; and I had for pleasant comrade the brawling river. I dismounted once to drink, and in that green haven of flowers and ferns I was struck sharply with a sense of folly. Here were we wretched creatures of men making for each other's throats, and outraging the good earth which God had made so fair a habitation.

I had resolved on a short cut to Umvelos', avoiding the neighbourhood of Sikitola's kraal, so when the river emerged from the glen I crossed it and struck into the bush. I had not gone far before I realized that something strange was going on. It was like the woods on the Berg a week before. I had the impression of many people moving in the bush, and now and then I caught a glimpse of them. My first thought was that I should be stopped, but soon it appeared that these folk had business of their own which did not concern me. I was conscious of being watched, yet it was clear that the bush folk were not there for the purpose of watching me.

For a little I kept my spirits, but as the hours passed with the same uncanny hurrying to and fro all about me my nerves began to suffer. Weeks of espionage at Blaauwildebeestefontein had made me jumpy. These people apparently meant me no ill, and had no time to spare on me. But the sensation of moving through them was like walking on a black-dark night with precipices all around. I felt odd quiverings between my shoulder blades where a spear might be expected to lodge. Overhead was a great blue sky and a blazing sun, and I could see the path running clear before me between the walls of scrub. But it was like midnight to me, a midnight of suspicion and unknown perils. I began to wish heartily I had never come.

I stopped for my midday meal at a place called Taqui, a grassy glade in the bush where a tiny spring of water crept out from below a big stone, only to disappear in the sand. Here I sat and smoked for half an hour, wondering what was going to become of me. The air was very still, but I could hear the rustle of movement somewhere within a hundred yards. The hidden folk were busy about their own ends, and I regretted that I had not taken the road by Sikitola's and seen how the kraals looked. They must be empty now, for the young men were already out on some mission. So nervous I got that I took my pocket-book and wrote down certain messages to my mother, which I implored whoever should find my body to transmit. Then, a little ashamed of my childishness, I pulled myself together, and remounted.

About three in the afternoon I came over a low ridge of bush and saw the corrugated iron roof of the store and the gleam of water from the Labongo. The sight encouraged me, for at any rate it meant the end of this disquieting ride. Here the bush changed to trees of some size, and after leaving the ridge the road plunged for a little into a thick shade. I had forgotten for a moment the folk in the bush, and when a man stepped out of the thicket I pulled up my horse with a start.

It was a tall native, who carried himself proudly, and after a glance at me, stalked along at my side. He wore curious clothes, for he had a kind of linen tunic, and around his waist hung a kilt of leopard-skin. In such a man one would have looked for a *ring-kop*,[1] but instead he had a mass of hair, not like a Kaffir's wool, but long and curled like some popular musician's. I should have been prepared for the face, but the sight of it sent a sudden chill of fright through my veins. For there was the curved nose, the deep flashing eyes, and the cruel lips of my enemy of the Kirkcaple shore.

Colin was deeply suspicious and followed his heels growling, but he never turned his head.

'The day is warm, father,' I said in Kaffir. 'Do you go far?'

He slackened his pace till he was at my elbow. 'But a short way, Baas,' he replied in English; 'I go to the store yonder.'

'Well met, then,' said I, 'for I am the storekeeper. You will find little in it, for it is newly built and not yet stocked. I have ridden over to see to it.'

He turned his face to me. 'That is bad news. I had hoped for food and drink yonder. I have travelled far, and in the chill nights I desire a cover for my head. Will the Baas allow me to sleep the night in an outhouse?'

By this time I had recovered my nerve, and was ready to play the part I had determined on. 'Willingly,' I said. 'You may sleep in the storeroom if you care. You will find sacks for bedding, and the place is snug enough on a cold night.'

He thanked me with a grave dignity which I had never seen in any Kaffir. As my eye fell on his splendid proportions I forgot all else in my admiration of the man. In his minister's clothes he had looked only a heavily built native, but now in his savage dress I saw how noble a figure he made. He must

---

[1] The circlet into which, with the aid of gum, Zulu warriors weave their hair.

have been at least six feet and a half, but his chest was so deep
and his shoulders so massive that one did not remark his
height. He put a hand on my saddle, and I remember noting
how slim and fine it was, more like a high-bred woman's than
a man's. Curiously enough he filled me with a certain confidence. 'I do not think you will cut my throat,' I said to myself.
'Your game is too big for common murder.'

The store at Umvelos' stood as I had left it. There was the
sjambok I had forgotten still lying on the window sill. I
unlocked the door, and a stifling smell of new paint came out
to meet me. Inside there was nothing but the chairs and
benches, and in a corner the pots and pans I had left against
my next visit. I unlocked the cupboard and got out a few
stores, opened the windows of the bedroom next door, and
flung my kaross on the cartel* which did duty as bed. Then I
went out to find Laputa standing patiently in the sunshine.

I showed him the outhouse where I had said he might sleep.
It was the largest room in the store, but wholly unfurnished.
A pile of barrels and packing-cases stood in the corner, and
there was enough sacking to make a sort of bed.

'I am going to make tea,' I said. 'If you have come far you
would maybe like a cup?'

He thanked me, and I made a fire in the grate and put on
the kettle to boil. Then I set on the table biscuits, and sardines,
and a pot of jam. It was my business now to play the fool, and
I believe I succeeded to admiration in the part. I blush to-day
to think of the stuff I talked.* First I made him sit on a chair
opposite me, a thing no white man in the country would have
done. Then I told him affectionately that I liked natives, that
they were fine fellows and better men than the dirty whites
round about. I explained that I was fresh from England, and
believed in equal rights for all men, white or coloured. God
forgive me, but I think I said I hoped to see the day when
Africa would belong once more to its rightful masters.

He heard me with an impassive face, his grave eyes studying
every line of me. I am bound to add that he made a hearty
meal, and drank three cups of strong tea of my brewing. I gave
him a cigar, one of a lot I had got from a Dutch farmer who
was experimenting with their manufacture—and all the while

I babbled of myself and my opinions. He must have thought me half-witted, and indeed before long I began to be of the same opinion myself. I told him that I meant to sleep the night here, and go back in the morning to Blaauwildebeestefontein, and then to Pietersdorp for stores. By-and-by I could see that he had ceased to pay any attention to what I said. I was clearly set down in his mind as a fool. Instead he kept looking at Colin, who was lying blinking in the doorway, one wary eye cocked on the stranger.

'You have a fine dog,' he observed.

'Yes,' I agreed, with one final effort of mendacity, 'he's fine to look at, but he has no grit in him. Any mongrel from a kraal can make him turn tail. Besides, he is a born fool and can't find his way home. I'm thinkng of getting rid of him.'

Laputa rose and his eye fell on the dog's back. I could see that he saw the lie of his coat, and that he did not agree with me.

'The food was welcome, Baas,' he said. 'If you will listen to me I can repay hospitality with advice. You are a stranger here. Trouble comes, and if you are wise you will go back to the Berg.'

'I don't know what you mean,' I said, with an air of cheerful idiocy. 'But back to the Berg I go the first thing in the morning. I hate these stinking plains.'

'It were wise to go to-night,' he said, with a touch of menace in his tone.

'I can't,' I said, and began to sing the chorus of a ridiculous music-hall song—

'There's no place like home—but'
I'm afraid to go home in the dark.'

Laputa shrugged his shoulders, stepped over the bristling Colin, and went out. When I looked after him two minutes later he had disappeared.

# CHAPTER IX

## THE STORE AT UMVELOS'

I SAT down on a chair and laboured to collect my thoughts. Laputa had gone, and would return sooner or later with Henriques. If I was to remain alive till morning, both of them must be convinced that I was harmless. Laputa was probably of that opinion, but Henriques would recognize me, and I had no wish to have that yellow miscreant investigating my character. There was only one way out of it—I must be incapably drunk. There was not a drop of liquor in the store, but I found an old whisky bottle half full of methylated spirits. With this I thought I might raise an atmosphere of bad whisky, and for the rest I must trust to my meagre gifts as an actor.

Supposing I escaped suspicion, Laputa and Henriques would meet in the outhouse, and I must find some means of overhearing them. Here I was fairly baffled. There was no window in the outhouse save in the roof, and they were sure to shut and bolt the door. I might conceal myself among the barrels inside; but apart from the fact that they were likely to search them before beginning their conference, it was quite certain that they would satisfy themselves that I was safe in the other end of the building before going to the outhouse.

Suddenly I thought of the cellar which we had built below the store. There was an entrance by a trap-door behind the counter, and another in the outhouse. I had forgotten the details, but my hope was that the second was among the barrels. I shut the outer door, prised up the trap, and dropped into the vault, which had been floored roughly with green bricks. Lighting match after match, I crawled to the other end and tried to lift the door. It would not stir, so I guessed that the barrels were on the top of it. Back to the outhouse I went, and found that sure enough a heavy packing-case was standing on a corner. I fixed it slightly open, so as to let me hear, and so arranged the odds and ends round about it that no one looking from the floor of the outhouse would guess at its existence. It occurred to me that the conspirators would want seats, so I placed two cases at the edge of the heap, that they might not be tempted to forage in the interior.

This done, I went back to the store and proceeded to rig myself out for my part. The cellar had made me pretty dirty, and I added some new daubs to my face. My hair had grown longish, and I ran my hands through it till it stood up like a cockatoo's crest. Then I cunningly disposed the methylated spirits in the places most likely to smell. I burned a little on the floor, I spilt some on the counter and on my hands, and I let it dribble over my coat. In five minutes I had made the room stink like a shebeen.* I loosened the collar of my shirt, and when I looked at myself in the cover of my watch I saw a specimen of debauchery which would have done credit to a Saturday night's police cell.

By this time the sun had gone down, but I thought it better to kindle no light. It was the night of the full moon—for which reason, I supposed, Laputa had selected it—and in an hour or two the world would be lit with that ghostly radiance. I sat on the counter while the minutes passed, and I confess I found the time of waiting very trying for my courage. I had got over my worst nervousness by having something to do, but whenever I was idle my fears returned. Laputa had a big night's work before him, and must begin soon. My vigil, I told myself, could not be long.

My pony was stalled in a rough shed we had built opposite the store. I could hear him shaking his head and stamping the ground above the croaking of the frogs by the Labongo. Presently it seemed to me that another sound came from behind the store—the sound of horses' feet and the ratttle of bridles. It was hushed for a moment, and then I heard human voices. The riders had tied up their horses to a tree and were coming nearer.

I sprawled gracefully on the counter, the empty bottle in my hand, and my eyes fixed anxiously on the square of the door, which was filled with the blue glimmer of the late twilight. The square darkened, and two men peered in. Colin growled from below the counter, but with one hand I held the scruff of his neck.

'Hullo,' I said, 'ish that my black friend? Awfly shorry, old man, but I've f'nish'd th' whisky. The bo-o-ottle shempty,' and I waved it upside down with an imbecile giggle.

Laputa said something which I did not catch. Henriques laughed an ugly laugh.

'We had better make certain of him,' he said.

The two argued for a minute, and then Laputa seemed to prevail. The door was shut and the key, which I had left in the lock, turned on me.

I gave them five minutes to get to the outhouse and settle to business. Then I opened the trap, got into the cellar, and crawled to the other end. A ray of light was coming through the partially raised door. By a blessed chance some old bricks had been left behind, and of these I made a footstool, which enabled me to get my back level with the door and look out. My laager* of barrels was intact, but through a gap I had left I could see the two men sitting on the two cases I had provided for them. A lantern was set between them, and Henriques was drinking out of a metal flask.

He took something—I could not see what—out of his pocket, and held it before his companion.

'Spoils of war,' he said. 'I let Sikitola's men draw first blood. They needed it to screw up their courage. Now they are as wild as Umbooni's.'

Laputa asked a question.

'It was the Dutchmen, who were out on the Koodoo Flats with their cattle. Man, it's no good being squeamish. Do you think you can talk over these surly black-veld fools? If we had not done it, the best of their horses would now be over the Berg to give warning. Besides, I tell you, Sikitola's men wanted blooding. I did for the old swine, Coetzee, with my own hands. Once he set his dogs on me, and I don't forget an injury.'

Laputa must have disapproved, for Henriques' voice grew high.

'Run the show the way you please,' he cried; 'but don't blame me if you make a hash of it. God, man, do you think you are going to work a revolution on skim milk? If I had my will, I would go in and stick a knife in the drunken hog next door.'

'He is safe enough,' Laputa replied. 'I gave him the chance of life, and he laughed at me. He won't get far on his road home.'

This was pleasant hearing for me, but I scarcely thought of myself. I was consumed with a passion of fury against the murdering yellow devil. With Laputa I was not angry; he was an open enemy, playing a fair game. But my fingers itched to get at the Portugoose—that double-dyed traitor to his race. As I thought of my kindly old friends, lying butchered with their kinsfolk out in the bush, hot tears of rage came to my eyes. Perfect love casteth out fear, the Bible says; but, to speak it reverently, so does perfect hate. Not for safety and a king's ransom would I have drawn back from the game. I prayed for one thing only, that God in His mercy would give me the chance of settling with Henriques.

I fancy I missed some of the conversation, being occupied with my own passion. At any rate, when I next listened the two were deep in plans. Maps were spread beside them, and Laputa's delicate forefinger was tracing a route. I strained my ears, but could catch only a few names. Apparently they were to keep in the plains till they had crossed the Klein Labongo and the Letaba. I thought I caught the name of the ford of the latter; it sounded like Dupree's Drift. After that the talk became plainer, for Laputa was explaining in his clear voice. The force would leave the bush, ascend the Berg by the glen of the Groot Letaba, and the first halt would be called at a place called Inanda's Kraal, where a promontory of the high-veld juts out behind the peaks called the Wolkberg or Cloud Mountains. All this was very much to the point, and the names sunk into my memory like a die into wax.

'Meanwhile,' said Laputa, 'there is the gathering at Ntaba-kaikonjwa.[1] It will take us three hours' hard riding to get there.'

Where on earth was Ntabakaikonjwa? It must be the native

[1] Literally, 'The Hill which is not to be pointed at'.

name for the Rooirand, for after all Laputa was not likely to use the Dutch word for his own sacred place.

'Nothing has been forgotten. The men are massed below the cliffs, and the chiefs and the great indunas will enter the Place of the Snake. The door will be guarded, and only the password will get a man through. That word is "Immanuel," which means, "God with us."'

'Well, when we get there, what happens?' Henriques asked with a laugh. 'What kind of magic will you spring on us?'

There was a strong contrast between the flippant tone of the Portugoose and the grave voice which answered him.

'The Keeper of the Snake will open the holy place, and bring forth the Isetembiso sami.[1] As the leader of my people, I will assume the collar of Umkulunkulu in the name of our God and the spirits of the great dead.'

'But you don't propose to lead the march in a necklace of rubies,' said Henriques, with a sudden eagerness in his voice.

Again Laputa spoke gravely, and, as it were, abstractedly. I heard the voice of one whose mind was fixed on a far horizon.

'When I am acclaimed king, I restore the Snake to its Keeper, and swear never to clasp it on my neck till I have led my people to victory.'

'I see,' said Henriques. 'What about the purification you mentioned?'

I had missed this before and listened earnestly.

'The vows we take in the holy place bind us till we are purged of them at Inanda's Kraal. Till then no blood must be shed and no flesh eaten. It was the fashion of our forefathers.'

'Well, I think you've taken on a pretty risky job,' Henriques said. 'You propose to travel a hundred miles, binding yourself not to strike a blow. It is simply putting yourself at the mercy of any police patrol.'

'There will be no patrol,' Laputa replied. 'Our march will be as secret and as swift as death. I have made my preparations.'

'But suppose you met with opposition,' the Portugoose persisted, 'would the rule hold?'

---

[1] Literally, 'Very sacred thing'.

'If any try to stop us, we shall tie them hand and foot, and carry them with us. Their fate will be worse than if they had been slain in battle.'

'I see,' said Henriques, whistling through his teeth. 'Well, before we start this vow business, I think I'll go back and settle that storekeeper.'

Laputa shook his head. 'Will you be serious and hear me? We have no time to knife harmless fools. Before we start for Ntabakaikonjwa I must have from you the figures of the arming in the south. That is the one thing which remains to be settled.'

I am certain these figures would have been most interesting, but I never heard them. My feet were getting cramped with standing on the bricks, and I inadvertently moved them. The bricks came down with a rattle, and unfortunately in slipping I clutched at the trap. This was too much for my frail prop, and the door slammed down with a great noise.

Here was a nice business for the eavesdropper! I scurried along the passage as stealthily as I could and clambered back into the store, while I heard the sound of Laputa and Henriques ferreting among the barrels. I managed to throttle Colin and prevent him barking, but I could not get the confounded trap to close behind me. Something had jammed in it, and it remained half a foot open.

I heard the two approaching the door, and I did the best thing that occurred to me. I pulled Colin over the trap, rolled on the top of him, and began to snore heavily as if in a drunken slumber.

The key was turned, and the gleam of a lantern was thrown on the wall. It flew up and down as its bearer cast the light into the corners.

'By God, he's gone,' I heard Henriques say. 'The swine was listening, and he has bolted now.'

'He won't bolt far,' Laputa said. 'He is here. He is snoring behind the counter.'

These were anxious moments for me. I had a firm grip on Colin's throat, but now and then a growl escaped, which was fortunately blended with my snores. I felt that a lantern was flashed on me, and that the two men were peering down at the heap on the half-opened trap. I think that was the worst minute I ever spent, for, as I have said, my courage was not so bad in action, but in a passive game it oozed out of my fingers.

'He is safe enough,' Laputa said, after what seemed to me an eternity. 'The noise was only the rats among the barrels.'

I thanked my Maker that they had not noticed the other trap-door.

'All the same I think I'll make him safer,' said Henriques.

Laputa seemed to have caught him by the arm.

'Come back and get to business,' he said. 'I've told you I'll have no more murder. You will do as I tell you, Mr Henriques.'

I did not catch the answer, but the two went out and locked the door. I patted the outraged Colin, and got to my feet with an aching side where the confounded lid of the trap had been pressing. There was no time to lose for the two in the outhouse would soon be setting out, and I must be before them.

With no better light than a ray of the moon through the window, I wrote a message on a leaf from my pocket-book. I told of the plans I had overheard, and especially I mentioned Dupree's Drift on the Letaba. I added that I was going to the Rooirand to find the secret of the cave, and in one final sentence implored Arcoll to do justice on the Portugoose. That was all, for I had no time for more. I carefully tied the paper with a string below the collar of the dog.

Then very quietly I went into the bedroom next door—the side of the store farthest from the outhouse. The place was flooded with moonlight, and the window stood open, as I had left it in the afternoon. As softly as I could I swung Colin over the sill and clambered after him. In my haste I left my coat behind me with my pistol in the pocket.

Now came a check. My horse was stabled in the shed, and that was close to the outhouse. The sound of leading him out would most certainly bring Laputa and Henriques to the door. In that moment I all but changed my plans. I thought of slipping back to the outhouse and trying to shoot the two men as they came forth. But I reflected that, before I could get them both, one or other would probably shoot me. Besides, I had a queer sort of compunction about killing Laputa. I understood now why Arcoll had stayed his hand from murder, and I was beginning to be of his opinion on our arch-enemy.

Then I remembered the horses tied up in the bush. One of them I could get with perfect safety. I ran round the end of the store and into the thicket, keeping on soft grass to dull my tread. There, tied up to a merula tree,* were two of the finest beasts I had seen in Africa. I selected the better, an Africander stallion of the *blaauw-schimmel*, or blue-roan type, which is famous for speed and endurance. Slipping his bridle from the branch, I led him a little way into the bush in the direction of the Rooirand.

Then I spoke to Colin. 'Home with you,' I said. 'Home, old man, as if you were running down a tsessebe.'[1]

The dog seemed puzzled. 'Home,' I said again, pointing west in the direction of the Berg. 'Home, you brute.'

And then he understood. He gave one low whine, and cast a reproachful eye on me and the blue roan. Then he turned, and with his head down set off with great lopes on the track of the road I had ridden in the morning.

A second later and I was in the saddle, riding hell-for-leather for the north.

---

[1] A species of buck, famous for its speed.

# CHAPTER X

## I GO TREASURE-HUNTING

FOR a mile or so I kept the bush, which was open and easy to ride through, and then turned into the path. The moon was high, and the world was all a dim dark green, with the track a golden ivory band before me. I had looked at my watch before I started, and seen that it was just after eight o'clock. I had a great horse under me, and less than thirty miles to cover. Midnight should see me at the cave. With the password I would gain admittance, and there would wait for Laputa and Henriques. Then, if my luck held, I should see the inner workings of the mystery which had puzzled me ever since the Kirkcaple shore. No doubt I should be roughly treated, tied up prisoner, and carried with the army when the march began. But till Inanda's Kraal my life was safe, and before that came the ford of the Letaba. Colin would carry my message to Arcoll, and at the Drift the tables would be turned on Laputa's men.

Looking back in cold blood, it seems the craziest chain of accidents to count on for preservation. A dozen possibilities might have shattered any link of it. The password might be wrong, or I might never get the length of those who knew it. The men in the cave might butcher me out of hand, or Laputa might think my behaviour a sufficient warrant for the breach of the solemnest vow. Colin might never get to Blaauwilde-beestefontein, Laputa might change his route of march, or Arcoll's men might fail to hold the Drift. Indeed, the other day at Portincross I was so overcome by the recollection of the perils I had dared and God's goodness towards me that I built a new hall for the parish kirk as a token of gratitude.*

Fortunately for mankind the brain in a life of action turns more to the matter in hand than to conjuring up the chances of the future. Certainly it was in no discomfort of mind that I swung along the moonlit path to the north. Truth to tell, I was almost happy. The first honours in the game had fallen to me.

I knew more about Laputa than any man living save Henriques; I had my finger on the central pulse of the rebellion. There was hid treasure ahead of me—a great necklace of rubies, Henriques had said. Nay, there must be more, I argued. This cave of the Rooirand was the headquarters of the rising, and there must be stored their funds—diamonds, and the gold they had been bartered for. I believe that every man has deep in his soul a passion for treasure-hunting, which will often drive a coward into prodigies of valour. I lusted for that treasure of jewels and gold. Once I had been high-minded, and thought of my duty to my country, but in that night ride I fear that what I thought of was my duty to enrich David Crawfurd. One other purpose simmered in my head. I was devoured with wrath against Henriques. Indeed, I think that was the strongest motive for my escapade, for even before I heard Laputa tell of the vows and the purification, I had it in my mind to go at all costs to the cave. I am a peaceable man at most times, but I think I would rather have had the Portugoose's throat in my hands than the collar of Prester John.

But behind my thoughts was one master-feeling, that Providence had given me my chance and I must make the most of it. Perhaps the Calvinism of my father's preaching had unconsciously taken grip of my soul. At any rate I was a fatalist in creed, believing that what was willed would happen, and that man was but a puppet in the hands of his Maker. I looked on the last months as a clear course which had been mapped out for me. Not for nothing had I been given a clue to the strange events which were coming. It was foreordained that I should go alone to Umvelos', and in the promptings of my own fallible heart I believed I saw the workings of Omnipotence. Such is our moral arrogance, and yet without such a belief I think that mankind would have ever been content to bide sluggishly at home.

I passed the spot where on my former journey I had met the horses, and knew that I had covered more than half the road. My ear had been alert for the sound of pursuit, but the bush was quiet as the grave. The man who rode my pony would find him a slow traveller, and I pitied the poor beast bucketed along by an angry rider. Gradually a hazy wall of purple began to shimmer before me, apparently very far off. I knew the ramparts of the Rooirand, and let my *schimmel* feel my knees in his ribs. Within an hour I should be at the cliff's foot.

I had trusted for safety to the password, but as it turned out I owed my life mainly to my horse. For, a mile or so from the cliffs, I came to the fringes of a great army. The bush was teeming with men, and I saw horses picketed in bunches, and a multitude of Cape-carts and light wagons. It was like a colossal gathering for *naachtmaal*[1] at a Dutch dorp, but every man was black. I saw through a corner of my eye that they were armed with guns, though many carried in addition their spears and shields. Their first impulse was to stop me. I saw guns fly to shoulders, and a rush towards the path. The boldest game was the safest, so I dug my heels into the *schimmel* and shouted for a passage. 'Make way!' I cried in Kaffir. 'I bear a message from the Inkulu.[2] Clear out, you dogs!'

They recognized the horse, and fell back with a salute. Had I but known it, the beast was famed from the Zambesi to the Cape. It was their king's own charger I rode, and who dared question such a warrant? I heard the word pass through the bush, and all down the road I got the salute. In that moment I fervently thanked my stars that I had got away first, for there would have been no coming second for me.

At the cliff-foot I found a double line of warriors who had the appearance of a royal guard, for all were tall men with leopard-skin cloaks. Their rifle-barrels glinted in the moon-light, and the sight sent a cold shiver down my back. Above them, among the scrub and along the lower slopes of the kranzes, I could see further lines with the same gleaming weapons. The Place of the Snake was in strong hands that night.

I dismounted and called for a man to take my horse. Two of the guards stepped forward in silence and took the bridle. This left the track to the cave open, and with as stiff a back as I could command, but a sadly fluttering heart, I marched through the ranks.

---

[1] The Communion Sabbath.
[2] A title applied only to the greatest chiefs.

The path was lined with guards, all silent and rigid as graven images. As I stumbled over the stones I felt that my appearance scarcely fitted the dignity of a royal messenger. Among those splendid men-at-arms I shambled along in old breeches and leggings, hatless, with a dirty face, dishevelled hair, and a torn flannel shirt. My mind was no better than my body, for now that I had arrived I found my courage gone. Had it been possible I would have turned tail and fled, but the boats were burned behind me, and I had no choice. I cursed my rash folly, and wondered at my exhilaration of an hour ago. I was going into the black mysterious darkness, peopled by ten thousand cruel foes. My knees rubbed against each other, and I thought that no man had even been in more deadly danger.

At the entrance to the gorge the guards ceased and I went on alone. Here there was no moonlight, and I had to feel my way by the sides. I moved very slowly, wondering how soon I should find the end my folly demanded. The heat of the ride had gone, and I remember feeling my shirt hang clammily on my shoulders.

Suddenly a hand was laid on my breast, and a voice demanded, 'The word?'

'Immanuel,'* I said hoarsely.

Then unseen hands took both my arms, and I was led farther into the darkness. My hopes revived for a second. The password had proved true, and at any rate I should enter the cave.

In the darkness I could see nothing, but I judged that we stopped before the stone slab which, as I remembered, filled the extreme end of the gorge. My guide did something with the right-hand wall, and I felt myself being drawn into a kind of passage. It was so narrow that two could not go abreast, and so low that the creepers above scraped my hair. Something clicked behind me like the turnstile at the gate of a show.

Then we began to ascend steps, still in utter darkness, and a great booming fell on my ear. It was the falling river which had scared me on my former visit, and I marvelled that I had not heard it sooner. Presently we came out into a gleam of moonlight, and I saw that we were inside the gorge and far above the slab. We followed a narrow shelf on its left side (or 'true right',* as mountaineers would call it) until we could go no farther. Then we did a terrible thing. Across the gorge, which here was at its narrowest, stretched a slab of stone. Far, far below I caught the moonlight on a mass of hurrying waters. This was our bridge, and though I have a good head for crags, I confess I grew dizzy as we turned to cross it. Perhaps it was broader than it looked; at any rate my guides seemed to have no fear, and strode across it as if it was a highway, while I followed in a sweat of fright. Once on the other side, I was handed over to a second pair of guides, who led me down a high passage running into the heart of the mountain.

The boom of the river sank and rose as the passage twined. Soon I saw a gleam of light ahead which was not the moon. It grew larger, until suddenly the roof rose and I found myself in a gigantic chamber. So high it was that I could not make out anything of the roof, though the place was brightly lit with torches stuck round the wall, and a great fire which burned at the farther end. But the wonder was on the left side, where the floor ceased in a chasm. The left wall was one sheet of water, where the river fell from the heights into the infinite depth below. The torches and the fire made the sheer stream glow and sparkle like the battlements of the Heavenly City. I have never seen any sight so beautiful or so strange, and for a second my breath stopped in admiration.

There were two hundred men or more in the chamber, but so huge was the place that they seemed only a little company. They sat on the ground in a circle, with their eyes fixed on the fire and on a figure which stood before it. The glow revealed the old man I had seen on that morning a month before moving towards the cave. He stood as if in a trance, straight as a tree, with his arms crossed on his breast. A robe of some shining white stuff fell from his shoulders, and was clasped round his middle by a broad circle of gold. His head was shaven, and on his forehead was bound a disc of carved gold. I saw from his gaze that his old eyes were blind.

'Who comes?' he asked as I entered.

'A messenger from the Inkulu,' I spoke up boldly. 'He follows soon with the white man, Henriques.'

Then I sat down in the back row of the circle to await

events. I noticed that my neighbour was the fellow 'Mwanga whom I had kicked out of the store. Happily I was so dusty that he could scarcely recognize me, but I kept my face turned away from him. What with the light and the warmth, the drone of the water, the silence of the folk, and my mental and physical stress, I grew drowsy and all but slept.

# CHAPTER XI

## THE CAVE OF THE ROOIRAND

I WAS roused by a sudden movement. The whole assembly stood up, and each man clapped his right hand to his brow and then raised it high. A low murmur of 'Inkulu' rose above the din of the water. Laputa strode down the hall, with Henriques limping behind him. They certainly did not suspect my presence in the cave, nor did Laputa show any ruffling of his calm. Only Henriques looked weary and cross. I guessed he had had to ride my pony.

The old man whom I took to be the priest advanced towards Laputa with his hands raised over his head. A pace before they met he halted, and Laputa went on his knees before him. He placed his hands on his head, and spoke some words which I could not understand. It reminded me, so queer are the tricks of memory, of an old Sabbath-school book I used to have which had a picture of Samuel ordaining Saul* as king of Israel. I think I had forgotten my own peril and was enthralled by the majesty of the place—the wavering torches, the dropping wall of green water, above all, the figures of Laputa and the Keeper of the Snake, who seemed to have stepped out of an antique world.

Laputa stripped off his leopard skin till he stood stark, a noble form of a man. Then the priest sprinkled some herbs on the fire, and a thin smoke rose to the roof. The smell was that I had smelled on the Kirkcaple shore, sweet, sharp, and strange enough to chill the marrow. And round the fire went the priest in widening and contracting circles, just as on that Sabbath evening in spring.

Once more we were sitting on the ground, all except Laputa and the Keeper. Henriques was squatting in the front row, a tiny creature among so many burly savages. Laputa stood with bent head in the centre.

Then a song began, a wild incantation in which all joined. The old priest would speak some words, and the reply came in barbaric music. The words meant nothing to me; they must

have been in some tongue long since dead. But the music told
its own tale. It spoke of old kings and great battles, of splendid
palaces and strong battlements, of queens white as ivory, of
death and life, love and hate, joy and sorrow. It spoke, too, of
desperate things, mysteries of horror long shut to the world.
No Kaffir ever forged that ritual. It must have come straight
from Prester John or Sheba's queen, or whoever ruled in
Africa when time was young.

I was horribly impressed. Devouring curiosity and a lurking
nameless fear filled my mind. My old dread had gone. I was
not afraid now of Kaffir guns, but of the black magic of which
Laputa had the key.

The incantation died away, but still herbs were flung on the
fire, till the smoke rose in a great cloud, through which the
priest loomed misty and huge. Out of the smoke-wreaths his
voice came high and strange. It was as if some treble stop had
been opened in a great organ, as against the bass drone of the
cataract.

He was asking Laputa questions, to which came answers in
that rich voice which on board the liner had preached the
gospel of Christ. The tongue I did not know, and I doubt if
my neighbours were in better case. It must have been some
old sacred language—Phoenician, Sabaean, I know not what—
which had survived in the rite of the Snake.

Then came silence while the fire died down and the smoke
eddied away in wreaths towards the river. The priest's lips
moved as if in prayer: of Laputa I saw only the back, and his
head was bowed.

Suddenly a rapt cry broke from the Keeper. 'God has
spoken,' he cried. 'The path is clear. The Snake returns to the
House of its Birth.'

An attendant led forward a black goat, which bleated feebly.
With a huge antique knife the old man slit its throat, catching
the blood in a stone ewer. Some was flung on the fire, which
had burned small and low.

'Even so,' cried the priest, 'will the king quench in blood the
hearth-fires of his foes.'

Then on Laputa's forehead and bare breast he drew a bloody
cross.

'I seal thee,' said the voice, 'priest and king of God's people.'

The ewer was carried round the assembly, and each dipped his finger in it and marked his forehead. I got a dab to add to the other marks on my face.

'Priest and king of God's people,' said the voice again, 'I call thee to the inheritance of John. Priest and king was he, king of kings, lord of hosts, master of the earth. When he ascended on high he left to his son the sacred Snake, the ark of his valour, to be God's dower and pledge to the people whom He has chosen.'

I could not make out what followed. It seemed to be a long roll of the kings who had borne the Snake. None of them I knew, but at the end I thought I caught the name of Tchaka the Terrible, and I remembered Arcoll's tale.

The Keeper held in his arms a box of curiously wrought ivory, about two feet long and one broad. He was standing beyond the ashes, from which, in spite of the blood, thin streams of smoke still ascended. He opened it, and drew out something which swung from his hand like a cascade of red fire.

'Behold the Snake,' cried the Keeper, and every man in the assembly, excepting Laputa and including me, bowed his head to the ground and cried 'Ow.'

'Ye who have seen the Snake,' came the voice, 'on you is the vow of silence and peace. No blood shall ye shed of man or beast, no flesh shall ye eat till the vow is taken from you. From the hour of midnight till sunrise on the second day ye are bound to God. Whoever shall break the vow, on him shall the curse fall. His blood shall dry in his veins, and his flesh shrink on his bones. He shall be an outlaw and accursed, and there shall follow him through life and death the Avengers of the Snake. Choose ye, my people; upon you is the vow.'

By this time we were all flat on our faces, and a great cry of assent went up. I lifted my head as much as I dared to see what would happen next.

The priest raised the necklace till it shone above his head like a halo of blood. I have never seen such a jewel, and I think there has never been another such on earth. Later I was to have the handling of it, and could examine it closely, though now I had only a glimpse. There were fifty-five rubies in it, the largest as big as a pigeon's egg, and the least not smaller than my thumbnail. In shape they were oval, cut on both sides *en cabochon,*\* and on each certain characters were engraved. No doubt this detracted from their value as gems, yet the characters might have been removed and the stones cut in facets, and these rubies would still have been the noblest in the world. I was no jewel merchant to guess their value, but I knew enough to see that here was wealth beyond human computation. At each end of the string was a great pearl and a golden clasp. The sight absorbed me to the exclusion of all fear. I, David Crawfurd, nineteen years of age, an assistant-storekeeper in a back-veld dorp, was privileged to see a sight to which no Portuguese adventurer had ever attained. There, floating on the smoke-wreaths, was the jewel which may once have burned in Sheba's hair.

As the priest held the collar aloft, the assembly rocked with a strange passion. Foreheads were rubbed in the dust, and then adoring eyes would be raised, while a kind of sobbing shook the worshippers. In that moment I learned something of the secret of Africa, of Prester John's empire and Tchaka's victories.

'In the name of God,' came the voice, 'I deliver to the heir of John the Snake of John.'

Laputa took the necklet and twined it in two loops round his neck till the clasp hung down over his breast. The position changed. The priest knelt before him, and received his hands on his head. Then I knew that, to the confusion of all talk about equality, God has ordained some men to be kings and others to serve. Laputa stood naked as when he was born. The rubies were dulled against the background of his skin, but they still shone with a dusky fire. Above the blood-red collar his face had the passive pride of a Roman emperor. Only his great eyes gloomed and burned as he looked on his followers.

'Heir of John,' he said, 'I stand before you as priest and king. My kingship is for the morrow. Now I am the priest to make intercession for my people.'

He prayed\*—prayed as I never heard man pray before—and to the God of Israel! It was no heathen fetich he was invoking, but the God of whom he had often preached in

Christian kirks. I recognized texts from Isaiah and the Psalms and the Gospels, and very especially from the two last chapters of Revelation. He pled with God to forget the sins of his people, to recall the bondage of Zion. It was amazing to hear these bloodthirsty savages consecrated by their leader to the meek service of Christ. An enthusiast may deceive himself, and I did not question his sincerity. I knew his heart, black with all the lusts of paganism. I knew that his purpose was to deluge the land with blood. But I knew also that in his eyes his mission was divine, and that he felt behind him all the armies of Heaven.

'*Thou hast been a strength to the poor,*' said the voice, '*a refuge from the storm, a shadow from the heat, when the blast of the Terrible Ones is as a storm against a wall.*

'*Thou shalt bring down the noise of strangers, as the heat in a dry place; ... the branch of the Terrible Ones shall be brought low.*

'*And in this mountain shall the Lord of Hosts make unto all people a feast of fat things, a feast of wines on the lees, of fat things full of marrow.*

'*And He will destroy in this mountain the face of the covering cast over all people, and the vail that is brought over all nations.*

'*And the rebuke of His people shall He take away from off all the earth; for the Lord hath spoken it.*'

I listened spellbound as he prayed. I heard the phrases familiar to me in my schooldays at Kirkcaple. He had some of the tones of my father's voice, and when I shut my eyes I could have believed myself a child again. So much he had got from his apprenticeship to the ministry. I wondered vaguely what the good folks who had listened to him in churches and halls at home would think of him now. But there was in the prayer more than the supplications of the quondam preacher. There was a tone of arrogant pride, the pride of the man to whom the Almighty is only another and greater Lord of Hosts. He prayed less as a suppliant than as an ally. A strange emotion tingled in my blood, half awe, half sympathy. As I have said, I understood that there are men born to kingship.

He ceased with a benediction. Then he put on his leopard-skin cloak and kilt, and received from the kneeling chief a

spear and shield. Now he was more king than priest, more
barbarian than Christian. It was as a king that he now spoke.

I had heard him on board the liner, and had thought his
voice the most wonderful I had ever met with. But now in that
great resonant hall the magic of it was doubled. He played
upon the souls of his hearers as on a musical instrument. At
will he struck the chords of pride, fury, hate, and mad joy.
Now they would be hushed in breathless quiet, and now the
place would echo with savage assent. I remember noticing that
the face of my neighbour, 'Mwanga, was running with tears.

He spoke of the great days of Prester John, and a hundred
names I had never heard of. He pictured the heroic age of his
nation, when every man was a warrior and hunter, and rich
kraals stood in the spots now desecrated by the white man, and
cattle wandered on a thousand hills. Then he told tales of
white infamy, lands snatched from their rightful possessors,
unjust laws which forced the Ethiopian to the bondage of a
despised caste, the finger of scorn everywhere, and the mocking word. If it be the part of an orator to rouse the passion of
his hearers, Laputa was the greatest on earth. 'What have ye
gained from the white man?' he cried. 'A bastard civilization
which has sapped your manhood; a false religion which would
rivet on you the chains of the slave. Ye, the old masters of the
land, are now the servants of the oppressor. And yet the
oppressors are few, and the fear of you is in their hearts. They
feast in their great cities, but they see the writing on the wall,
and their eyes are anxiously turning lest the enemy be at their
gates.' I cannot hope in my prosaic words to reproduce that
amazing discourse. Phrases which the hearers had heard at
mission schools now suddenly appeared, not as the white man's
learning, but as God's message to His own. Laputa fitted the
key to the cipher, and the meaning was clear. He concluded, I
remember, with a picture of the overthrow of the alien, and
the golden age which would dawn for the oppressed. Another
Ethiopian empire would arise, so majestic that the white man
everywhere would dread its name, so righteous that all men
under it would live in ease and peace.

By rights, I suppose, my blood should have been boiling at
this treason. I am ashamed to confess that it did nothing of the

sort. My mind was mesmerized by this amazing man. I could not refrain from shouting with the rest. Indeed I was a convert, if there can be conversion when the emotions are dominant and there is no assent from the brain. I had a mad desire to be of Laputa's party. Or rather, I longed for a leader who should master me and make my soul his own, as this man mastered his followers. I have already said that I might have made a good subaltern soldier, and the proof is that I longed for such a general.

As the voice ceased there was a deep silence. The hearers were in a sort of trance, their eyes fixed glassily on Laputa's face. It was the quiet of tense nerves and imagination at white-heat. I had to struggle with a spell which gripped me equally with the wildest savage. I forced myself to look round at the strained faces, the wall of the cascade, the line of torches. It was the sight of Henriques that broke the charm. Here was one who had no part in the emotion. I caught his eye fixed on the rubies, and in it I read only a devouring greed. It flashed through my mind that Laputa had a foe in his own camp, and the Prester's collar a votary whose passion was not that of worship.

The next thing I remember was a movement among the first ranks. The chiefs were swearing fealty. Laputa took off the collar and called God to witness that it should never again encircle his neck till he had led his people to victory. Then one by one the great chiefs and indunas advanced, and swore allegiance with their foreheads on the ivory box. Such a collection of races has never been seen. There were tall Zulus and Swazis with *ringkops** and feather head-dresses. There were men from the north with heavy brass collars and anklets; men with quills in their ears, and earrings and nose-rings; shaven heads, and heads with wonderfully twisted hair; bodies naked or all but naked, and bodies adorned with skins and necklets. Some were light in colour, and some were black as coal; some had squat negro features, and some thin, high-boned Arab faces. But in all there was the air of mad enthusiasm. For a day they were forsworn from blood, but their wild eyes and twitching hands told their future purpose.

For an hour or two I had been living in a dream-world.

Suddenly my absorption was shattered, for I saw that my time to swear was coming. I sat in the extreme back row at the end nearest the entrance, and therefore I should naturally be the last to go forward. The crisis was near when I should be discovered, for there was no question of my shirking the oath.

Then for the first time since I entered the cave I realized the frightful danger in which I stood. My mind had been strung so high by the ritual that I had forgotten all else. Now came the rebound, and with shaky nerves I had to face discovery and certain punishment. In that moment I suffered the worst terror of my life. There was much to come later, but by that time my senses were dulled. Now they had been sharpened by what I had seen and heard, my nerves were already quivering and my fancy on fire. I felt every limb shaking as 'Mwanga went forward. The cave swam before my eyes, heads were multiplied giddily, and I was only dimly conscious when he rose to return.

Nothing would have made me advance, had I not feared Laputa less than my neighbours. They might rend me to pieces, but to him the oath was inviolable. I staggered crazily to my feet, and shambled forwards. My eye was fixed on the ivory box, and it seemed to dance before me and retreat.

Suddenly I heard a voice—the voice of Henriques—cry, 'By God, a spy!' I felt my throat caught, but I was beyond resisting.

It was released, and I was pinned by the arms. I must have stood vacantly, with a foolish smile, while unchained fury raged round me. I seemed to hear Laputa's voice saying, 'It is the storekeeper.' His face was all that I could see, and it was unperturbed. There was a mocking ghost of a smile about his lips.

Myriad hands seemed to grip me and crush my breath, but above the clamour I heard a fierce word of command.

After that I fainted.

# CHAPTER XII

## CAPTAIN ARCOLL SENDS A MESSAGE

I ONCE read—I think in some Latin writer*—the story of a
man who was crushed to a jelly by the mere repeated touch of
many thousand hands. His murderers were not harsh, but an
infinite repetition of the gentlest handling meant death. I do
not suppose that I was very brutally manhandled in the cave.
I was trussed up tight and carried out to the open, and left in
the care of the guards. But when my senses returned I felt as
if I had been cruelly beaten in every part. The raw-hide bonds
chafed my wrists and ankle and shoulders, but they were the
least part of my aches. To be handled by a multitude of Kaffirs
is like being shaken by some wild animal. Their skins are
insensible to pain, and I have seen a Zulu stand on a piece of
red-hot iron without noticing it till he was warned by the smell
of burning hide. Anyhow, after I had been bound by Kaffir
hands and tossed on Kaffir shoulders, I felt as if I had been in
a scrimmage of mad bulls.

I found myself lying looking up at the moon. It was the edge
of the bush, and all around was the stir of the army getting
ready for the road. You know how a native babbles and
chatters over any work he has to do. It says much for Laputa's
iron hand that now everything was done in silence. I heard the
nickering of horses and the jolt of carts as they turned from the
bush into the path. There was the sound of hurried whisper-
ing, and now and then a sharp command. And all the while I
lay, staring at the moon and wondering if I was going to keep
my reason.

If he who reads this doubts the discomfort of bonds let him
try them for himself. Let him be bound foot and hand and left
alone, and in half an hour he will be screaming for release.
The sense of impotence is stifling, and I felt as if I were buried
in some landslip instead of lying under the open sky, with the
night wind fanning my face. I was in the second stage of panic,
which is next door to collapse. I tried to cry, but could only

raise a squeak like a bat. A wheel started to run round in my head, and, when I looked at the moon, I saw that it was rotating in time. Things were very bad with me.

It was 'Mwanga who saved me from lunacy. He had been appointed my keeper, and the first I knew of it was a violent kick in the ribs. I rolled over on the grass down a short slope. The brute squatted beside me, and prodded me with his gun-barrel.

'Ha, Baas,' he said in his queer English. 'Once you ordered me out of your store and treated me like a dog. It is 'Mwanga's turn now. You are 'Mwanga's dog, and he will skin you with a sjambok soon.'

My wandering wits were coming back to me. I looked into his bloodshot eyes and saw what I had to expect. The cheerful savage went on to discuss just the kind of beating I should get from him. My bones were to be uncovered till the lash curled round my heart. Then the jackals would have the rest of me.

This was ordinary Kaffir brag, and it made me angry. But I thought it best to go cannily.

'If I am to be your slave,' I managed to say, 'it would be a pity to beat me so hard. You would get no more work out of me.'

'Mwanga grinned wickedly. 'You are my slave for a day and a night. After that we kill you—slowly. You will burn till your legs fall off and your knees are on the ground, and then you will be chopped small with knives.'

Thank God, my courage and common sense were coming back to me.

'What happens to me to-morrow,' I said, 'is the Inkulu's business, not yours. I am *his* prisoner. But if you lift your hand on me to-day so as to draw one drop of blood the Inkulu will make short work of you. The vow is upon you, and if you break it you know what happens.' And I repeated, in a fair imitation of the priest's voice, the terrible curse he had pronounced in the cave.

You should have seen the change in that cur's face. I had guessed he was a coward, as he was most certainly a bully, and now I knew it. He shivered, and drew his hand over his eyes.

'Nay, Baas,' he pleaded, 'it was but a joke. No harm shall

come on you to-day. But tomorrow—' and his ugly face grew
more cheerful.

'To-morrow we shall see what we shall see,' I said stoically,
and a loud drum-beat sounded through the camp.

It was the signal for moving, for in the east a thin pale line
of gold was beginning to show over the trees. The bonds at my
knees and ankles were cut, and I was bundled on to the back
of a horse. Then my feet were strapped firmly below its belly.
The bridle of my beast was tied to 'Mwanga's, so that there
was little chance of escape even if I had been unshackled.

My thoughts were very gloomy. So far all had happened as
I planned, but I seemed to have lost my nerve, and I could not
believe in my rescue at the Letaba, while I thought of Inanda's
Kraal with sheer horror. Last night I had looked into the heart
of darkness,* and the sight had terrified me. What part should
I play in the great purification? Most likely that of the Biblical
scapegoat.* But the dolour of my mind was surpassed by the
discomfort of my body. I was broken with pains and weariness,
and I had a desperate headache. Also, before we had gone a
mile, I began to think that I should split in two. The paces of
my beast were uneven, to say the best of it, and the bump-
bump was like being on the rack. I remembered that the saints
of the Covenant used to journey to prison this way, especially
the great Mr Peden,* and I wondered how they liked it. When
I hear of a man doing a brave deed, I always want to discover
whether at the time he was well and comfortable in body.
That, I am certain, is the biggest ingredient in courage, and
those who plan and execute great deeds in bodily weakness
have my homage as truly heroic. For myself, I had not the
spirit of a chicken as I jogged along at 'Mwanga's side. I
wished he would begin to insult me, if only to distract my
mind, but he kept obstinately silent. He was sulky, and I think
rather afraid of me.

As the sun got up I could see something of the host around
me. I am no hand at guessing numbers, but I should put the
fighting men I saw at not less than twenty thousand. Every
man of them was on this side his prime, and all were armed
with good rifles and bandoliers. There were none of your old

*roers*[1] and decrepit Enfields, which I had seen signs of in Kaffir kraals. These guns were new, serviceable Mausers, and the men who bore them looked as if they knew how to handle them. There must have been long months of training behind this show, and I marvelled at the man who had organized it. I saw no field-guns, and the little transport they had was evidently for food only. We did not travel in ranks like an orthodox column. About a third of the force was mounted, and this formed the centre. On each wing the infantry straggled far afield, but there was method in their disorder, for in the bush close ranks would have been impossible. At any rate we kept wonderfully well together, and when we mounted a knoll the whole army seemed to move in one piece. I was well in the rear of the centre column, but from the crest of a slope I sometimes got a view in front. I could see nothing of Laputa, who was probably with the van, but in the very heart of the force I saw the old priest of the Snake, with his treasure carried in the kind of litter which the Portuguese call a *machila*, between rows of guards. A white man rode beside him, whom I judged to be Henriques. Laputa trusted this fellow, and I wondered why. I had not forgotten the look on his face while he had stared at the rubies in the cave. I had a notion that the Portugoose might be an unsuspected ally of mine, though for blackguard reasons.

About ten o'clock, as far as I could judge by the sun, we passed Umvelos', and took the right bank of the Labongo. There was nothing in the store to loot, but it was overrun by Kaffirs, who carried off the benches for firewood. It gave me an odd feeling to see the remains of the meal at which I had entertained Laputa in the hands of a dozen warriors. I thought of the long sunny days when I had sat by my *nachtmaal* while the Dutch farmers rode in to trade. Now these men were all dead, and I was on my way to the same bourne.*

Soon the blue line of the Berg rose in the west, and through the corner of my eye, as I rode, I could see the gap of the Klein Labongo. I wondered if Arcoll and his men were up

---

[1] Boer elephant guns.

there watching us. About this time I began to be so wretched in body that I ceased to think of the future. I had had no food for seventeen hours, and I was dropping from lack of sleep. The ache of my bones was so great that I found myself crying like a baby. What between pain and weakness and nervous exhaustion, I was almost at the end of my tether, and should have fainted dead away if a halt had not been called. But about midday, after we had crossed the track from Blaauwildebees-tefontein to the Portuguese frontier, we came to the broad, shallow drift of the Klein Labongo. It is the way of the Kaffirs to rest at noon, and on the other side of the drift we encamped. I remember the smell of hot earth and clean water as my horse scrambled up the bank. Then came the smell of wood-smoke as fires were lit. It seemed an age after we stopped before my feet were loosed and I was allowed to fall over on the ground. I lay like a log where I fell, and was asleep in ten seconds.

I awoke two hours later much refreshed, and with a raging hunger. My ankles and knees had been tied again, but the sleep had taken the worst stiffness out of my joints. The natives were squatting in groups round their fires, but no one came near me. I satisfied myself by straining at my bonds that this solitude gave no chance of escape. I wanted food, and I shouted on 'Mwanga, but he never came. Then I rolled over into the shadow of a *wacht-en-beetje*\* bush to get out of the glare.

I saw a Kaffir on the other side of the bush who seemed to be grinning at me. Slowly he moved round to my side, and stood regarding me with interest.

'For God's sake get me some food,' I said.

'Ja, Baas,' was the answer; and he disappeared for a minute, and returned with a wooden bowl of hot mealie-meal porridge, and a calabash full of water.

I could not use my hands, so he fed me with the blade of his knife. Such porridge without salt or cream is beastly food, but my hunger was so great that I could have eaten a vat of it.

Suddenly it appeared that the Kaffir had something to say to me. As he fed me he began to speak in a low voice in English.

'Baas,' he said, 'I come from Ratitswan, and I have a message for you.'

I guessed that Ratitswan was the native name for Arcoll. There was no one else likely to send a message.

'Ratitswan says,' he went on, '"Look out for Dupree's Drift." I will be near you and cut your bonds; then you must swim across when Ratitswan begins to shoot.'

The news took all the weight of care from my mind. Colin had got home, and my friends were out for rescue. So volatile is the mood of 19 that I veered round from black despair to an unwarranted optimism. I saw myself already safe, and Laputa's rising scattered. I saw my hands on the treasure, and Henriques' ugly neck below my heel.

'I don't know your name,' I said to the Kaffir, 'but you are a good fellow. When I get out of this business I won't forget you.'

'There is another message, Baas,' he said. 'It is written on paper in a strange tongue. Turn your head to the bush, and see, I will hold it inside the bowl, that you may read it.'

I did as I was told, and found myself looking at a dirty half-sheet of notepaper, marked by the Kaffir's thumbs. Some words were written on it in Wardlaw's hand; and, characteristically, in Latin, which was not a bad cipher. I read—

*'Henricus de Letaba transeunda apud Duprei vada jam nos certiores fecit.'*[1]

I had guessed rightly. Henriques was a traitor to the cause he had espoused. Arcoll's message had given me new heart, but Wardlaw's gave me information of tremendous value. I repented that I had ever underrated the schoolmaster's sense. He did not come out of Aberdeen for nothing.

I asked the Kaffir how far it was to Duprec's Drift, and was told three hours' march. We should get there after the darkening. It seemed he had permission to ride with me instead of 'Mwanga, who had no love for the job. How he managed this I do not know; but Arcoll's men had their own ways of doing things. He undertook to set me free when the first shot was

[1] 'Henriques has already told us about the crossing at Dupree's Drift.'

fired at the ford. Meantime I bade him leave me, to avert suspicion.

There is a story of one of King Arthur's knights—Sir Percival,* I think—that once, riding through a forest, he found a lion fighting with a serpent. He drew his sword and helped the lion, for he thought it was the more natural beast of the two. To me Laputa was the lion, and Henriques the serpent; and though I had no good will to either, I was determined to spoil the serpent's game. He was after the rubies, as I had fancied; he had never been after anything else. He had found out about Arcoll's preparations, and had sent him a warning, hoping, no doubt, that, if Laputa's force was scattered on the Letaba, he would have a chance of getting off with the necklace in the confusion. If he succeeded, he would go over the Lebombo to Mozambique, and whatever happened afterwards in the rising would be no concern of Mr Henriques. I determined that he should fail; but how to manage it I could not see. Had I had a pistol, I think I would have shot him; but I had no weapon of any kind. I could not warn Laputa, for that would seal my own fate, even if I were believed. It was clear that Laputa must go to Dupree's Drift, for otherwise I could not escape; and it was equally clear that I must find the means of spoiling the Portugoose's game.

A shadow fell across the sunlight, and I looked up to see the man I was thinking of standing before me. He had a cigarette in his mouth, and his hands in the pockets of his riding-breeches. He stood eyeing me with a curious smile on his face.

'Well, Mr Storekeeper,' he said, 'you and I have met before under pleasanter circumstances.'

I said nothing, my mind being busy with what to do at the drift.

'We were shipmates, if I am not mistaken,' he said. 'I dare say you found it nicer work smoking on the after-deck than lying here in the sun.'

Still I said nothing. If the man had come to mock me, he would get no change out of David Crawfurd.

'Tut, tut, don't be sulky. You have no quarrel with me.

Between ourselves,' and he dropped his voice, 'I tried to save you; but you had seen rather too much to be safe. What devil prompted you to steal a horse and go to the cave? I don't blame you for overhearing us; but if you had had the sense of a louse you would have gone off to the Berg with your news. By the way, how did you manage it? A cellar, I suppose. Our friend Laputa was a fool not to take better precautions; but I must say you acted the drunkard pretty well.'

The vanity of 19 is an incalculable thing. I rose to the fly.

'I know the kind of precaution you wanted to take,' I muttered.

'You heard that too? Well, I confess I am in favour of doing a job thoroughly when I take it up.'

'In the Koodoo Flats, for example,' I said.

He sat down beside me, and laughed softly. 'You heard my little story? You are clever, Mr Storekeeper, but not quite clever enough. What if I can act a part as well as yourself?' And he thrust his yellow face close to mine.

I saw his meaning, and did not for a second believe him; but I had the sense to temporize.

'Do you mean to say that you did not kill the Dutchmen, and did not mean to knife me?'

'I mean to say that I am not a fool,' he said, lighting another cigarette.

'I am a white man, Mr Storekeeper, and I play the white man's game. Why do you think I am here? Simply because I was the only man in Africa who had the pluck to get to the heart of this business. I am here to dish Laputa, and by God I am going to do it.'

I was scarcely prepared for such incredible bluff. I knew every word was a lie, but I wanted to hear more, for the man fascinated me.

'I suppose you know what will happen to you,' he said, flicking the ashes from his cigarette. 'To-morrow at Inanda's Kraal, when the vow is over, they will give you a taste of Kaffir habits. Not death, my friend—that would be simple enough—but a slow death with every refinement of horror. You have broken into their sacred places, and you will be sacrificed to

Laputa's god. I have seen native torture before, and his own
mother would run away shrieking from a man who had
endured it.'

I said nothing, but the thought made my flesh creep.

'Well,' he went on, 'you're in an awkward plight, but I think
I can help you. What if I can save your life, Mr Storekeeper?
You are trussed up like a fowl, and can do nothing. I am the
only man alive who can help you. I am willing to do it, too—
on my own terms.'

I did not wait to hear those terms, for I had a shrewd guess
what they would be. My hatred of Henriques rose and choked
me. I saw murder and trickery in his mean eyes and cruel
mouth. I could not, to be saved from the uttermost horror,
have made myself his ally.

'Now listen, Mr Portugoose,' I cried. 'You tell me you are a
spy. What if I shout that through the camp? There will be
short shrift for you if Laputa hears it.'

He laughed loudly. 'You are a bigger fool than I took you
for. Who would believe you, my friend. Not Laputa. Not any
man in this army. It would only mean tighter bonds for these
long legs of yours.'

By this time I had given up all thought of diplomacy. 'Very
well, you yellow-faced devil, you will hear my answer. I would
not take my freedom from you, though I were to be boiled
alive. I know you for a traitor to the white man's cause, a dirty
I.D.B. swindler, whose name is a byword among honest men.
By your own confession you are a traitor to this idiot rising.
You murdered the Dutchmen and God knows how many
more, and you would fain have murdered me. I pray to Heaven
that the men whose cause you have betrayed and the men
whose cause you would betray may join to stamp the life out
of you and send your soul to hell. I know the game you would
have me join in, and I fling your offer in your face. But I tell
you one thing—you are damned yourself. The white men are
out, and you will never get over the Lebombo. From black or
white you will get justice before many hours, and your carcass
will be left to rot in the bush. Get out of my sight, you swine.'

In that moment I was so borne up in my passion that I
forgot my bonds and my grave danger. I was inspired like a

prophet with a sense of approaching retribution. Henriques heard me out; but his smile changed to a scowl, and a flush rose on his sallow cheek.

'Stew in your own juice,' he said, and spat in my face. Then he shouted in Kaffir that I had insulted him, and demanded that I should be bound tighter and gagged.

It was Arcoll's messenger who answered his summons. That admirable fellow rushed at me with a great appearance of savagery. He made a pretence of swathing me up in fresh rawhide ropes, but his knots were loose and the thing was a farce. He gagged me with what looked like a piece of wood, but was in reality a chunk of dry banana. And all the while, till Henriques was out of hearing, he cursed me with a noble gift of tongues.

The drums beat for the advance, and once more I was hoisted on my horse, while Arcoll's Kaffir tied my bridle to his own. A Kaffir cannot wink, but he has a way of slanting his eyes which does as well, and as we moved on he would turn his head to me with this strange grimace.

Henriques wanted me to help him to get the rubies—that I presumed was the offer he had meant to make. Well, thought I, I will perish before the jewel reaches the Portuguese's hands. He hoped for a stampede when Arcoll opposed the crossing of the river, and in the confusion intended to steal the casket. My plan must be to get as near the old priest as possible before we reached the ford. I spoke to my warder and told him what I wanted. He nodded, and in the first mile we managed to edge a good way forward. Several things came to aid us. As I have said, we of the centre were not marching in close ranks, but in a loose column, and often it was possible by taking a short cut on rough ground to join the column some distance ahead. There was a *vlei*,* too, which many circumvented, but we swam, and this helped our lead. In a couple of hours we were so near the priest's litter that I could have easily tossed a cricket ball on the head of Henriques who rode beside it.

Very soon the twilight of the winter day began to fall. The far hills grew pink and mulberry in the sunset, and strange shadows stole over the bush. Still creeping forward, we found ourselves not twenty yards behind the litter, while far ahead I

saw a broad, glimmering space of water with a high woody
bank beyond.

'Dupree's Drift;' whispered my warder. 'Courage, Inkoos;[1]
in an hour's time you will be free.'

[1] Great chief.

# CHAPTER XIII

## THE DRIFT OF THE LETABA

THE dusk was gathering fast as we neared the stream. From the stagnant reaches above and below a fine white mist was rising, but the long shallows of the ford were clear. My heart was beginning to flutter wildly, but I kept a tight grip on myself and prayed for patience. As I stared into the evening my hopes sank. I had expected, foolishly enough, to see on the far bank some sign of my friends, but the tall bush was dead and silent.

The drift slants across the river at an acute angle, roughly S.S.W. I did not know this at the time, and was amazed to see the van of the march turn apparently up stream. Laputa's great voice rang out in some order which was repeated down the column, and the wide flanks of the force converged on the narrow cart-track which entered the water. We had come to a standstill while the front ranks began the passage.

I sat shaking with excitement, my eyes straining into the gloom. Water holds the evening light for long, and I could make out pretty clearly what was happening. The leading horsemen rode into the stream with Laputa in front. The ford is not the best going, so they had to pick their way, but in five or ten minutes they were over. Then came some of the infantry of the flanks, who crossed with the water to their waists, and their guns held high above their heads. They made a portentous splashing, but not a sound came from their throats. I shall never know how Laputa imposed silence on the most noisy race on earth. Several thousand footmen must have followed the riders, and disappeared into the far bush. But not a shot came from the bluffs in front.

I watched with a sinking heart. Arcoll had failed, and there was to be no check at the drift. There remained for me only the horrors at Inanda's Kraal. I resolved to make a dash for freedom, at all costs, and was in the act of telling Arcoll's man to cut my bonds, when a thought occurred to me.

Henriques was after the rubies, and it was his interest to get Laputa across the river before the attack began. It was Arcoll's business to split the force, and above all to hold up the leader. Henriques would tell him, and for that matter he must have assumed himself, that Laputa would ride in the centre of the force. Therefore there would be no check till the time came for the priest's litter to cross.

It was well that I had not had my bonds cut. Henriques came riding towards me, his face sharp and bright as a ferret's. He pulled up and asked if I were safe. My Kaffir showed my strapped elbows and feet, and tugged at the cords to prove their tightness.

'Keep him well,' said Henriques, 'or you will answer to Inkulu. Forward with him now and get him through the water.' Then he turned and rode back.

My warder, apparently obeying orders, led me out of the column and into the bush on the right hand. Soon we were abreast of the litter and some twenty yards to the west of it. The water gleamed through the trees a few paces in front. I could see the masses of infantry converging on the drift, and the churning like a cascade which they made in the passage.

Suddenly from the far bank came an order. It was Laputa's voice, thin and high-pitched, as the Kaffir cries when he wishes his words to carry a great distance. Henriques repeated it, and the infantry halted. The riders of the column in front of the litter began to move into the stream.

We should have gone with them, but instead we pulled our horses back into the darkness of the bush. It seemed to me that odd things were happening around the priest's litter. Henriques had left it, and dashed past me so close that I could have touched him. From somewhere among the trees a pistol-shot cracked into the air.

As if in answer to a signal the high bluff across the stream burst into a sheet of fire. 'A sheet of fire' sounds odd enough for scientific warfare. I saw that my friends were using shot-guns and firing with black powder into the mob in the water. It was humane and it was good tactics, for the flame in the grey dusk had the appearance of a heavy battery of ordnance.

Once again I heard Henriques' voice. He was turning the

column to the right. He shouted to them to get into cover, and take the water higher up. I thought, too, that from far away I heard Laputa.

These were maddening seconds. We had left the business of cutting my bonds almost too late. In the darkness of the bush the strips of hide could only be felt for, and my Kaffir had a woefully blunt knife. *Reims\** are always tough to sever, and mine had to be sawn through. Soon my arms were free, and I was plucking at my other bonds. The worst were those on my ankles below the horse's belly. The Kaffir fumbled away in the dark, and pricked my beast so that he reared and struck out. And all the while I was choking with impatience, and gabbling prayers to myself.

The men on the other side had begun to use ball-cartridge. I could see through a gap the centre of the river, and it was filled with a mass of struggling men and horses. I remember that it amazed me that no shot was fired in return. Then I remembered the vow, and was still more amazed at the power of a ritual on that savage horde.

The column was moving past me to the right. It was a disorderly rabble which obeyed Henriques' orders. Bullets began to sing through the trees, and one rider was hit in the shoulder and came down with a crash. This increased the confusion, for most of them dismounted and tried to lead their horses in the cover. The infantry coming in from the wings collided with them, and there was a struggle of excited beasts and men in the thickets of thorn and mopani. And still my Kaffir was trying to get my ankles loose as fast as a plunging horse would let him.

At last I was free, and dropped stiffly to the ground. I fell prone on my face with cramp, and when I got up I rolled like a drunk man. Here I made a great blunder. I should have left my horse with my Kaffir, and bidden him follow me. But I was too eager to be cautious, so I let it go, and crying to the Kaffir to await me, I ran towards the litter.

Henriques had laid his plans well. The column had abandoned the priest, and by the litter were only the two bearers. As I caught sight of them one fell with a bullet in his chest. The other, wild with fright, kept turning his head to every quarter of the compass. Another bullet passed close to his head. This was too much for him, and with a yell he ran away.

As I broke through the thicket I looked to the quarter whence the bullets had come. These, I could have taken my oath, were not fired by my friends on the farther bank. It was close-quarter shooting, and I knew who had done it. But I saw nobody. The last few yards of the road were clear, and only out in the water was the struggling shouting mass of humanity. I saw a tall man on a big horse plunge into the river on his way back. It must be Laputa returning to command the panic.

My business was not with Laputa but with Henriques. The old priest in the litter, who had been sleeping, had roused himself, and was looking vacantly round him. He did not look long. A third bullet, fired from a dozen yards away, drilled a hole in his forehead. He fell back dead, and the ivory box, which lay on his lap, tilted forward on the ground.

I had no weapon of any kind, and I did not want the fourth bullet for myself. Henriques was too pretty a shot to trifle with. I waited quietly on the edge of the shade till the Portugoose came out of the thicket. I saw him running forward with a rifle in his hand. A whinny from a horse told me that somewhere near his beast was tied up. It was all but dark, but it seemed to me that I could see the lust of greed in his eyes as he rushed to the litter.

Very softly I stole behind him. He tore off the lid of the box, and pulled out the great necklace. For a second it hung in his hands, but only for a second. So absorbed was he that he did not notice me standing full before him. Nay, he lifted his head, and gave me the finest chance of my life. I was something of a boxer, and all my accumulated fury went into the blow. It caught him on the point of the chin, and his neck cricked like the bolt of a rifle. He fell limply on the ground and the jewels dropped from his hand.

I picked them up and stuffed them into my breeches pocket.

Then I pulled the pistol out of his belt. It was six-chambered, and I knew that only three had been emptied. I remembered feeling extraordinarily cool and composed, and yet my wits must have been wandering or I would have never taken the course I did.

The right thing to do—on Arcoll's instructions—was to make for the river and swim across to my friends. But Laputa was coming back, and I dreaded meeting him. Laputa seemed to my heated fancy omnipresent. I thought of him as covering the whole bank of the river, whereas I might easily have crossed a little farther down, and made my way up the other bank to my friends. It was plain that Laputa intended to evade the patrol, not to capture it, and there, consequently, I should be safe. The next best thing was to find Arcoll's Kaffir, who was not twenty yards away, get some sort of horse, and break for the bush. Long before morning we should have been over the Berg and in safety. Nay, if I wanted a mount, there was Henriques' whinnying a few paces off.

Instead I did the craziest thing of all. With the jewels in one pocket, and the Portugoose's pistol in the other, I started running back the road we had come.

# CHAPTER XIV

## I CARRY THE COLLAR OF PRESTER JOHN

I RAN till my breath grew short, for some kind of swift motion I had to have or choke. The events of the last few minutes had inflamed my brain. For the first time in my life I had seen men die by violence—nay, by brutal murder. I had put my soul into the blow which laid out Henriques, and I was still hot with the pride of it. Also I had in my pocket the fetich of the whole black world; I had taken their Ark of the Covenant,* and soon Laputa would be on my trail. Fear, pride, and a blind exultation all throbbed in my veins. I must have run three miles before I came to my sober senses.

I put my ear to the ground, but heard no sound of pursuit. Laputa, I argued, would have enough to do for a little, shepherding his flock over the water. He might surround and capture the patrol, or he might evade it; the vow prevented him from fighting it. On the whole I was clear that he would ignore it and push on for the rendezvous. All this would take time, and the business of the priest would have to wait. When Henriques came to he would no doubt have a story to tell, and the scouts would be on my trail. I wished I had shot the Portugoose while I was at the business. It would have been no murder, but a righteous execution.

Meanwhile I must get off the road. The sand had been disturbed by an army, so there was little fear of my steps being traced. Still it was only wise to leave the track which I would be assumed to have taken, for Laputa would guess I had fled back the way to Blaauwildebeestefontein. I turned into the bush, which here was thin and sparse like whins on a common.

The Berg must be my goal. Once on the plateau I would be inside the white man's lines. Down here in the plains I was in the country of my enemies. Arcoll meant to fight on the uplands when it came to fighting. The black man might rage as he pleased in his own flats, but we stood to defend the gates of the hills. Therefore over the Berg I must be before morning, or there would be a dead man with no tales to tell.

I think that even at the start of that night's work I realized the exceeding precariousnesss of my chances. Some twenty miles of bush and swamp separated me from the foot of the mountains. After that there was the climbing of them, for at the point opposite where I now stood the Berg does not descend sharply on the plain, but is broken into foot-hills around the glens of the Klein Letaba and the Letsitela. From the spot where these rivers emerge on the flats to the crown of the plateau is ten miles at the shortest. I had a start of an hour or so, but before dawn I had to traverse thirty miles of unknown and difficult country. Behind me would follow the best trackers in Africa, who knew every foot of the wilderness. It was a wild hazard, but it was my only hope. At this time I was feeling pretty courageous. For one thing I had Henriques' pistol close to my leg, and for another I still thrilled with the satisfaction of having smitten his face.

I took the rubies, and stowed them below my shirt and next my skin. I remember taking stock of my equipment and laughing at the humour of it. One of the heels was almost twisted off my boots, and my shirt and breeches were old at the best and ragged from hard usage. The whole outfit would have been dear at five shillings, or seven-and-six with the belt thrown in. Then there was the Portugoose's pistol, costing, say, a guinea; and last, the Prester's collar, worth several millions.

What was more important than my clothing was my bodily strength. I was still very sore from the bonds and the jog of that accursed horse, but exercise was rapidly suppling my joints. About five hours ago I had eaten a filling, though not very sustaining, meal, and I thought I could go on very well till morning. But I was still badly in arrears with my sleep, and there was no chance of my snatching a minute till I was over the Berg. It was going to be a race against time, and I swore that I would drive my body to the last ounce of strength.

Moonrise was still an hour or two away, and the sky was bright with myriad stars. I knew now what starlight meant, for there was ample light to pick my way by. I steered by the Southern Cross, for I was aware that the Berg ran north and south, and with that constellation on my left hand I was bound to reach it sooner or later. The bush closed around me with its mysterious dull green shades, and trees, which in the daytime were thin scrub, now loomed like tall timber. It was very eerie moving, a tiny fragment of mortality, in that great wide silent wilderness, with the starry vault, like an impassive celestial audience, watching with many eyes. They cheered me, those stars. In my hurry and fear and passion they spoke of the old calm dignities of man. I felt less alone when I turned my face to the lights which were slanting alike on this uncanny bush and on the homely streets of Kirkcaple.

The silence did not last long. First came the howl of a wolf,* to be answered by others from every quarter of the compass. This serenade went on for a bit, till the jackals chimed in with their harsh bark. I had been caught by darkness before this when hunting on the Berg, but I was not afraid of wild beasts. That is one terror of the bush which travellers' tales have put too high. It was true that I might meet a hungry lion, but the chance was remote, and I had my pistol. Once indeed a huge animal bounded across the road a little in front of me. For a moment I took him for a lion, but on reflection I was inclined to think him a very large bush-pig.

By this time I was out of the thickest bush and into a piece of parkland with long, waving tambuki* grass, which the Kaffirs would burn later. The moon was coming up, and her faint rays silvered the flat tops of the mimosa trees. I could hear and feel around me the rustling of animals. Once or twice a big buck—an eland or a koodoo—broke cover, and at the sight of me went off snorting down the slope. Also there were droves of smaller game—rhebok and springbok and duikers*— which brushed past at full gallop without even noticing me.

The sight was so novel that it set me thinking. That shy wild things should stampede like this could only mean that they had been thoroughly scared. Now obviously the thing that scared them must be on this side of the Letaba. This must mean that Laputa's army, or a large part of it, had not crossed at Dupree's Drift, but had gone up the stream to some higher ford. If that was so, I must alter my course; so I bore away to the right for a mile or two, making a line due north-west.

In about an hour's time the ground descended steeply, and I saw before me the shining reaches of a river. I had the chief features of the countryside clear in my mind, both from old porings over maps, and from Arcoll's instructions. This stream must be the Little Letaba, and I must cross it if I would get to the mountains. I remembered that Majinje's kraal stood on its left bank, and higher up in its valley in the Berg 'Mpefu lived. At all costs the kraals must be avoided. Once across it I must make for the Letsitela, another tributary of the Great Letaba, and by keeping the far bank of that stream I should cross the mountains to the place on the plateau of the Wood Bush which Arcoll had told me would be his headquarters.

It is easy to talk about crossing a river, and looking to-day at the slender streak on the map I am amazed that so small a thing should have given me such ugly tremors. Yet I have rarely faced a job I liked so little. The stream ran yellow and sluggish under the clear moon. On the near side a thick growth of bush clothed the bank, but on the far side I made out a swamp with tall bulrushes. The distance across was no more than fifty yards, but I would have swum a mile more readily in deep water. The place stank of crocodiles. There was no ripple to break the oily flow except where a derelict branch swayed with the current. Something in the stillness, the eerie light on the water, and the rotting smell of the swamp made that stream seem unhallowed and deadly.

I sat down and considered the matter. Crocodiles had always terrified me more than any created thing, and to be dragged by iron jaws to death in that hideous stream seemed to me the most awful of endings. Yet cross it I must if I were to get rid of my human enemies. I remembered a story of an escaped prisoner during the war who had only the Komati River between him and safety. But he dared not enter it, and was recaptured by a Boer commando. I was determined that such cowardice should not be laid to my charge. If I was to die, I would at least have given myself every chance of life. So I braced myself as best I could, and looked for a place to enter.

The veld-craft I had mastered had taught me a few things. One was that wild animals drink at night, and that they have regular drinking places. I thought that the likeliest place for crocodiles was at or around such spots, and, therefore, I resolved to take the water away from a drinking place. I went up the bank, noting where the narrow bush-paths emerged on the water-side. I scared away several little buck, and once the violent commotion in the bush showed that I had frightened some bigger animal, perhaps a hartebeest. Still following the bank I came to a reach where the undergrowth was unbroken and the water looked deeper.

Suddenly—I fear I must use this adverb often, for all the happenings on that night were sudden—I saw a biggish animal break through the reeds on the far side. It entered the water and, whether wading or swimming I could not see, came out a little distance. Then some sense must have told it of my presence, for it turned and with a grunt made its way back.

I saw that it was a big wart-hog, and began to think. Pig, unlike other beasts, drink not at night, but in the daytime. The hog had, therefore, not come to drink, but to swim across. Now, I argued, he would choose a safe place, for the wart-hog, hideous though he is, is a wise beast. What was safe for him would, therefore, in all likelihood be safe for me.

With this hope to comfort me I prepared to enter. My first care was the jewels, so, feeling them precarious in my shirt, I twined the collar round my neck and clasped it. The snake-clasp was no flimsy device of modern jewellery, and I had no fear but that it would hold. I held the pistol between my teeth, and with a prayer to God slipped into the muddy waters.

I swam in the wild way of a beginner who fears cramp. The current was light and the water moderately warm, but I seemed to go very slowly, and I was cold with apprehension. In the middle it suddenly shallowed, and my breast came against a mudshoal. I thought it was a crocodile, and in my confusion the pistol dropped from my mouth and disappeared.

I waded a few steps and then plunged into deep water again. Almost before I knew, I was among the bulrushes, with my feet in the slime of the bank. With feverish haste I scrambled through the reeds and up through roots and undergrowth to the hard soil. I was across, but, alas, I had lost my only weapon.

The swim and the anxiety had tired me considerably, and though it meant delay, I did not dare to continue with the weight of water-logged clothes to impede me. I found a dry sheltered place in the bush and stripped to the skin. I emptied my boots and wrung out my shirt and breeches, while the Prester's jewels were blazing on my neck. Here was a queer counterpart to Laputa in the cave!

The change revived me, and I continued my way in better form. So far there had been no sign of pursuit. Before me the Letsitela was the only other stream, and from what I remembered of its character near the Berg I thought I should have little trouble. It was smaller than the Klein Letaba, and a rushing torrent where shallows must be common.

I kept running till I felt my shirt getting dry on my back. Then I restored the jewels to their old home, and found their cool touch on my breast very comforting. The country was getting more broken as I advanced. Little kopjes* with thickets of wild bananas took the place of the dead levels. Long before I reached the Letsitela, I saw that I was right in my guess. It ran, a brawling mountain stream, in a narrow rift in the bush. I crossed it almost dry-shod on the boulders above a little fall, stopping for a moment to drink and lave my brow.

After that the country changed again. The wood was now getting like that which clothed the sides of the Berg. There were tall timber-trees—yellowwood, sneezewood, essenwood, stinkwood*—and the ground was carpeted with thick grass and ferns. The sight gave me my first earnest of safety. I was approaching my own country. Behind me was heathendom and the black fever flats. In front were the cool mountains and bright streams, and the guns of my own folk.

As I struggled on—for I was getting very footsore and weary—I became aware of an odd sound in my rear. It was as if something were following me. I stopped and listened with a sudden dread. Could Laputa's trackers have got up with me already? But the sound was not of human feet. It was as if some heavy animal were plunging through the undergrowth. At intervals came the soft pad of its feet on the grass.

It must be the hungry lion of my nightmare, and Henriques' pistol was in the mud of the Klein Letaba! The only thing was a tree, and I had sprung for one and scrambled wearily into the first branches when a great yellow animal came into the moonlight.

Providence had done kindly in robbing me of my pistol. The next minute I was on the ground with Colin leaping on me and baying with joy. I hugged that blessed hound and buried my head in his shaggy neck, sobbing like a child. How he had traced me I can never tell. The secret belongs only to the Maker of good and faithful dogs.

With him by my side I was a new man. The awesome loneliness had gone. I felt as if he were a message from my own people to take me safely home. He clearly knew the business afoot, for he padded beside me with never a glance to right or left. Another time he would have been snowking* in every thicket; but now he was on duty, a serious, conscientious dog with no eye but for business.

The moon went down, and the starry sky was our only light. The thick gloom which brooded over the landscape pointed to the night being far gone. I thought I saw a deeper blackness ahead which might be the line of the Berg. Then came that period of utter stillness when every bush sound is hushed and the world seems to swoon. I felt almost impious hurrying through that profound silence, when not even the leaves stirred or a frog croaked.

Suddenly as we came over a rise a little wind blew on the back of my head, and a bitter chill came into the air. I knew from nights spent in the open that it was the precursor of dawn. Sure enough, as I glanced back, far over the plain a pale glow was stealing upwards into the sky. In a few minutes the pall melted into an airy haze, and above me I saw the heavens shot with tremors of blue light. Then the foreground began to clear, and there before me, with their heads still muffled in vapour, were the mountains.

Xenophon's Ten Thousand* did not hail the sea more gladly than I welcomed those frowning ramparts of the Berg.

Once again my weariness was eased. I cried to Colin, and together we ran down into the wide, shallow trough which lies at the foot of the hills. As the sun rose above the horizon, the black masses changed to emerald and rich umber, and the fleecy mists of the summits opened and revealed beyond shining spaces of green. Some lines of Shakespeare ran in my head, which I have always thought the most beautiful of all poetry:

> 'Night's candles are burned out, and jocund day
> Walks tiptoe on the misty mountain tops.'*

Up there among the clouds was my salvation. Like the Psalmist, I lifted my eyes to the hills from whence came my aid.

Hope is a wonderful restorative. To be near the hills, to smell their odours, to see at the head of the glens the lines of the plateau where were white men and civilization—all gave me new life and courage. Colin saw my mood, and spared a moment now and then to inspect a hole or a covert. Down in the shallow trough I saw the links of a burn, the Machudi, which flowed down the glen it was my purpose to ascend. Away to the north in the direction of Majinje's were patches of Kaffir tillage, and I thought I discerned the smoke from fires. Majinje's womankind would be cooking their morning meal. To the south ran a thick patch of forest, but I saw beyond it the spur of the mountain over which runs the highroad to Wesselsburg. The clear air of dawn was like wine in my blood. I was not free, but I was on the threshold of freedom.* If I could only reach my friends with the Prester's collar in my shirt, I would have performed a feat which would never be forgotten. I would have made history by my glorious folly. Breakfastless and footsore, I was yet a proud man as I crossed the hollow to the mouth of Machudi's glen.

My chickens had been counted too soon, and there was to be no hatching. Colin grew uneasy, and began to sniff up wind. I was maybe a quarter of a mile from the glen foot, plodding through the long grass of the hollow, when the behaviour of the dog made me stop and listen. In that still air sounds carry far, and I seemed to hear the noise of feet brushing through cover. The noise came both from north and south, from the forest and from the lower course of the Machudi.

I dropped into shelter, and running with bent back got to the summit of a little bush-clad knoll. It was Colin who first caught sight of my pursuers. He was staring at a rift in the trees, and suddenly gave a short bark. I looked and saw two men, running hard, cross the grass and dip into the bed of the stream. A moment later I had a glimpse of figures on the edge of the forest, moving fast to the mouth of the glen. The pursuit had not followed me; it had waited to cut me off. Fool that I was, I had forgotten the wonders of Kaffir telegraphy. It had been easy for Laputa to send word thirty miles ahead to stop any white man who tried to cross the Berg.

And then I knew that I was very weary.

# CHAPTER XV

## MORNING IN THE BERG

I WAS perhaps half a mile the nearer to the glen, and was likely to get there first. And after that? I could see the track winding by the waterside and then crossing a hill-shoulder which diverted the stream. It was a road a man could scarcely ride, and a tired man would have a hard job to climb. I do not think that I had any hope. My exhilaration had died as suddenly as it had been born. I saw myself caught and carried off to Laputa, who must now be close on the rendezvous at Inanda's Kraal. I had no weapon to make a fight for it. My foemen were many and untired. It must be only a matter of minutes till I was in their hands.

More in a dogged fury of disappointment than with any hope of escape I forced my sore legs up the glen. Ten minutes ago I had been exulting in the glories of the morning, and now the sun was not less bright or the colours less fair, but the heart had gone out of the spectator. At first I managed to get some pace out of myself, partly from fear and partly from anger. But I soon found that my body had been tried too far. I could plod along, but to save my life I could not have hurried. Any healthy savage could have caught me in a hundred yards.

The track, I remember, was overhung with creepers, and often I had to squeeze through thickets of tree-ferns. Countless little brooks ran down from the hillside, threads of silver among the green pastures. Soon I left the stream and climbed up on the shoulder, where the road was not much better than a precipice. Every step was a weariness. I could hardly drag one foot after the other, and my heart was beating like the fanners* of a mill. I had spasms of acute sickness, and it took all my resolution to keep me from lying down by the roadside.

At last I was at the top of the shoulder and could look back. There was no sign of anybody on the road so far as I could see. Could I have escaped them? I had been in the shadow of the trees for the first part, and they might have lost sight of me and concluded that I had avoided the glen or tried one of the faces. Before me, I remember, there stretched the upper glen, a green cup-shaped hollow with the sides scarred by ravines. There was a high waterfall in one of them which was white as snow against the red rocks. My wits must have been shaky, for I took the fall for a snowdrift, and wondered sillily why the Berg had grown so Alpine.

A faint spasm of hope took me into that green cup. The bracken was as thick as on the Pentlands, and there was a multitude of small lovely flowers in the grass. It was like a water-meadow at home, such a place as I had often in boyhood searched for moss-cheepers'* and corncrakes' eggs. Birds were crying round me as I broke this solitude, and one small buck— a klipspringer*—rose from my feet and dashed up one of the gullies. Before me was a steep green wall with the sky blue above it. Beyond it was safety, but as my sweat-dimmed eyes looked at it I knew that I could never reach it.

Then I saw my pursuers. High up on the left side, and rounding the rim of the cup, were little black figures. They had not followed my trail, but, certain of my purpose, had gone forward to intercept me. I remember feeling a puny weakling compared with those lusty natives who could make such good going on steep mountains.* They were certainly no men of the plains, but hillmen, probably some remnants of old Machudi's tribe who still squatted in the glen. Machudi* was a blackguard chief whom the Boers long ago smashed in one of their native wars. He was a fierce old warrior and had put up a good fight to the last, till a hired impi of Swazis had surrounded his hiding-place in the forest and destroyed him. A Boer farmer on the plateau had his skull, and used to drink whisky out of it when he was merry.

The sight of the pursuit was the last straw. I gave up hope, and my intentions were narrowed to one frantic desire—to hide the jewels. Patriotism, which I had almost forgotten, flickered up in that crisis. At any rate Laputa should not have the Snake. If he drove out the white man, he should not clasp the Prester's rubies on his great neck.

There was no cover in the green cup, so I turned up the

ravine on the right side. The enemy, so far as I could judge,
were on the left and in front, and in the gully I might find a
pot-hole to bury the necklet in. Only a desperate resolution
took me through the tangle of juniper bushes into the red
screes of the gully. At first I could not find what I sought. The
stream in the ravine slid down a long slope like a mill-race, and
the sides were bare and stony. Still I plodded on, helping
myself with a hand on Colin's back, for my legs were numb
with fatigue. By-and-by the gully narrowed, and I came to a
flat place with a long pool. Beyond was a little fall, and up this
I climbed into a network of tiny cascades. Over one pool hung
a dead tree-fern, and a bay from it ran into a hole of the rock.
I slipped the jewels far into the hole, where they lay on the
firm sand, showing odd lights through the dim blue water.
Then I scrambled down again to the flat space and the pool,
and looked round to see if any one had reached the edge of the
ravine. There was no sign as yet of the pursuit, so I dropped
limply on the shingle and waited. For I had suddenly con-
ceived a plan.

As my breath came back to me my wits came back from
their wandering. These men were not there to kill me, but to
capture me. They could know nothing of the jewels, for Laputa
would never have dared to make the loss of the sacred Snake
public. Therefore they would not suspect what I had done,
and would simply lead me to Laputa at Inanda's Kraal. I
began to see the glimmerings of a plan for saving my life, and
by God's grace, for saving my country from the horrors of
rebellion. The more I thought the better I liked it. It
demanded a bold front, and it might well miscarry, but I had
taken such desperate hazards during the past days that I was
less afraid of fortune. Anyhow, the choice lay between certain
death and a slender chance of life, and it was easy to decide.

Playing football, I used to notice how towards the end of a
game I might be sore and weary, without a kick in my body;
but when I had a straight job of tackling a man my strength
miraculously returned. It was even so now. I lay on my side,
luxuriating in being still, and slowly a sort of vigour crept back
into my limbs. Perhaps a half-hour of rest was given me before,
on the lip of the gully, I saw figures appear. Looking down I

saw several men who had come across from the opposite side of the valley, scrambling up the stream. I got to my feet, with Colin bristling beside me, and awaited them with the stiffest face I could muster.

As I expected, they were Machudi's men. I recognized them by the red ochre in their hair and their copper-wire necklets. Big fellows they were, long-legged and deep in the chest, the true breed of mountaineers. I admired their light tread on the slippery rock. It was hopeless to think of evading such men in their own hills.

The men from the side joined the men in front, and they stood looking at me from about twelve yards off. They were armed only with knobkerries,* and very clearly were no part of Laputa's army. This made their errand plain to me.

'Halt!' I said in Kaffir, as one of them made a hesitating step to advance. 'Who are you and what do you seek?'

There was no answer, but they looked at me curiously. Then one made a motion with his stick. Colin gave a growl, and would have been on him if I had not kept a hand on his collar. The rash man drew back, and all stood stiff and perplexed.

'Keep your hands by your side,' I said, 'or the dog, who has a devil, will devour you. One of you speak for the rest and tell me your purpose.'

For a moment I had a wild notion that they might be friends, some of Arcoll's scouts, and out to help me. But the first words shattered the fancy.

'We are sent by Inkulu,' the biggest of them said. 'He bade us bring you to him.'

'And what if I refuse to go?'

'Then, Baas, we must take you to him. We are under the vow of the Snake.'

'Vow of fiddlestick!' I cried. 'Who do you think is the bigger chief, the Inkulu or Ratitswan? I tell you Ratitswan is now driving Inkulu before him as a wind drives rotten leaves. It will be well for you, men of Machudi, to make peace with Ratitswan and take me to him on the Berg. If you bring me to him, I and he will reward you; but if you do Inkulu's bidding you will soon be hunted like buck out of your hills.'

They grinned at one another, but I could see that my words had no effect. Laputa had done his business too well.

The spokesman shrugged his shoulders in the way the Kaffirs have.

'We wish you no ill, Baas, but we have been bidden to take you to Inkulu. We cannot disobey the command of the Snake.'

My weakness was coming on me again, and I could talk no more. I sat down plump on the ground, almost falling into the pool. 'Take me to Inkulu,' I stammered with a dry throat, 'I do not fear him;' and I rolled half-fainting on my back.

These clansmen of Machudi were decent fellows. One of them had some Kaffir beer in a calabash, which he gave me to drink. The stuff was thin and sickly, but the fermentation in it did me good. I had the sense to remember my need of sleep. 'The day is young,' I said, 'and I have come far. I ask to be allowed to sleep for an hour.'

The men made no difficulty, and with my head between Colin's paws I slipped into dreamless slumber.

When they wakened me the sun was beginning to climb the sky. I judged it to be about eight o'clock. They had made a little fire and roasted mealies. Some of the food they gave me, and I ate it thankfully. I was feeling better, and I think a pipe would have almost completed my cure.

But when I stood up I found that I was worse than I had thought. The truth is, I was leg-weary, which you often see in horses, but rarely in men. What the proper explanation is I do not know, but the muscles simply refuse to answer the direction of the will. I found my legs sprawling like a child's who is learning to walk.

'If you want me to go to the Inkulu, you must carry me,' I said, as I dropped once more on the ground.

The men nodded, and set to work to make a kind of litter out of their knobkerries and some old ropes they carried. As they worked and chattered I looked idly at the left bank of the ravine—that is, the left as you ascend it. Some of Machudi's men had come down there, and, though the place looked sheer and perilous, I saw how they had managed it. I followed out bit by bit the track upwards, not with any thought of escape, but merely to keep my mind under control. The right road was from the foot of the pool up a long shelf to a clump of juniper. Then there was an easy chimney; then a piece of good hand-and-foot climbing; and last, another ledge which led by an easy gradient to the top. I figured all this out as I have heard a condemned man will count the windows of the houses on his way to the scaffold.

Presently the litter was ready, and the men made signs to me to get into it. They carried me down the ravine and up the Machudi burn to the green walls at its head. I admired their bodily fitness, for they bore me up those steep slopes with never a halt, zigzagging in the proper style of mountain transport. In less than an hour we had topped the ridge, and the plateau was before me.

It looked very homelike and gracious, rolling in gentle undulations to the western horizon, with clumps of wood in its hollows. Far away I saw smoke rising from what should be the village of the Iron Kranz. It was the country of my own people, and my captors behoved to go cautiously. They were old hands at veld-craft, and it was wonderful the way in which they kept out of sight even on the bare ridges. Arcoll could have taught them nothing in the art of scouting. At an incredible pace they hurried me along, now in a meadow by a stream side, now through a patch of forest, and now skirting a green shoulder of hill.

Once they clapped down suddenly, and crawled into the lee of some thick bracken. Then very quietly they tied my hands and feet, and, not urgently, wound a dirty length of cotton over my mouth. Colin was meantime held tight and muzzled with a kind of bag strapped over his head. To get this over his snapping jaws took the whole strength of the party. I guessed that we were nearing the highroad which runs from the plateau down the Great Letaba valley to the mining township of Wesselsburg, away out on the plain. The police patrols must be on this road, and there was risk in crossing. Sure enough I seemed to catch a jingle of bridles as if from some company of men riding in haste.

We lay still for a little till the scouts came back and reported the coast clear. Then we made a dart for the road, crossed it, and got into cover on the other side, where the ground sloped down to the Letaba glen. I noticed in crossing that the dust of the highway was thick with the marks of shod horses. I was very near and yet very far from my own people.

Once in the rocky gorge of the Letaba we advanced with less care. We scrambled up a steep side gorge and came on to the small plateau from which the Cloud Mountains rise. After that I was so tired that I drowsed away, heedless of the bumping of the litter. We went up and up, and when I next opened my eyes we had gone through a pass into a hollow of the hills. There was a flat space a mile or two square, and all round it stern black ramparts of rock. This must be Inanda's Kraal, a strong place if ever one existed, for a few men could defend all the approaches. Considering that I had warned Arcoll of this rendezvous, I marvelled that no attempt had been made to hold the entrance. The place was impregnable unless guns were brought up to the heights. I remember thinking of a story I had heard—how in the war Beyers* took his guns into the Wolkberg,* and thereby saved them from our troops. Could Arcoll be meditating the same exploit?

Suddenly I heard the sound of loud voices, and my litter was dropped roughly on the ground. I woke to clear consciousness in the midst of pandemonium.

# CHAPTER XVI

## INANDA'S KRAAL

THE vow was at an end. In place of the silent army of yesterday a mob of maddened savages surged around me. They were chanting a wild song, and brandishing spears and rifles to its accompaniment. From their bloodshot eyes stared the lust of blood, the fury of conquest, and all the aboriginal passions on which Laputa had laid his spell. In my mind ran a fragment from Laputa's prayer in the cave about the 'Terrible Ones.' Machudi's men—stout fellows, they held their ground as long as they could—were swept out of the way, and the wave of black savagery seemed to close over my head.

I thought my last moment had come. Certainly it had but for Colin. The bag had been taken from his head, and the fellow of Machudi's had dropped the rope round his collar. In a red fury of wrath the dog leaped at my enemies. Though every man of them was fully armed, they fell back, for I have noticed always that Kaffirs are mortally afraid of a white man's dog. Colin had the sense to keep beside me. Growling like a thunderstorm he held the ring around my litter.

The breathing space would not have lasted long, but it gave me time to get to my feet. My wrists and feet had been unbound long before, and the rest had cured my leg-weariness. I stood up in that fierce circle with the clear knowledge that my life hung by a hair.

'Take me to Inkulu,' I cried. 'Dogs and fools, would you despise his orders? If one hair of my head is hurt, he will flay you alive. Show me the way to him, and clear out of it.'

I dare say there was a break in my voice, for I was dismally frightened, but there must have been sufficient authority to get me a hearing. Machudi's men closed up behind me, and repeated my words with flourishes and gestures. But still the circle held. No man came nearer me, but none moved so as to give me passage.

Then I screwed up my courage, and did the only thing possible. I walked straight into the circle, knowing well that I was running no light risk. My courage, as I have already explained, is of little use unless I am doing something. I could not endure another minute of sitting still with those fierce eyes on me.

The circle gave way. Sullenly they made a road for me, closing up behind on my guards, so that Machudi's men were swallowed in the mob. Alone I stalked forward with all that huge yelling crowd behind me.

I had not far to go. Inanda's Kraal was a cluster of kyas* and rondavels,* shaped in a half-moon, with a flat space between the houses, where grew a big merula* tree. All around was a medley of little fires, with men squatted beside them. Here and there a party had finished their meal, and were swaggering about with a great shouting. The mob into which I had fallen was of this sort, and I saw others within the confines of the camp. But around the merula tree there was a gathering of chiefs, if I could judge by the comparative quiet and dignity of the men, who sat in rows on the ground. A few were standing, and among them I caught sight of Laputa's tall figure. I strode towards it, wondering if the chiefs would let me pass.

The hubbub of my volunteer attendants brought the eyes of the company round to me. In a second it seemed every man was on his feet. I could only pray that Laputa would get to me before his friends had time to spear me. I remember I fixed my eyes on a spur of hill beyond the kraal, and walked on with the best resolution I could find. Already I felt in my breast some of the long thin assegais of Umbooni's men.

But Laputa did not intend that I should be butchered. A word from him brought his company into order, and the next thing I knew I was facing him, where he stood in front of the biggest kya, with Henriques beside him, and some of the northern indunas. Henriques looked ghastly in the clear morning light, and he had a linen rag bound round his head and jaw, as if he suffered from toothache. His face was more livid, his eyes more bloodshot, and at the sight of me his hand went to his belt, and his teeth snapped. But he held his peace, and it was Laputa who spoke. He looked straight through me, and addressed Machudi's men.

'You have brought back the prisoner. That is well, and your service will be remembered. Go to 'Mpefu's camp on the hill there, and you will be given food.'

The men departed, and with them fell away the crowd which had followed me. I was left, very giddy and dazed, to confront Laputa and his chiefs. The whole scene was swimming before my eyes. I remember there was a clucking of hens from somewhere behind the kraal, which called up ridiculous memories. I was trying to remember the plan I had made in Machudi's glen. I kept saying to myself like a parrot: 'The army cannot know about the jewels. Laputa must keep his loss secret. I can get my life from him if I offer to give them back.' It had sounded a good scheme three hours before, but with the man's hard face before me, it seemed a frail peg to hang my fate on.

Laputa's eye fell on me, a clear searching eye with a question in it.

There was something he was trying to say to me which he dared not put into words. I guessed what the something was, for I saw his glance run over my shirt and my empty pockets.

'You have made little of your treachery,' he said. 'Fool, did you think to escape me? I could bring you back from the ends of the earth.'

'There was no treachery,' I replied. 'Do you blame a prisoner for trying to escape? When shooting began I found myself free, and I took the road for home. Ask Machudi's men and they will tell you that I came quietly with them, when I saw that the game was up.'

He shrugged his shoulders. 'It matters very little what you did. You are here now.—Tie him up and put him in my kya,' he said to the bodyguard. 'I have something to say to him before he dies.'

As the men laid hands on me, I saw the exultant grin on Henriques' face. It was more than I could endure.

'Stop,' I said. 'You talk of traitors, Mr Laputa. There is the biggest and blackest at your elbow. That man sent word to

Arcoll about your crossing at Dupree's Drift. At our outspan at noon yesterday he came to me and offered me my liberty if I would help him. He told me he was a spy, and I flung his offer in his face. It was he who shot the Keeper by the river side, and would have stolen the Snake if I had not broken his head. You call me a traitor, and you let that thing live, though he has killed your priest and betrayed your plans. Kill me if you like, but by God let him die first.'

I do not know how the others took the revelation, for my eyes were only for the Portugoose. He made a step towards me, his hands twitching by his sides.

'You lie,' he screamed in that queer broken voice which much fever gives. 'It was this English hound that killed the Keeper, and felled me when I tried to save him. The man who insults my honour is dead.' And he plucked from his belt a pistol.

A good shot does not miss at two yards. I was never nearer my end than in that fraction of time while the weapon came up to the aim. It was scarcely a second, but it was enough for Colin. The dog had kept my side, and had stood docilely by me while Laputa spoke. The truth is, he must have been as tired as I was. As the Kaffirs approached to lay hands on me he had growled menacingly, but when I spoke again he had stopped. Henriques' voice had convinced him of a more urgent danger, and so soon as the trigger hand of the Portugoose rose, the dog sprang. The bullet went wide, and the next moment dog and man were struggling on the ground.

A dozen hands held me from going to Colin's aid, but oddly enough no one stepped forward to help Henriques. The ruffian kept his head, and though the dog's teeth were in his shoulder, he managed to get his right hand free. I saw what would happen, and yelled madly in my apprehension. The yellow wrist curved, and the pistol barrel was pressed below the dog's shoulder. Thrice he fired, the grip relaxed, and Colin rolled over limply, fragments of shirt still hanging from his jaw. The Portugoose rose slowly with his hand to his head, and a thin stream of blood dripping from his shoulder.

As I saw the faithful eyes glazing in death, and knew that I had lost the best of all comrades, I went clean berserk mad.

The cluster of men round me, who had been staring open-eyed at the fight, were swept aside like reeds. I went straight for the Portugoose, determined that, pistol or no pistol, I would serve him as he had served my dog.

For my years I was a well-set-up lad, long in the arms and deep in the chest. But I had not yet come to my full strength, and in any case I could not hope to fight the whole of Laputa's army. I was flung back and forwards like a shuttlecock. They played some kind of game with me, and I could hear the idiotic Kaffir laughter. It was blind man's buff, so far as I was concerned, for I was blind with fury. I struck out wildly left and right, beating the air often, but sometimes getting in a solid blow on hard black flesh. I was soundly beaten myself, pricked with spears, and made to caper for savage sport. Suddenly I saw Laputa before me, and hurled myself madly at his chest. Some one gave me a clout on the head, and my senses fled.

When I came to myself, I was lying on a heap of mealie-stalks in a dark room. I had a desperate headache, and a horrid nausea, which made me fall back as soon as I tried to raise myself.

A voice came out of the darkness as I stirred—a voice speaking English.

'Are you awake, Mr Storekeeper?'

The voice was Laputa's, but I could not see him. The room was pitch dark, except for a long ray of sunlight on the floor.

'I'm awake,' I said. 'What do you want with me?'

Some one stepped out of the gloom and sat down near me. A naked black foot broke the belt of light on the floor.

'For God's sake get me a drink,' I murmured.

The figure rose and fetched a pannikin of water from a pail. I could hear the cool trickle of the drops on the metal. A hand put the dish to my mouth, and I drank water with a strong dash of spirits. This brought back my nausea, and I collapsed on the mealie-stalks till the fit passed.

Again the voice spoke, this time from close at hand.

'You are paying the penalty of being a fool, Mr Storekeeper. You are young to die, but folly is common in youth. In an hour you will regret that you did not listen to my advice at Umvelos'.'

I clawed at my wits and strove to realize what he was saying. He spoke of death within an hour. If it only came sharp and sudden, I did not mind greatly. The plan I had made had slipped utterly out of my mind. My body was so wretched, that I asked only for rest. I was very lightheaded and foolish at that moment.

'Kill me if you like,' I whispered. 'Some day you will pay dearly for it all. But for God's sake go away and leave me alone.'

Laputa laughed. It was a horrid sound in the darkness.

'You are brave, Mr Storekeeper, but I have seen a brave man's courage ebb very fast when he saw the death which I have arranged for you. Would you like to hear something of it by way of preparation?'

In a low gentle voice he began to tell me mysteries of awful cruelty. At first I scarcely heard him, but as he went on my brain seemed to wake from its lethargy. I listened with freezing blood. Not in my wildest nightmares had I imagined such a fate. Then in despite of myself a cry broke from me.

'It interests you?' Laputa asked. 'I could tell you more, but something must be left to the fancy. Yours should be an active one,' and his hand gripped my shaking wrist and felt my pulse.

'Henriques will see that the truth does not fall short of my forecast,' he went on. 'For I have appointed Henriques your executioner.'

The name brought my senses back to me.

'Kill me,' I said, 'but for God's sake kill Henriques too. If you did justice you would let me go and roast the Portugoose alive. But for me the Snake would be over the Lebombo by this time in Henriques' pocket.'

'But it is not, my friend. It was stolen by a storekeeper, who will shortly be wishing he had died in his mother's womb.'

My plan was slowly coming back to me.

'If you value Prester John's collar, you will save my life. What will your rising be without the Snake? Would they follow you a yard if they suspected you had lost it?'

'So you would threaten me,' Laputa said very gently. Then

in a burst of wrath he shouted, 'They will follow me to hell for my own sake. Imbecile, do you think my power is built on a trinket? When you are in your grave, I will be ruling a hundred millions from the proudest throne on earth.'

He sprang to his feet, and pulled back a shutter of the window, letting a flood of light into the hut. In that light I saw that he had in his hands the ivory box which had contained the collar.

'I will carry the casket through the wars,' he cried, 'and if I choose never to open it, who will gainsay me? You besotted fool, to think that any theft of yours could hinder my destiny!'

He was the blustering savage again, and I preferred him in the part. All that he said might be true, but I thought I could detect in his voice a keen regret, and in his air a touch of disquiet. The man was a fanatic, and like all fanatics had his superstitions.

'Yes,' I said, 'but when you mount the throne you speak of, it would be a pity not to have the rubies on your neck after all your talk in the cave.'

I thought he would have throttled me. He glowered down at me with murder in his eyes. Then he dashed the casket on the floor with such violence that it broke into fragments.

'Give me back the Ndhlondhlo,' he cried, like a petted child. 'Give me back the collar of John.'

This was the moment I had been waiting for.

'Now see here, Mr Laputa,' I said. 'I am going to talk business. Before you started this rising, you were a civilized man with a good education. Well, just remember that education for a minute, and look at the matter in a sensible light. I'm not like the Portugoose. I don't want to steal your rubies. I swear to God that what I have told you is true. Henriques killed the priest, and would have bagged the jewels if I had not laid him out. I ran away because I was going to be killed to-day, and I took the collar to keep it out of Henriques' hands. I tell you I would never have shot the old man myself. Very well, what happened? Your men overtook me, and I had no choice but to surrender. Before they reached me, I hid the collar in a place I know of. Now, I am going to make you a fair and square business proposition. You may be able to get on

without the Snake, but I can see you want it back. I am in a
tight place and want nothing so much as my life. I offer to
trade with you. Give me my life, and I will take you to the
place and put the jewels in your hand. Otherwise you may kill
me, but you will never see the collar of John again.'

I still think that was a pretty bold speech for a man to make
in a predicament like mine. But it had its effect. Laputa ceased
to be the barbarian king, and talked like a civilized man.

'That is, as you call it, a business proposition. But supposing
I refuse it? Supposing I take measures here—in this kraal—to
make you speak, and then send for the jewels.'

'There are several objections,' I said, quite cheerfully, for I
felt that I was gaining ground. 'One is that I could not explain
to any mortal soul how to find the collar. I know where it is,
but I could not impart the knowledge. Another is that the
country between here and Machudi's is not very healthy for
your people. Arcoll's men are all over it, and you cannot have
a collection of search parties rummaging about in the glen for
long. Last and most important, if you send any one for the
jewels, you confess their loss. No, Mr Laputa, if you want
them back, you must go yourself and take me with you.'

He stood silent for a little, with his brows knit in thought.
Then he opened the door and went out. I guessed that he had
gone to discover from his scouts the state of the country
between Inanda's Kraal and Machudi's glen. Hope had come
back to me, and I sat among the mealie-stalks trying to plan
the future. If he made a bargain I believed he would keep it.
Once set free at the head of Machudi's, I should be within an
hour or two of Arcoll's posts. So far, I had done nothing for
the cause. My message had been made useless by Henriques'
treachery, and I had stolen the Snake only to restore it. But if
I got off with my life, there would be work for me to do in the
Armageddon which I saw approaching. Should I escape, I
wondered. What would hinder Laputa from setting his men to
follow me, and seize me before I could get into safety? My
only chance was that Arcoll might have been busy this day,
and the countryside too full of his men to let Laputa's Kaffirs
through. But if this was so, Laputa and I should be stopped,
and then Laputa would certainly kill me. I wished—and yet I

did not wish—that Arcoll should hold all approaches. As I reflected, my first exhilaration died away. The scales were still heavily weighted against me.

Laputa returned, closing the door behind him.

'I will bargain with you on my own terms. You shall have your life, and in return you will take me to the place where you hid the collar, and put it into my hands. I will ride there, and you will run beside me, tied to my saddle. If we are in danger from the white men, I will shoot you dead. Do you accept?'

'Yes,' I said, scrambling to my feet, and ruefully testing my shaky legs. 'But if you want me to get to Machudi's you must go slowly, for I am nearly foundered.'

Then he brought out a Bible, and made me swear on it that I would do as I promised.

'Swear to me in turn,' I said, 'that you will give me my life if I restore the jewels.'

He swore, kissing the book like a witness in a police-court. I had forgotten that the man called himself a Christian.

'One thing more I ask,' I said. 'I want my dog decently buried.'

'That has been already done,' was the reply. 'He was a brave animal, and my people honour bravery.'

# CHAPTER XVII

## A DEAL AND ITS CONSEQUENCES

My eyes were bandaged tight, and a thong was run round my right wrist and tied to Laputa's saddle-bow. I felt the glare of the afternoon sun on my head, and my shins were continually barked by stones and trees; but these were my only tidings of the outer world. By the sound of his paces Laputa was riding the *schimmel*, and if any one thinks it easy to go blindfold by a horse's side I hope he will soon have the experience. In the darkness I could not tell the speed of the beast. When I ran I overshot it and was tugged back; when I walked my wrist was dislocated with the tugs forward.

For an hour or more I suffered this breakneck treatment. We were descending. Often I could hear the noise of falling streams, and once we splashed through a mountain ford. Laputa was taking no risks, for he clearly had in mind the possibility of some accident which would set me free, and he had no desire to have me guiding Arcoll to his camp.

But as I stumbled and sprawled down these rocky tracks I was not thinking of Laputa's plans. My whole soul was filled with regret for Colin, and rage against his murderer. After my first mad rush I had not thought about my dog. He was dead, but so would I be in an hour or two, and there was no cause to lament him. But at the first revival of hope my grief had returned. As they bandaged my eyes I was wishing that they would let me see his grave. As I followed beside Laputa I told myself that if ever I got free, when the war was over I would go to Inanda's Kraal, find the grave, and put a tombstone over it in memory of the dog that saved my life. I would also write that the man who shot him was killed on such and such a day at such and such a place by Colin's master. I wondered why Laputa had not the wits to see the Portugoose's treachery and to let me fight him. I did not care what were the weapons—knives or guns, or naked fists—I would certainly kill him, and afterwards the Kaffirs could do as they pleased with me. Hot tears of rage and weakness wet the bandage on my eyes, and the sobs which came from me were not only those of weariness.

At last we halted. Laputa got down and took off the bandage, and I found myself in one of the hill-meadows which lie among the foothills of the Wolkberg. The glare blinded me, and for a little I could only see the marigolds growing at my feet. Then I had a glimpse of the deep gorge of the Great Letaba below me, and far to the east the flats running out to the hazy blue line of the Lebombo hills. Laputa let me sit on the ground for a minute or two to get my breath and rest my feet. 'That was a rough road,' he said. 'You can take it easier now, for I have no wish to carry you.' He patted the *schimmel*, and the beautiful creature turned his mild eyes on the pair of us. I wondered if he recognized his rider of two nights ago.

I had seen Laputa as the Christian minister, as the priest and king in the cave, as the leader of an army at Dupree's Drift, and at the kraal we had left as the savage with all self-control flung to the winds. I was to see this amazing man in a further part. For he now became a friendly and rational companion. He kept his horse at an easy walk, and talked to me as if we were two friends out for a trip together. Perhaps he had talked thus to Arcoll, the half-caste who drove his Cape-cart.

The wooded bluff above Machudi's glen* showed far in front. He told me the story of the Machudi war,* which I knew already, but he told it as a saga. There had been a stratagem by which one of the Boer leaders—a Grobelaar, I think—got some of his men into the enemy's camp by hiding them in a captured forage wagon.

'Like the Trojan horse,' I said involuntarily.

'Yes,' said my companion, 'the same old device,' and to my amazement he quoted some lines of Virgil.*

'Do you understand Latin?' he asked.

I told him that I had some slight knowledge of the tongue, acquired at the university of Edinburgh. Laputa nodded. He mentioned the name of a professor there, and commented on his scholarship.

'O man!' I cried, 'what in God's name are you doing in this business? You that are educated and have seen the world, what makes you try to put the clock back? You want to wipe out the civilization of a thousand years, and turn us all into savages. It's the more shame to you when you know better.'

'You misunderstand me,' he said quietly. 'It is because I have sucked civilization dry that I know the bitterness of the fruit. I want a simpler and better world, and I want that world for my own people. I am a Christian, and will you tell me that your civilization pays much attention to Christ? You call yourself a patriot? Will you not give me leave to be a patriot in turn?'

'If you are a Christian, what sort of Christianity is it to deluge the land with blood?'

'The best,' he said. 'The house must be swept and garnished* before the man of the house can dwell in it. You have read history. Such a purging has descended on the Church at many times, and the world has awakened to a new hope. It is the same in all religions. The temples grow tawdry and foul and must be cleansed, and, let me remind you, the cleanser has always come out of the desert.'

I had no answer, being too weak and forlorn to think. But I fastened on his patriotic plea.

'Where are the patriots in your following? They are all red Kaffirs crying for blood and plunder. Supposing you were Oliver Cromwell you could make nothing out of such a crew.'

'They are my people,' he said simply.

By this time we had forded the Great Letaba, and were making our way through the clumps of forest to the crown of the plateau. I noticed that Laputa kept well in cover, preferring the tangle of wooded undergrowth to the open spaces of the water-meadows. As he talked, his wary eyes were keeping a sharp look-out over the landscape. I thrilled with the thought that my own folk were near at hand.

Once Laputa checked me with his hand as I was going to speak, and in silence we crossed the kloof of a little stream. After that we struck a long strip of forest and he slackened his watch.

'If you fight for a great cause,' I said, 'why do you let a miscreant like Henriques have a hand in it? You must know that the man's only interest in you is the chance of loot. I am for you against Henriques, and I tell you plain that if you don't break the snake's back it will sting you.'

Laputa looked at me with an odd, meditative look.

'You misunderstand again, Mr Storekeeper. The Portuguese is what you call a "mean white." His only safety is among us. I am campaigner enough to know that an enemy, who has a burning grievance against my other enemies, is a good ally. You are too hard on Henriques. You and your friends have treated him as a Kaffir, and a Kaffir he is in everything but Kaffir virtues. What makes you so anxious that Henriques should not betray me?'

'I'm not a mean white,' I said, 'and I will speak the truth. I hope, in God's name, to see you smashed; but I want it done by honest men, and not by a yellow devil who has murdered my dog and my friends. Sooner or later you will find him out; and if he escapes you, and there's any justice in heaven, he won't escape me.'

'Brave words,' said Laputa, with a laugh, and then in one second he became rigid in the saddle. We had crossed a patch of meadow and entered a wood, beyond which ran the highway. I fancy he was out in his reckoning, and did not think the road so near. At any rate, after a moment he caught the sound of horses, and I caught it too. The wood was thin, and there was no room for retreat, while to recross the meadow would bring us clean into the open. He jumped from his horse, untied with amazing quickness the rope halter from its neck, and started to gag me by winding the thing round my jaw.

I had no time to protest that I would keep faith, and my right hand was tethered to his pommel. In the grip of these great arms I was helpless, and in a trice was standing dumb as a lamp-post; while Laputa, his left arm round both of mine, and his right hand over the *schimmel*'s eyes, strained his ears like a sable antelope who has scented danger.

There was never a more brutal gagging. The rope crushed my nose and drove my lips down on my teeth, besides gripping my throat so that I could scarcely breathe. The pain was so great that I became sick, and would have fallen but for Laputa. Happily I managed to get my teeth apart, so that one coil slipped between, and eased the pain of the jaws. But the rest was bad enough to make me bite frantically on the tow, and I think in a little my sharp front teeth would have severed it. All this discomfort prevented me seeing what happened. The wood, as I have said, was thin, and through the screen of leaves I had a confused impression of men and horses passing interminably. There can only have been a score at the most; but the momemts drag if a cord is gripping your throat. When Laputa at length untied me, I had another fit of nausea, and leaned helplessly against a tree.

Laputa listened till the sound of the horses had died away; then silently we stole to the edge of the road, across, and into the thicker evergreen bush on the far side. At a pace which forced me to run hard, we climbed a steepish slope, till ahead of us we saw the bald green crown of the meadowland. I noticed that his face had grown dark and sullen again. He was in an enemy's country, and had the air of the hunted instead of the hunter. When I stopped he glowered at me, and once, when I was all but overcome with fatigue, he lifted his hand in a threat. Had he carried a sjambok, it would have fallen on my back.

If he was nervous, so was I. The fact that I was out of the Kaffir country and in the land of my own folk was a kind of qualified liberty. At any moment, I felt, Providence might intervene to set me free. It was in the bond that Laputa should shoot me if we were attacked; but a pistol might miss. As far as my shaken wits would let me, I began to forecast the future. Once he got the jewels my side of the bargain was complete. He had promised me my life, but there had been nothing said about my liberty; and I felt assured that Laputa would never allow one who had seen so much to get off to Arcoll with his tidings. But back to that unhallowed kraal I was resolved I would not go. He was armed, and I was helpless; he was strong, and I was dizzy with weakness; he was mounted, and I was on foot: it seemed a poor hope that I should get away. There was little chance from a wandering patrol, for I knew if we were followed I should have a bullet in my head, while Laputa got off on the *schimmel*. I must wait and bide events. At the worst, a clean shot on the hillside in a race for life was better than the unknown mysteries of the kraal. I prayed earnestly to God to show me His mercy, for if ever man was sore bested by the heathen it was I.

To my surprise, Laputa chose to show himself on the green hill-shoulder. He looked towards the Wolkberg and raised his hands. It must have been some signal. I cast my eyes back on the road we had come, and I thought I saw some figures a mile back, on the edge of the Letaba gorge. He was making sure of my return.

By this time it was about four in the afternoon, and as heavenly weather as the heart of man could wish. The meadows were full of aromatic herbs, which, as we crushed them, sent up a delicate odour. The little pools and shallows of the burns were as clear as a Lothian trout-stream. We were now going at a good pace, and I found that my earlier weariness was growing less. I was being keyed up for some great crisis, for in my case the spirit acts direct on the body, and fatigue grows and ebbs with hope. I knew that my strength was not far from breaking-point; but I knew also that so long as a chance was left me I should have enough for a stroke.

Before I realized where we were we had rounded the hill, and were looking down on the green cup of the upper Machudi's glen. Far down, I remember, where the trees began, there was a cloud of smoke. Some Kaffir—or maybe Arcoll—had fired the forest. The smoke was drifting away under a light west wind over the far plains, so that they were seen through a haze of opal.

Laputa bade me take the lead. I saw quite clear the red kloof on the far side, where the collar was hid. To get there we might have ridden straight into the cup, but a providential instinct made me circle round the top till we were on the lip of the ravine. This was the road some of Machudi's men had taken, and unthinkingly I followed them. Twenty minutes' riding brought us to the place, and all the while I had no kind of plan of escape. I was in the hands of my Maker, watching, like the Jews of old, for a sign.

Laputa dismounted and looked down into the gorge.

'There is no road there,' I said. 'We must go down to the foot and come up the stream-side. It would be better to leave your horse here.'

He started down the cliff, which from above looks a sheer precipice. Then he seemed to agree with me, took the rope from the *schimmel*'s neck, and knee-haltered his beast. And at that moment I had an inspiration.

With my wrist-rope in his hand, he preceded me down the hill till we got to the red screes at the foot of the kloof. Then, under my guidance, we turned up into the darkness of the gorge. As we entered I looked back, and saw figures coming over the edge of the green cup—Laputa's men, I guessed. What I had to do must be done quickly.

We climbed up the burn, over the succession of little cataracts, till we came to the flat space of shingle and the long pool where I had been taken that morning. The ashes of the fire which Machudi's men had made were plain on the rock. After that I had to climb a waterfall to get to the rocky pool where I had bestowed the rubies.

'You must take off this thong,' I said. 'I must climb to get the collar. Cover me with a pistol if you like. I won't be out of sight.'

Laputa undid the thong and set me free. From his belt he took a pistol, cocked it, and held it over his left hand. I had seen this way of shooting adopted by indifferent shots, and it gave me a wild hope that he might not be much of a marksman.

It did not take me long to find the pool, close against the blackened stump of a tree-fern. I thrust in my hand and gathered up the jewels from the cool sand. They came out glowing like living fires, and for a moment I thrilled with a sense of reverence. Surely these were no common stones which held in them the very heart of hell. Clutching them tightly, I climbed down to Laputa.

At the sight of the great Snake he gave a cry of rapture. Tearing it from me, he held it at arm's length, his face lit with a passionate joy. He kissed it, he raised it to the sky; nay, he was on his knees before it. Once more he was the savage transported in the presence of his fetich. He turned to me with burning eyes.

'Down on your knees,' he cried, 'and reverence the Ndhlon-dhlo. Down, you impious dog, and seek pardon for your sacrilege.'

'I won't,' I said. 'I won't bow to any heathen idol.'

He pointed his pistol at me.

'In a second I shoot where your head is now. Down, you fool, or perish.'

'You promised me my life,' I said stubbornly, though Heaven knows why I chose to act thus.

He dropped the pistol and flung himself on me. I was helpless as a baby in his hands. He forced me to the ground and rolled my face in the sand; then he pulled me to my feet and tossed me backward, till I almost staggered into the pool. I saved myself, and staggered instead into the shallow at the foot of it, close under the ledge of the precipice.

That morning, when Machudi's men were cooking breakfast, I had figured out a route up the cliff. This route was now my hope of escape. Laputa had dropped his pistol, and the collar had plunged him in an ecstasy of worship. Now, if ever, was my time. I must get on the shelf which ran sideways up the cliff, and then scramble for dear life.

I pretended to be dazed and terrified.

'You promised me my life,' I whimpered.

'Your life,' he cried. 'Yes, you shall have your life; and before long you will pray for death.'

'But I saved the Collar,' I pleaded. 'Henriques would have stolen it. I brought it safe here, and now you have got it.'

Meantime I was pulling myself up on the shelf, and loosening with one hand a boulder which overhung the pool.

'You have been repaid,' he said savagely. 'You will not die.'

'But my life is no use without liberty,' I said, working at the boulder till it lay loose in its niche.

He did not answer, being intent on examining the Collar to see if it had suffered any harm.

'I hope it isn't scratched,' I said. 'Henriques trod on it when I hit him.'

Laputa peered at the gems like a mother at a child who has had a fall. I saw my chance and took it. With a great heave I pulled the boulder down into the pool. It made a prodigious splash, sending a shower of spray over Laputa and the Collar. In cover of it I raced up the shelf, straining for the shelter of the juniper tree.

A shot rang out and struck the rock above me. A second later I had reached the tree and was scrambling up the crack beyond it.

Laputa did not fire again. He may have distrusted his shooting, or seen a better way of it. He dashed through the stream and ran up the shelf like a klipspringer after me. I felt rather than saw what was happening, and with my heart in my mouth I gathered my dregs of energy for the last struggle.

You know the nightmare when you are pursued by some awful terror, and, though sick with fear, your legs have a strange numbness, and you cannot drag them in obedience to the will. Such was my feeling in the crack above the juniper tree. In truth, I had passed the bounds of my endurance. Last night I had walked fifty miles, and all day I had borne the torments of a dreadful suspense. I had been bound and gagged and beaten till the force was out of my limbs. Also, and above all, I had had little food, and I was dizzy with want of sleep. My feet seemed leaden, my hands had no more grip than putty. I do not know how I escaped falling into the pool, for my head was singing and my heart thumping in my throat. I seemed to feel Laputa's great hand every second clawing at my heels.

I had reason for my fears. He had entered the crack long before I had reached the top, and his progress was twice as fast as mine. When I emerged on the topmost shelf he was scarcely a yard behind me. But an overhang checked his bulky figure and gave me a few seconds' grace. I needed it all, for these last steps on the shelf were the totterings of an old man. Only a desperate resolution and an extreme terror made me drag one foot after the other. Blindly I staggered on to the top of the ravine, and saw before me the *schimmel* grazing in the light of the westering sun.

I forced myself into a sort of drunken run, and crawled into the saddle. Behind me, as I turned, I could see Laputa's shoulders rising over the edge. I had no knife to cut the knee-halter, and the horse could not stir.

Then the miracle happened. When the rope had gagged me, my teeth must have nearly severed it at one place, and this Laputa had not noticed when he used it as a knee-halter. The shock of my entering the saddle made the *schimmel* fling up his head violently, and the rope snapped. I could not find the stirrups, but I dug my heels into his sides, and he leaped forward.

At the same moment Laputa began to shoot. It was a foolish move, for he might have caught me by running, since I had neither spurs nor whip, and the horse was hampered by the loose end of rope at his knee. In any case, being an indifferent shot, he should have aimed at the *schimmel*, not at me; but I suppose he wished to save his charger. One bullet sang past my head; a second did my business for me. It passed over my shoulder, as I lay low in the saddle, and grazed the beast's right ear. The pain maddened him, and, rope-end and all, he plunged into a wild gallop. Other shots came, but they fell far short. I saw dimly a native or two—the men who had followed us—rush to intercept me, and I think a spear was flung. But in a flash we were past them, and their cries faded behind me. I found the bridle, reached for the stirrups, and galloped straight for the sunset and for freedom.

# CHAPTER XVIII

### HOW A MAN MAY SOMETIMES PUT HIS TRUST
### IN A HORSE

I HAD long passed the limit of my strength. Only constant fear and wild alternations of hope had kept me going so long, and now that I was safe I became light-headed in earnest. The wonder is that I did not fall off. Happily the horse was good and the ground easy, for I was powerless to do any guiding. I simply sat on his back in a silly glow of comfort, keeping a line for the dying sun, which I saw in a nick of the Iron Crown Mountain. A sort of childish happiness possessed me. After three days of imminent peril, to be free was to be in fairyland. To be swishing through the long bracken or plunging among the breast-high flowers of the meadowland, in a world of essential lights and fragrances, seemed scarcely part of mortal experience. Remember that I was little more than a lad, and that I had faced death so often of late that my mind was all adrift. To be able to hope once more, nay, to be allowed to cease both from hope and fear, was like a deep and happy opiate to my senses. Spent and frail as I was, my soul swam in blessed waters of ease.

The mood did not last long. I came back to earth with a shock, as the *schimmel* stumbled at the crossing of a stream. I saw that the darkness was fast falling, and with the sight panic returned to me. Behind me I seemed to hear the sound of pursuit. The noise was in my ears, but when I turned it ceased, and I saw only the dusky shoulders of hills.

I tried to remember what Arcoll had told me about his headquarters, but my memory was wiped clean. I thought they were on or near the highway, but I could not remember where the highway was. Besides, he was close to the enemy, and I wanted to get back into the towns, far away from the battle-line. If I rode west I must come in time to villages, where I could hide myself. These were unworthy thoughts, but my excuse must be my tattered nerves. When a man comes out of great danger, he is apt to be a little deaf to the call of duty.

Suddenly I became ashamed. God had preserved me from deadly perils, but not that I might cower in some shelter. I had a mission as clear as Laputa's. For the first time I became conscious to what a little thing I owed my salvation. That matter of the broken halter was like the finger of Divine Providence.* I had been saved for a purpose, and unless I fulfilled that purpose I should again be lost. I was always a fatalist, and in that hour of strained body and soul I became something of a mystic. My panic ceased, my lethargy departed, and a more manly resolution took their place. I gripped the *schimmel* by the head and turned him due left. Now I remembered where the highroad ran, and I remembered something else.

For it was borne in on me that Laputa had fallen into my hands. Without any subtle purpose I had played a master game. He was cut off from his people, without a horse, on the wrong side of the highroad which Arcoll's men patrolled. Without him the rising would crumble. There might be war, even desperate war, but we should fight against a leaderless foe. If he could only be shepherded to the north, his game was over, and at our leisure we could mop up the scattered concentrations.

I was now as eager to get back into danger as I had been to get into safety. Arcoll must be found and warned, and that at once, or Laputa would slip over to Inanda's Kraal under cover of dark. It was a matter of minutes, and on these minutes depended the lives of thousands. It was also a matter of ebbing strength, for with my return to common sense I saw very clearly how near my capital was spent. If I could reach the highroad, find Arcoll or Arcoll's men, and give them my news, I would do my countrymen a service such as no man in Africa could render. But I felt my head swimming, I was swaying crazily in the saddle, and my hands had scarcely the force of a child's. I could only lie limply on the horse's back, clutching at his mane with trembling fingers. I remember that my head was full of a text from the Psalms* about not putting one's trust in horses. I prayed that this one horse might be an exception, for he carried more than Caesar and his fortunes.*

My mind is a blank about those last minutes. In less than an hour after my escape I struck the highway, but it was an hour which in the retrospect unrolls itself into unquiet years. I was dimly conscious of scrambling through a ditch and coming to a ghostly white road. The *schimmel* swung to the right, and the next I knew some one had taken my bridle and was speaking to me.

At first I thought it was Laputa and screamed. Then I must have tottered in the saddle, for I felt an arm slip round my middle. The rider uncorked a bottle with his teeth and forced some brandy down my throat. I choked and coughed, and then looked up to see a white policeman staring at me. I knew the police by the green shoulder-straps.

'Arcoll,' I managed to croak. 'For God's sake take me to Arcoll.'

The man whistled shrilly on his fingers, and a second rider came cantering down the road. As he came up I recognized his face, but could not put a name to it.

'Losh, it's the lad Crawfurd,' I heard a voice say. 'Crawfurd, man, d'ye no mind me at Lourenço Marques? Aitken?'

The Scotch tongue worked a spell with me. It cleared my wits and opened the gates of my past life. At last I knew I was among my own folk.

'I must see Arcoll. I have news for him—tremendous news. O man, take me to Arcoll and ask me no questions. Where is he? Where is he?'

'As it happens, he's about two hundred yards off,' Aitken said. 'That light ye see at the top of the brae is his camp.'

They helped me up the road, a man on each side of me, for I could never have kept in the saddle without their support. My message to Arcoll kept humming in my head as I tried to put it into words, for I had a horrid fear that my wits would fail me and I should be dumb when the time came. Also I was in a fever of haste. Every minute I wasted increased Laputa's chance of getting back to the kraal. He had men with him every bit as skilful as Arcoll's trackers. Unless Arcoll had a big force and the best horses there was no hope. Often in looking back at this hour I have marvelled at the strangeness of my behaviour. Here was I just set free from the certainty of a hideous death, and yet I had lost all joy in my security. I was more fevered at the thought of Laputa's escape than I had been at the prospect of David Crawfurd's end.

The next thing I knew I was being lifted off the *schimmel* by what seemed to me a thousand hands. Then came a glow of light, a great moon, in the centre of which I stood blinking. I was forced to sit down on a bed, while I was given a cup of hot tea, far more reviving than any spirits. I became conscious that some one was holding my hands, and speaking very slowly and gently.

'Davie,' the voice said, 'you're back among friends, my lad. Tell me, where have you been?'

'I want Arcoll,' I moaned. 'Where is Ratitswan?' There were tears of weakness running down my cheeks.

'Arcoll is here,' said the voice; 'he is holding your hands, Davie. Quiet, lad, quiet. Your troubles are all over now.'

I made a great effort, found the eyes to which the voice belonged, and spoke to them.

'Listen. I stole the collar of Prester John at Dupree's Drift. I was caught in the Berg and taken to the kraal—I forget its name—but I had hid the rubies.'

'Yes,' the voice said, 'you hid the rubies,—and then?'

'Inkulu wanted them back, so I made a deal with him. I took him to Machudi's and gave him the collar, and then he fired at me and I climbed and climbed . . . I climbed on a horse,' I concluded childishly.

I heard the voice say 'Yes?' again inquiringly, but my mind ran off at a tangent.

'Beyers took guns up into the Wolkberg,' I cried shrilly. 'Why the devil don't you do the same? You have the whole Kaffir army in a trap.'

I saw a smiling face before me.

'Good lad. Colles told me you weren't wanting in intelligence. What if we have done that very thing, Davie?'

But I was not listening. I was trying to remember the thing I most wanted to say, and that was not about Beyers and his guns. Those were nightmare minutes. A speaker who has lost

the thread of his discourse, a soldier who with a bayonet at his
throat has forgotten the password—I felt like them, and worse.
And to crown all I felt my faintness coming back, and my head
dropping with heaviness. I was in a torment of impotence.

Arcoll, still holding my hands, brought his face close to
mine, so that his clear eyes mastered and constrained me.

'Look at me, Davie,' I heard him say. 'You have something
to tell me, and it is very important. It is about Laputa, isn't it?
Think, man. You took him to Machudi's and gave him the
collar. He has gone back with it to Inanda's Kraal. Very well,
my guns will hold him there.'

I shook my head. 'You can't. You may split the army, but
you can't hold Laputa. He will be over the Olifants before you
fire a shot.'

'We will hunt him down before he crosses. And if not, we
will catch him at the railway.'

'For God's sake, hurry then,' I cried. 'In an hour he will be
over it and back in the kraal.'

'But the river is a long way.'

'River?' I repeated hazily. 'What river? The Letaba is not
the place. It is the road I mean.'

Arcoll's hands closed firmly on my wrists.

'You left Laputa at Machudi's and rode here without stopping. That would take you an hour. Had Laputa a horse?'

'Yes; but I took it,' I stammered. 'You can see it behind
me.'

Arcoll dropped my hands and stood up straight.

'By God, we've got him!' he said, and he spoke to his
companions. A man turned and ran out of the tent.

Then I remembered what I wanted to say. I struggled from
the bed and put my hands on his shoulders.

'Laputa is our side of the highroad. Cut him off from his
men, and drive him north—north—away up to the Rooirand.
Never mind the Wolkberg and the guns, for they can wait. I
tell you Laputa *is* the Rising, and he has the collar. Without
him you can mop up the Kaffirs at your leisure. Line the highroad with every man you have, for he must cross it or perish.
Oh, hurry, man, hurry; never mind me. We're saved if we can
chivy Laputa till morning. Quick, or I'll have to go myself.'

The tent emptied, and I lay back on the bed with a dim feeling that my duty was done and I could rest. Henceforth the affair was in stronger hands than mine. I was so weak that I could not lift my legs up to the bed, but sprawled half on and half off.

Utter exhaustion defeats sleep. I was in a fever, and my eyes would not close. I lay and drowsed while it seemed to me that the outside world was full of men and horses. I heard voices and the sound of hoofs and the jingle of bridles, but above all I heard the solid tramp of an army. The whole earth seemed to be full of war. Before my mind was spread the ribbon of the great highway. I saw it run white through the meadows of the plateau, then in a dark corkscrew down the glen of the Letaba, then white again through the vast moonlit bush of the plains, till the shanties of Wesselsburg rose at the end of it. It seemed to me to be less a road than a rampart, built of shining marble,* the Great Wall of Africa. I saw Laputa come out of the shadows and try to climb it, and always there was the sound of a rifle-breech clicking, a summons, and a flight. I began to take a keen interest in the game. Down in the bush were the dark figures of the hunted, and on the white wall were my own people—horse, foot, and artillery, the squadrons of our defence. What a general Arcoll was, and how great a matter had David Crawfurd kindled!

A man came in—I suppose a doctor. He took off my leggings and boots, cutting them from my bleeding feet, but I knew no pain. He felt my pulse and listened to my heart. Then he washed my face and gave me a bowl of hot milk. There must have been a drug in the milk, for I had scarcely drunk it before a tide of sleep seemed to flow over my brain. The white rampart faded from my eyes and I slept.

# CHAPTER XIX

## ARCOLL'S SHEPHERDING

WHILE I lay in a drugged slumber great things were happening. What I have to tell is no experience of my own, but the story as I pieced it together afterwards from talks with Arcoll and Aitken. The history of the Rising has been compiled. As I write I see before me on the shelves two neat blue volumes in which Mr Alexander Upton,* sometime correspondent of the *Times*, has told for the edification of posterity the tale of the war between the Plains and the Plateau. To him the Kaffir hero is Umbooni, a half-witted ruffian, whom we afterwards caught and hanged. He mentions Laputa only in a footnote as a renegade Christian who had something to do with fomenting discontent. He considers that the word 'Inkulu,' which he often heard, was a Zulu name for God. Mr Upton is a picturesque historian, but he knew nothing of the most romantic incident of all. This is the tale of the midnight shepherding of the 'heir of John' by Arcoll and his irregulars.

At Bruderstroom, where I was lying unconscious, there were two hundred men of the police; sixty-three Basuto scouts under a man called Stephen, who was half native in blood and wholly native in habits; and three commandoes of the farmers, each about forty strong. The commandoes were really companies of the North Transvaal Volunteers, but the old name had been kept and something of the old loose organization. There were also two four-gun batteries of volunteer artillery, but these were out on the western skirts of the Wolkberg following Beyers's historic precedent. Several companies of regulars were on their way from Pietersdorp, but they did not arrive till the next day. When they came they went to the Wolkberg to join the artillery. Along the Berg at strategic points were pickets of police with native trackers, and at Blaauwildebeestefontein there was a strong force with two field guns, for there was some fear of a second Kaffir army marching by that place to Inanda's Kraal. At Wesselsburg out on the plain there was a biggish police patrol, and a system of small patrols along the road, with a fair number of Basuto scouts. But the road was picketed, not held; for Arcoll's patrols were only a branch of his Intelligence Department. It was perfectly easy, as I had found myself, to slip across in a gap of the pickets.

Laputa would be in a hurry,* and therefore he would try to cross at the nearest point. Hence it was Arcoll's first business to hold the line between the defile of the Letaba and the camp at Bruderstroom. A detachment of the police who were well mounted galloped at racing speed for the defile, and behind them the rest lined out along the road. The farmers took a line at right angles to the road, so as to prevent an escape on the western flank. The Basutos were sent into the woods as a sort of advanced post to bring tidings of any movement there. Finally a body of police with native runners at their stirrups rode on to the drift where the road crosses the Letaba. The place is called Main Drift, and you will find it on the map. The natives were first of all to locate Laputa, and prevent him getting out on the south side of the triangle of hill and wood between Machudi's, the road, and the Letaba. If he failed there, he must try to ford the Letaba below the drift, and cross the road between the drift and Wesselsburg. Now Arcoll had not men enough to watch the whole line, and therefore if Laputa were once driven below the drift, he must shift his men farther down the road. Consequently it was of the first importance to locate Laputa's whereabouts, and for this purpose the native trackers were sent forward. There was just a chance of capturing him, but Arcoll knew too well his amazing veld-craft and great strength of body to build much hope on that.

We were none too soon. The advance men of the police rode into one of the Kaffirs from Inanda's Kraal, whom Laputa had sent forward to see if the way was clear. In two minutes more he would have been across and out of our power, for we had no chance of overtaking him in the woody ravines of the Letaba. The Kaffir, when he saw us, dived back into the grass on the north side of the road, which made it clear that Laputa was still there.

After that nothing happened for a little. The police reached their drift, and all the road west of that point was strongly held. The flanking commandoes joined hands with one of the police posts farther north, and moved slowly to the scarp of the Berg. They saw nobody; from which Arcoll could deduce that his man had gone down the Berg into the forests.

Had the Basutos been any good at woodcraft we should have had better intelligence. But living in a bare mountain country they are apt to find themselves puzzled in a forest. The best men among the trackers were some renegades of 'Mpefu, who sent back word by a device known only to Arcoll that five Kaffirs were in the woods a mile north of Main Drift. By this time it was after ten o'clock, and the moon was rising. The five men separated soon after, and the reports became confused. Then Laputa, as the biggest of the five, was located on the banks of the Great Letaba about two miles below Main Drift.

The question was as to his crossing. Arcoll had assumed that he would swim the river and try to get over the road between Main Drift and Wesselsburg. But in this assumption he underrated the shrewdness of his opponent. Laputa knew perfectly well that we had not enough men to patrol the whole countryside, but that the river enabled us to divide the land into two sections and concentrate strongly on one or the other. Accordingly he left the Great Letaba unforded and resolved to make a long circuit back to the Berg. One of his Kaffirs swam the river, and when word of this was brought Arcoll began to withdraw his posts farther down the road. But as the men were changing 'Mpefu's fellows got wind of Laputa's turn to the left, and in great haste Arcoll countermanded the move and waited in deep perplexity at Main Drift.

The salvation of his scheme was the farmers on the scarp of the Berg. They lit fires and gave Laputa the notion of a great army. Instead of going up the glen of Machudi or the Letsitela he bore away to the north for the valley of the Klein Letaba. The pace at which he moved must have been amazing. He had a great physique, hard as nails from long travelling, and in his own eyes he had an empire at stake. When I look at the map and see the journey which with vast fatigue I completed from

Dupree's Drift to Machudi's, and then look at the huge spaces of country over which Laputa's legs took him on that night, I am lost in admiration of the man.

About midnight he must have crossed the Letsitela. Here he made a grave blunder. If he had tried the Berg by one of the faces he might have got on to the plateau and been at Inanda's Kraal by the dawning. But he over-estimated the size of the commandoes, and held on to the north, where he thought there would be no defence. About one o'clock Arcoll, tired of inaction and conscious that he had misread Laputa's tactics, resolved on a bold stroke. He sent half his police to the Berg to reinforce the commandoes, bidding them get into touch with the post at Blaauwildebeestefontein.

A little after two o'clock a diversion occurred. Henriques succeeded in crossing the road three miles east of Main Drift. He had probably left the kraal early in the night and had tried to cross farther west, but had been deterred by the patrols. East of Main Drift, where the police were fewer, he succeeded; but he had not gone far till he was discovered by the Basuto scouts. The find was reported to Arcoll, who guessed at once who this traveller was. He dared not send out any of his white men, but he bade a party of the scouts follow the Portugoose's trail. They shadowed him to Dupree's Drift, where he crossed the Letaba. There he lay down by the roadside to sleep, while they kept him company. A hard fellow Henriques was, for he could slumber peacefully on the very scene of his murder.

Dawn found Laputa at the head of the Klein Letaba glen, not far from 'Mpefu's kraal. He got food at a hut, and set off at once up the wooded hill above it, which is a promontory of the plateau. By this time he must have been weary, or he would not have blundered as he did right into a post of the farmers. He was within an ace of capture, and to save himself was forced back from the scarp. He seems, to judge from reports, to have gone a little way south in the thicker timber, and then to have turned north again in the direction of Blaauwildebeestefontein. After that his movements are obscure. He was seen on the Klein Labongo, but the sight of the post at Blaauwildebeestefontein must have convinced him

that a korhaan* could not escape that way. The next we heard
of him was that he had joined Henriques.

After daybreak Arcoll, having got his reports from the
plateau, and knowing roughly the direction in which Laputa
was shaping, decided to advance his lines. The farmers,
reinforced by three more commandoes from the Pietersdorp
district, still held the plateau, but the police were now on the
line of the Great Letaba. It was Arcoll's plan to hold that river
and the long neck of land between it and the Labongo. His
force was hourly increasing, and his mounted men would be
able to prevent any escape on the flank to the east of
Wesselsburg.

So it happened that while Laputa was being driven east
from the Berg, Henriques was travelling north, and their lines
intersected. I should like to have seen the meeting. It must
have told Laputa what had always been in the Portugoose's
heart. Henriques, I fancy, was making for the cave in the
Rooirand. Laputa, so far as I can guess at his mind, had a plan
for getting over the Portuguese border, fetching a wide circuit,
and joining his men at any of the concentrations between there
and Amsterdam.

The two were seen at midday going down the road which
leads from Blaauwildebeestefontein to the Lebombo. Then
they struck Arcoll's new front, which stretched from the
Letaba to the Labongo. This drove them north again, and
forced them to swim the latter stream. From there to the
eastern extremity of the Rooirand, which is the Portuguese
frontier, the country is open and rolling, with a thin light
scrub in the hollows. It was bad cover for the fugitives, as they
found to their cost. For Arcoll had purposely turned his police
into a flying column. They no longer held a line; they scoured
a country. Only Laputa's incomparable veld-craft and great
bodily strength prevented the two from being caught in half an
hour. They doubled back, swam the Labongo again, and got
into the thick bush on the north side of the Blaauwildebeestefontein road. The Basuto scouts were magnificent in the open,
but in the cover they were again at fault. Laputa and Henriques
fairly baffled them, so that the pursuit turned to the west in

the belief that the fugitives had made for Majinje's kraal. In reality they had recrossed the Labongo and were making for Umvelos'.

All this I heard afterwards, but in the meantime I lay in Arcoll's tent in deep unconsciousness. While my enemies were being chased like partridges, I was reaping the fruits of four days' toil and terror. The hunters had become the hunted, the wheel had come full circle, and the woes of David Crawfurd were being abundantly avenged.

I slept till midday of the next day. When I awoke the hot noontide sun had made the tent like an oven. I felt better, but very stiff and sore, and I had a most ungovernable thirst. There was a pail of water with a tin pannikin beside the tent pole, and out of this I drank repeated draughts. Then I lay down again, for I was still very weary.

But my second sleep was not like my first. It was haunted by wild nightmares. No sooner had I closed my eyes than I began to live and move in a fantastic world. The whole bush of the plains lay before me, and I watched it as if from some view-point in the clouds. It was midday, and the sandy patches shimmered under a haze of heat. I saw odd little movements in the bush—a buck's head raised, a paauw* stalking solemnly in the long grass, a big crocodile rolling off a mudbank in the river. And then I saw quite clearly Laputa's figure going east.

In my sleep I did not think about Arcoll's manœuvres. My mind was wholly set upon Laputa. He was walking wearily, yet at a good pace, and his head was always turning, like a wild creature snuffing the wind. There was something with him, a shapeless shadow, which I could not see clearly. His neck was bare, but I knew well that the collar was in his pouch.

He stopped, turned west, and I lost him. The bush world for a space was quite silent, and I watched it eagerly as an aeronaut would watch the ground for a descent. For a long time I could see nothing. Then in a wood near a river there seemed to be a rustling. Some guinea-fowl flew up as if startled, and a stembok* scurried out. I knew that Laputa must be there.

Then, as I looked at the river, I saw a head swimming. Nay,

I saw two, one some distance behind the other. The first man landed on the far bank, and I recognized Laputa. The second was a slight short figure, and I knew it was Henriques.

I remember feeling very glad that these two had come together. It was certain now that Henriques would not escape. Either Laputa would find out the truth and kill him, or I would come up with him and have my revenge. In any case he was outside the Kaffir pale, adventuring on his own.

I watched the two till they halted near a ruined building. Surely this was the store I had built at Umvelos'. The thought gave me a horrid surprise. Laputa and Henriques were on their way to the Rooirand!

I woke with a start to find my forehead damp with sweat. There was some fever on me, I think, for my teeth were chattering. Very clear in my mind was the disquieting thought that Laputa and Henriques would soon be in the cave.

One of two things must happen—either Henriques would kill Laputa, get the collar of rubies, and be in the wilds of Mozambique before I could come up with his trail; or Laputa would outwit him, and have the handling himself of the treasure of gold and diamonds which had been laid up for the rising. If he thought there was a risk of defeat, I knew he would send my gems to the bottom of the Labongo, and all my weary work would go for nothing. I had forgotten all about patriotism. In that hour the fate of the country was nothing to me, and I got no satisfaction from the thought that Laputa was severed from his army. My one idea was that the treasure would be lost, the treasure for which I had risked my life.

There is a kind of courage which springs from bitter anger and disappointment. I had thought that I had bankrupted my spirit, but I found that there was a new passion in me to which my past sufferings taught no lesson. My uneasiness would not let me rest a moment longer. I rose to my feet, holding on by the bed, and staggered to the tent pole. I was weak, but not so very weak that I could not make one last effort. It maddened me that I should have done so much and yet fail at the end.

From a nail on the tent pole hung a fragment of looking-glass which Arcoll used for shaving. I caught a glimpse of my face in it, white and haggard and lined, with blue bags below the eyes. The doctor the night before had sponged it, but he had not got rid of all the stains of travel. In particular there was a faint splash of blood on the left temple. I remembered that this was what I had got from the basin of goat's blood that night in the cave.

I think that the sight of that splash determined me. Whether I willed it or not, I was sealed of Laputa's men. I must play the game to the finish, or never again know peace of mind on earth. These last four days had made me very old.

I found a pair of Arcoll's boots, roomy with much wearing, into which I thrust my bruised feet. Then I crawled to the door, and shouted for a boy to bring my horse. A Basuto appeared, and, awed by my appearance, went off in a hurry to see to the *schimmel*. It was late afternoon, about the same time of day as had yesterday seen me escaping from Machudi's. The Bruderstroom camp was empty, though sentinels were posted at the approaches. I beckoned the only white man I saw, and asked where Arcoll was. He told me that he had no news, but added that the patrols were still on the road as far as Wesselsburg. From this I gathered that Arcoll must have gone far out into the bush in his chase. I did not want to see him; above all, I did not want him to find Laputa. It was my private business that I rode on, and I asked for no allies.

Somebody brought me a cup of thick coffee, which I could not drink, and helped me into the saddle. The *schimmel* was fresh, and kicked freely as I cantered off the grass into the dust of the highroad. The whole world, I remember, was still and golden in the sunset.

# CHAPTER XX

## MY LAST SIGHT OF THE REVEREND JOHN LAPUTA

IT was dark before I got into the gorge of the Letaba. I passed many patrols, but few spoke to me, and none tried to stop me. Some may have known me, but I think it was my face and figure which tied their tongues. I must have been pale as death, with tangled hair and fever burning in my eyes. Also on my left temple was the splash of blood.

At Main Drift I found a big body of police holding the ford. I splashed through and stumbled into one of their camp-fires. A man questioned me, and told me that Arcoll had got his quarry. 'He's dead, they say. They shot him out on the hills when he was making for the Limpopo.' But I knew that this was not true. It was burned on my mind that Laputa was alive, nay, was waiting for me, and that it was God's will that we should meet in the cave.

A little later I struck the track of the Kaffirs' march. There was a broad, trampled way through the bush, and I followed it, for it led to Duprec's Drift. All this time I was urging the *schimmel* with all the vigour I had left in me. I had quite lost any remnant of fear. There were no terrors left for me either from Nature or man. At Dupree's Drift I rode the ford without a thought of crocodiles. I looked placidly at the spot where Henriques had slain the Keeper and I had stolen the rubies. There was no interest or imagination lingering in my dull brain. My nerves had suddenly become things of stolid, untempered iron. Each landmark I passed was noted down as one step nearer to my object. At Umvelos' I had not the leisure to do more than glance at the shell which I had built. I think I had forgotten all about that night when I lay in the cellar and heard Laputa's plans. Indeed, my doings of the past days were all hazy and trivial in my mind. I only saw one sight clearly— two men, one tall and black, the other little and sallow, slowly creeping nearer to the Rooirand, and myself, a midget on a horse, spurring far behind through the bush on their trail. I saw the picture as continuously and clearly as if I had been looking at a scene on the stage. There was only one change in the setting; the three figures seemed to be gradually closing together.

I had no exhilaration in my quest. I do not think I had even much hope, for something had gone numb and cold in me and killed my youth. I told myself that treasure-hunting was an enterprise accursed of God, and that I should most likely die. That Laputa and Henriques would die I was fully certain. The three of us would leave our bones to bleach among the diamonds, and in a little the Prester's collar would glow amid a little heap of human dust. I was quite convinced of all this, and quite apathetic. It really did not matter so long as I came up with Laputa and Henriques, and settled scores with them. That mattered everything in the world, for it was my destiny.

I had no means of knowing how long I took, but it was after midnight before I passed Umvelos', and ere I got to the Rooirand there was a fluttering of dawn in the east. I must have passed east of Arcoll's men, who were driving the bush towards Majinje's. I had ridden the night down and did not feel so very tired. My horse was stumbling, but my own limbs scarcely pained me. To be sure I was stiff and nerveless as if hewn out of wood, but I had been as bad when I left Bruderstroom. I felt as if I could go on riding to the end of the world.

At the brink of the bush I dismounted and turned the *schimmel* loose. I had brought no halter, and I left him to graze and roll. The light was sufficient to let me see the great rock face rising in a tower of dim purple. The sky was still picked out with stars, but the moon had long gone down, and the east was flushing. I marched up the path to the cave, very different from the timid being who had walked the same road three nights before. Then my terrors were all to come: now I had conquered terror and seen the other side of fear. I was centuries older.

But beside the path lay something which made me pause. It was a dead body, and the head was turned away from me. I did not need to see the face to know who it was. There had been only two men in my vision, and one of them was immortal.

I stopped and turned the body over. There was no joy in my heart, none of the lust of satisfied vengeance or slaked hate. I had forgotten about the killing of my dog and all the rest of Henriques' doings. It was only with curiosity that I looked down on the dead face, swollen and livid in the first light of morning.

The man had been strangled. His neck, as we say in Scotland, was 'thrawn',* and that was why he had lain on his back yet with his face turned away from me. He had been dead probably since before midnight. I looked closer, and saw that there was blood on his shirt and hands, but no wound. It was not his blood, but some other's. Then a few feet off on the path I found a pistol with two chambers empty.

What had happened was very plain. Henriques had tried to shoot Laputa at the entrance of the cave for the sake of the collar and the treasure within. He had wounded him—gravely, I thought, to judge from the amount of blood—but the quickness and marksmanship of the Portuguese had not availed to save his life from those terrible hands. After two shots Laputa had got hold of him and choked his life out as easily as a man twists a partridge's neck. Then he had gone into the cave.

I saw the marks of blood on the road, and hastened on. Laputa had been hours in the cave, enough to work havoc with the treasure. He was wounded, too, and desperate. Probably he had come to the Rooirand looking for sanctuary and rest for a day or two, but if Henriques had shot straight he might find a safer sanctuary and a longer rest. For the third time in my life I pushed up the gully between the straight high walls of rock, and heard from the heart of the hills the thunder of the imprisoned river.

There was only the faintest gleam of light in the cleft, but it sufficed to show me that the way to the cave was open. The hidden turnstile in the right wall stood ajar; I entered, and carelessly swung it behind me. The gates clashed into place with a finality which told me that they were firmly shut. I did not know the secret of them, so how should I get out again?

These things troubled me less than the fact that I had no light at all now. I had to go on my knees to ascend the stair, and I could feel that the steps were wet. It must be Laputa's blood.

Next I was out on the gallery which skirted the chasm. The sky above me was growing pale with dawn, and far below the tossing waters were fretted with light. A light fragrant wind was blowing on the hills, and a breath of it came down the funnel. I saw that my hands were all bloody with the stains on the steps, and I rubbed them on the rock to clean them. Without a tremor I crossed the stone slab over the gorge, and plunged into the dark alley which led to the inner chamber.

As before, there was a light in front of me, but this time it was a pin-point and not the glare of many torches. I felt my way carefully by the walls of the passage, though I did not really fear anything. It was by the stopping of these lateral walls that I knew I was in the cave, for the place had only one single speck of light. The falling wall of water stood out grey green and ghostly on the left, and I noticed that higher up it was lit as if from the open air. There must be a great funnel in the hillside in that direction. I walked a few paces, and then I made out that the spark in front was a lantern.

My eyes were getting used to the half-light, and I saw what was beside the lantern. Laputa knelt on the ashes of the fire which the Keeper had kindled three days before. He knelt before, and half leaned on, a rude altar of stone. The lantern stood by him on the floor, and its faint circle lit something which I was not unprepared for. Blood was welling from his side, and spreading in a dark pool over the ashes.

I had no fear, only a great pity—pity for lost romance, for vain endeavour, for fruitless courage. 'Greeting, Inkulu!' I said in Kaffir, as if I had been one of his indunas.

He turned his head and slowly and painfully rose to his feet. The place, it was clear, was lit from without, and the daylight was growing. The wall of the river had become a sheet of jewels, passing from pellucid diamond above to translucent emerald below. A dusky twilight sought out the extreme corners of the cave. Laputa's tall figure stood swaying above the white ashes, his hand pressed to his side.

'Who is it?' he said, looking at me with blind eyes.

'It is the storekeeper from Umvelos',' I answered.

'The storekeeper of Umvelos',' he repeated. 'God has used the weak things of the world to confound the strong. A king dies because a pedlar is troublesome. What do they call you, man? You deserve to be remembered.'

I told him 'David Crawfurd.'

'Crawfurd,' he repeated, 'you have been the little reef on which a great vessel has foundered. You stole the collar and cut me off from my people, and then when I was weary the Portuguese killed me.'

'No,' I cried, 'it was not me. You trusted Henriques, and you got your fingers on his neck too late. Don't say I didn't warn you.'

'You warned me, and I will repay you. I will make you rich, Crawfurd. You are a trader, and want money. I am a king, and want a throne. But I am dying, and there will be no more kings in Africa.'

The mention of riches did not thrill me as I had expected, but the last words awakened a wild regret. I was hypnotized by the man. To see him going out was like seeing the fall of a great mountain.

He stretched himself, gasping, and in the growing light I could see how broken he was. His cheeks were falling in, and his sombre eyes had shrunk back in their sockets. He seemed an old worn man standing there among the ashes, while the blood, which he made no effort to staunch, trickled down his side till it dripped on the floor. He had ceased to be the Kaffir king, or the Christian minister, or indeed any one of his former parts. Death was stripping him to his elements, and the man Laputa stood out beyond and above the characters he had played, something strange, and great, and moving, and terrible.

'We met for the first time three days ago,' he said, 'and now you will be the last to see the Inkulu.'

'Umvelos' was not our first meeting,' said I. 'Do you mind the Sabbath eight years since when you preached in the Free Kirk at Kirkcaple? I was the boy you chased from the shore, and I flung the stone that blacked your eye. Besides, I came out from England with you and Henriques, and I was in the boat which took you from Durban to Delagoa Bay. You and I have been long acquaint, Mr Laputa.'

'It is the hand of God,' he said solemnly. 'Your fate has been twisted with mine, and now you will die with me.'

I did not understand this talk about dying. I was not mortally wounded like him, and I did not think Laputa had the strength to kill me even if he wished. But my mind was so impassive that I scarcely regarded his words.

'I will make you rich,' he cried. 'Crawfurd, the storekeeper, will be the richest man in Africa. We are scattered, and our wealth is another's. He shall have the gold and the diamonds— all but the Collar, which goes with me.'

He staggered into a dark recess, one of many in the cave, and I followed him. There were boxes there, tea chests, cartridge cases, and old brass-ribbed Portuguese coffers. Laputa had keys at his belt, and unlocked them, his fingers fumbling with weakness. I peered in and saw gold coin and little bags of stones.

'Money and diamonds,' he cried. 'Once it was the war chest of a king, and now it will be the hoard of a trader. No, by the Lord! The trader's place is with the Terrible Ones.' An arm shot out, and my shoulder was fiercely gripped.

'You stole my horse. That is why I am dying. But for you I and my army would be over the Olifants. I am going to kill you, Crawfurd,' and his fingers closed in to my shoulder blades.

Still I was unperturbed. 'No, you are not. You cannot. You have tried to and failed. So did Henriques, and he is lying dead outside. I am in God's keeping, and cannot die before my time.'

I do not know if he heard me, but at any rate the murderous fit passed. His hand fell to his side and his great figure tottered out into the cave. He seemed to be making for the river, but he turned and went through the door I had entered by. I heard him slipping in the passage, and then there was a minute of silence.

Suddenly there came a grinding sound, followed by the kind of muffled splash which a stone makes when it falls into a deep well. I thought Laputa had fallen into the chasm, but when I reached the door his swaying figure was coming out of the corridor. Then I knew what he had done. He had used the remnant of his giant strength to break down the bridge of stone across the gorge, and so cut off my retreat.

I really did not care. Even if I had got over the bridge I should probably have been foiled by the shut turnstile. I had quite forgotten the meaning of fear of death.

I found myself giving my arm to the man who had tried to destroy me.

'I have laid up for you treasure in heaven,' he said. 'Your earthly treasure is in the boxes, but soon you will be seeking incorruptible jewels in the deep deep water. It is cool and quiet down there, and you forget the hunger and pain.'

The man was getting very near his end. The madness of despair came back to him, and he flung himself among the ashes.

'We are going to die together, Crawfurd,' he said. 'God has twined our threads, and there will be only one cutting. Tell me what has become of my army.'

'Arcoll has guns on the Wolkberg,' I said. 'They must submit or perish.'

'I have other armies . . . No, no, they are nothing. They will all wander and blunder and fight and be beaten. There is no leader anywhere . . . And I am dying.'

There was no gainsaying the signs of death. I asked him if he would like water, but he made no answer. His eyes were fixed on vacancy, and I thought I could realize something of the bitterness of that great regret. For myself I was as cold as a stone. I had no exultation of triumph, still less any fear of my own fate. I stood silent, the half-remorseful spectator of a fall like the fall of Lucifer.

'I would have taught the world wisdom.' Laputa was speaking English in a strange, thin, abstracted voice. 'There would have been no king like me since Charlemagne,' and he strayed into Latin which I have been told since was an adaptation of the Epitaph of Charles the Great. '*Sub hoc conditorio,*' he crooned, '*situm est corpus Joannis, magni et orthodoxi Imperatoris, qui imperium Africanum nobiliter ampliavit, et multos*

*per annos mundum feliciter rexit*.'[1] He must have chosen this
epitaph long ago.

He lay for a few seconds with his head on his arms, his
breast heaving with agony.

'No one will come after me. My race is doomed, and in a
little they will have forgotten my name. I alone could have
saved them. Now they go the way of the rest, and the warriors
of John become drudges and slaves.'

Something clicked in his throat, he gasped and fell forward,
and I thought he was dead. Then he struggled as if to rise. I
ran to him, and with all my strength aided him to his feet.

'Unarm, Eros,' he cried. 'The long day's task is done.'* With
the strange power of a dying man he tore off his leopard-skin
and belt till he stood stark as on the night when he had been
crowned. From his pouch he took the Prester's Collar. Then
he staggered to the brink of the chasm where the wall of green
water dropped into the dark depth below.

I watched, fascinated, as with the weak hands of a child he
twined the rubies round his neck and joined the clasp. Then
with a last effort he stood straight up on the brink, his eyes
raised to the belt of daylight from which the water fell. The
light caught the great gems and called fires from them, the
flames of the funeral pyre of a king.

Once more his voice, restored for a moment to its old vigour,
rang out through the cave above the din of the cascade. His
words were those which the Keeper had used three nights
before. With his hands held high and the Collar burning on
his neck he cried, 'The Snake returns to the House of its
Birth.'

'Come,' he cried to me. 'The Heir of John is going home.'

Then he leapt into the gulf. There was no sound of falling,
so great was the rush of water. He must have been whirled
into the open below where the bridge used to be, and then
swept into the underground deeps, where the Labongo

[1] 'Under this stone is laid the body of John, the great and orthodox Emperor,
who nobly enlarged the African realm, and for many years happily ruled the
world.'

drowses for thirty miles. Far from human quest he sleeps his last sleep, and perhaps on a fragment of bone washed into a crevice of rock there may hang the jewels that once gleamed in Sheba's hair.

# CHAPTER XXI

## I CLIMB THE CRAGS A SECOND TIME

I REMEMBER that I looked over the brink into the yeasty abyss with a mind hovering between perplexity and tears. I wanted to sit down and cry—why, I did not know, except that some great thing had happened. My brain was quite clear as to my own position. I was shut in this place, with no chance of escape and with no food. In a little I must die of starvation, or go mad and throw myself after Laputa. And yet I did not care a rush. My nerves had been tried too greatly in the past week. Now I was comatose, and beyond hoping or fearing.

I sat for a long time watching the light play on the fretted sheet of water and wondering where Laputa's body had gone. I shivered and wished he had not left me alone, for the darkness would come in time and I had no matches. After a little I got tired of doing nothing, and went groping among the treasure chests. One or two were full of coin—British sovereigns, Kruger sovereigns, Napoleons, Spanish and Portuguese gold pieces, and many older coins ranging back to the Middle Ages and even to the ancients. In one handful there was a splendid gold stater,* and in another a piece of Antoninus Pius.* The treasure had been collected for many years in many places, contributions of chiefs from ancient hoards as well as the cash received from I.D.B. I untied one or two of the little bags of stones and poured the contents into my hands. Most of the diamonds were small, such as a labourer might secrete on his person. The larger ones—and some were very large—were as a rule discoloured, looking more like big cairngorms.* But one or two bags had big stones which even my inexperienced eye told me were of the purest water. There must be some new pipe, I thought, for these could not have been stolen from any known mine.

After that I sat on the floor again and looked at the water. It exercised a mesmeric influence on me, soothing all care. I was quite happy to wait for death, for death had no meaning to me. My hate and fury were both lulled into a trance, since the passive is the next stage to the overwrought.

It must have been full day outside now, for the funnel was bright with sunshine, and even the dim cave caught a reflected radiance. As I watched the river I saw a bird flash downward, skimming the water. It turned into the cave and fluttered among its dark recesses. I heard its wings beating the roof as it sought wildly for an outlet. It dashed into the spray of the cataract and escaped again into the cave. For maybe twenty minutes it fluttered, till at last it found the way it had entered by. With a dart it sped up the funnel of rock into light and freedom.

I had begun to watch the bird in idle lassitude, I ended in keen excitement. The sight of it seemed to take a film from my eyes. I realized the zest of liberty, the passion of life again. I felt that beyond this dim underworld there was the great joyous earth, and I longed for it. I wanted to live now. My memory cleared, and I remembered all that had befallen me during the last few days. I had played the chief part in the whole business, and I had won. Laputa was dead and the treasure was mine, while Arcoll was crushing the Rising at his ease. I had only to be free again to be famous and rich. My hopes had returned, but with them came my fears. What if I could not escape? I must perish miserably by degrees, shut in the heart of a hill, though my friends were out for rescue. In place of my former lethargy I was now in a fever of unrest.

My first care was to explore the way I had come. I ran down the passage to the chasm which the slab of stone had spanned. I had been right in my guess, for the thing was gone. Laputa was in truth a Titan, who in the article of death could break down a bridge which would have taken any three men an hour to shift. The gorge was about seven yards wide, too far to risk a jump, and the cliff fell sheer and smooth to the imprisoned waters two hundred feet below. There was no chance of circuiting it, for the wall was as smooth as if it had been chiselled. The hand of man had been at work to make the sanctuary inviolable.

It occurred to me that sooner or later Arcoll would track Laputa to this place. He would find the bloodstains in the gully, but the turnstile would be shut and he would never find the trick of it. Nor could he have any Kaffirs with him who knew the secret of the Place of the Snake. Still if Arcoll knew I was inside he would find some way to get to me even though he had to dynamite the curtain of rock. I shouted, but my voice seemed to be drowned in the roar of the water. It made but a fresh chord in the wild orchestra, and I gave up hopes in that direction.

Very dolefully I returned to the cave. I was about to share the experience of all treasure-hunters—to be left with jewels galore and not a bite to sustain life. The thing was too commonplace to be endured. I grew angry, and declined so obvious a fate. 'Ek sal'n plan maak,'* I told myself in the old Dutchman's words. I had come through worse dangers, and a way I should find. To starve in the cave was no ending for David Crawfurd. Far better to join Laputa in the depths in a manly hazard for liberty.

My obstinacy and irritation cheered me. What had become of the lack-lustre young fool who had mooned here a few minutes back. Now I was as tense and strung for effort as the day I had ridden from Blaauwildebeestefontein to Umvelos'. I felt like a runner in the last lap of a race. For four days I had lived in the midst of terror and darkness. Daylight was only a few steps ahead, daylight and youth restored and a new world.

There were only two outlets from that cave—the way I had come, and the way the river came. The first was closed, the second a sheer staring impossibility. I had been into every niche and cranny, and there was no sign of a passage. I sat down on the floor and looked at the wall of water. It fell, as I have already explained, in a solid sheet, which made up the whole of the wall of the cave. Higher than the roof of the cave I could not see what happened, except that it must be the open air, for the sun was shining on it. The water was about three yards distant from the edge of the cave's floor, but it seemed to me that high up, level with the roof, this distance decreased to little more than a foot.

I could not see what the walls of the cave were like, but they looked smooth and difficult. Supposing I managed to climb up to the level of the roof close to the water, how on earth was I to get outside on to the wall of the ravine? I knew from my old days of rock-climbing what a complete obstacle the overhang of a cave is.

While I looked, however, I saw a thing which I had not noticed before. On the left side of the fall the water sluiced down in a sheet to the extreme edge of the cave, almost sprinkling the floor with water. But on the right side the force of water was obviously weaker, and a little short of the level of the cave roof there was a spike of rock which slightly broke the fall. The spike was covered, but the covering was shallow, for the current flowed from it in a rose-shaped spray. If a man could get to that spike and could get a foot on it without being swept down, it might be possible—just possible—to do something with the wall of the chasm above the cave. Of course I knew nothing about the nature of that wall. It might be as smooth as a polished pillar.

The result of these cogitations was that I decided to prospect the right wall of the cave close to the waterfall. But first I went rummaging in the back part to see if I could find anything to assist me. In one corner there was a rude cupboard with some stone and metal vessels. Here, too, were the few domestic utensils of the dead Keeper. In another were several locked coffers on which I could make no impression. There were the treasure-chests too, but they held nothing save treasure, and gold and diamonds were no manner of use to me. Other odds and ends I found—spears, a few skins, and a broken and notched axe. I took the axe in case there might be cutting to do.

Then at the back of a bin my hand struck something which brought the blood to my face. It was a rope, an old one, but still in fair condition and forty or fifty feet long. I dragged it out into the light and straightened its kinks. With this something could be done, assuming I could cut my way to the level of the roof.

I began the climb in my bare feet, and at the beginning it was very bad. Except on the very edge of the abyss there was scarcely a handhold. Possibly in floods the waters may have swept the wall in a curve, smoothing down the inner part and leaving the outer to its natural roughness. There was one place where I had to hang on by a very narrow crack while I scraped with the axe a hollow for my right foot. And then about twelve feet from the ground I struck the first of the iron pegs.

To this day I cannot think what these pegs were for. They were old square-headed things which had seen the wear of centuries. They cannot have been meant to assist a climber, for the dwellers of the cave had clearly never contemplated this means of egress. Perhaps they had been used for some kind of ceremonial curtain in a dim past. They were rusty and frail, and one of them came away in my hand, but for all that they marvellously assisted my ascent.

I had been climbing slowly, doggedly and carefully, my mind wholly occupied with the task; and almost before I knew I found my head close under the roof of the cave. It was necessary now to move towards the river, and the task seemed impossible. I could see no footholds, save two frail pegs, and in the corner between the wall and the roof was a rough arch too wide for my body to jam itself in. Just below the level of the roof—say two feet—I saw the submerged spike of rock. The waters raged around it, and could not have been more than an inch deep on the top. If I could only get my foot on that I believed I could avoid being swept down, and stand up and reach for the wall above the cave.

But how to get to it? It was no good delaying, for my frail holds might give at any moment. In any case I would have the moral security of the rope, so I passed it through a fairly staunch pin close to the roof, which had an upward tilt that almost made a ring of it. One end of the rope was round my body, the other was loose in my hand, and I paid it out as I moved. Moral support is something. Very gingerly I crawled like a fly along the wall, my fingers now clutching at a tiny knob, now clawing at a crack which did little more than hold my nails. It was all hopeless insanity, and yet somehow I did it. The rope and the nearness of the roof gave me confidence and balance.

Then the holds ceased altogether a couple of yards from the water. I saw my spike of rock a trifle below me. There was nothing for it but to risk all on a jump. I drew the rope out of the hitch, twined the slack round my waist, and leaped for the spike.

It was like throwing oneself on a line of spears. The solid wall of water hurled me back and down, but as I fell my arms closed on the spike. There I hung while my feet were towed outwards by the volume of the stream as if they had been dead leaves. I was half-stunned by the shock of the drip on my head, but I kept my wits, and presently got my face outside the falling sheet and breathed.

To get to my feet and stand on the spike while all the fury of water was plucking at me was the hardest physical effort I have ever made. It had to be done very circumspectly, for a slip would send me into the abyss. If I moved an arm or leg an inch too near the terrible dropping wall I knew I should be plucked from my hold. I got my knees on the outer face of the spike, so that all my body was removed as far as possible from the impact of the water. Then I began to pull myself slowly up.

I could not do it. If I got my feet on the rock the effort would bring me too far into the water, and that meant destruction. I saw this clearly in a second while my wrists were cracking with the strain. But if I had a wall behind me I could reach back with one hand and get what we call in Scotland a 'stell.' I knew there was a wall, but how far I could not judge. The perpetual hammering of the stream had confused my wits.

It was a horrible moment, but I had to risk it. I knew that if the wall was too far back I should fall, for I had to let my weight go till my hand fell on it. Delay would do no good, so with a prayer I flung my right hand back, while my left hand clutched the spike.

I found the wall—it was only a foot or two beyond my reach. With a heave I had my foot on the spike, and turning, had both hands on the opposite wall. There I stood, straddling like a Colossus* over a waste of white waters, with the cave floor far below me in the gloom, and my discarded axe lying close to a splash of Laputa's blood.

The spectacle made me giddy, and I had to move on or fall. The wall was not quite perpendicular, but as far as I could see a slope of about sixty degrees. It was ribbed and terraced pretty fully, but I could see no ledge within reach which offered standing room. Once more I tried the moral support of the rope, and as well as I could dropped a noose on the spike which might hold me if I fell. Then I boldly embarked on a hand traverse, pulling myself along a little ledge till I was right in the angle of the fall. Here, happily, the water was shallower and less violent, and with my legs up to the knees in foam I managed to scramble into a kind of corner. Now at last I was on the wall of the gully, and above the cave. I had achieved by amazing luck one of the most difficult of all mountaineering operations. I had got out of a cave to the wall above.

My troubles were by no means over, for I found the cliff most difficult to climb. The great rush of the stream dizzied my brain, the spray made the rock damp, and the slope steepened as I advanced. At one overhang my shoulder was almost in the water again. All this time I was climbing doggedly, with terror somewhere in my soul, and hope lighting but a feeble lamp. I was very distrustful of my body, for I knew that at any moment my weakness might return. The fever of three days of peril and stress is not allayed by one night's rest.

By this time I was high enough to see that the river came out of the ground about fifty feet short of the lip of the gully, and some ten feet beyond where I stood. Above the hole whence the waters issued was a loose slope of slabs and screes. It looked an ugly place, but there I must go, for the rock-wall I was on was getting unclimbable.

I turned the corner a foot or two above the water, and stood on a slope of about fifty degrees, running from the parapet of stone to a line beyond which blue sky appeared. The first step I took the place began to move. A boulder crashed into the fall, and tore down into the abyss with a shattering thunder. I lay flat and clutched desperately at every hold, but I had loosened an avalanche of earth, and not till my feet were sprayed by the water did I get a grip of firm rock and check my descent. All this frightened me horribly, with the kind of despairing angry fear which I had suffered at Bruderstroom, when I dreamed that the treasure was lost. I could not bear the notion of death when I had won so far.

After that I advanced, not by steps, but by inches. I felt more poised and pinnacled in the void than when I had stood on the spike of rock, for I had a substantial hold neither for foot nor hand. It seemed weeks before I made any progress away from the lip of the waterhole. I dared not look down, but kept my eyes on the slope before me, searching for any patch of ground which promised stability. Once I found a scrog of juniper with firm roots, and this gave me a great lift. A little further, however, I lit on a bank of screes which slipped with me to the right, and I lost most of the ground the bush had gained me. My whole being, I remember, was filled with a devouring passion to be quit of this gully and all that was in it.

Then, not suddenly as in romances, but after hard striving and hope long deferred, I found myself on a firm outcrop of weathered stone. In three strides I was on the edge of the plateau. Then I began to run, and at the same time to lose the power of running. I cast one look behind me, and saw a deep cleft of darkness out of which I had climbed. Down in the cave it had seemed light enough, but in the clear sunshine of the top the gorge looked a very pit of shade. For the first and last time in my life I had vertigo. Fear of falling back, and a mad craze to do it, made me acutely sick. I managed to stumble a few steps forward on the mountain turf, and then flung myself on my face.

When I raised my head I was amazed to find it still early morning. The dew was yet on the grass, and the sun was not far up the sky. I had thought that my entry into the cave, my time in it, and my escape had taken many hours, whereas at the most they had occupied two. It was little more than dawn, such a dawn as walks only on the hilltops. Before me was the shallow vale with its bracken and sweet grass, and farther on the shining links of the stream, and the loch still grey in the shadow of the beleaguering hills. Here was a fresh, clean land, a land for homesteads and orchards and children. All of a sudden I realized that at last I had come out of savagery.

The burden of the past days slipped from my shoulders. I

felt young again, and cheerful and brave. Behind me was the black night, and the horrid secrets of darkness. Before me was my own country, for that loch and that bracken might have been on a Scotch moor. The fresh scent of the air and the whole morning mystery put song into my blood. I remembered that I was not yet twenty.

My first care was to kneel there among the bracken and give thanks to my Maker, who in very truth had shown me 'His goodness in the land of the living.'*

After a little I went back to the edge of the cliff. There where the road came out of the bush was the body of Henriques, lying sprawled on the sand, with two dismounted riders looking hard at it. I gave a great shout, for in the men I recognized Aitken and the schoolmaster Wardlaw.

# CHAPTER XXII

## A GREAT PERIL AND A GREAT SALVATION

I MUST now take up some of the ragged ends which I have left behind me. It is not my task, as I have said, to write the history of the great Rising. That has been done by abler men, who were at the centre of the business, and had some knowledge of strategy and tactics; whereas I was only a raw lad who was privileged by fate to see the start. If I could, I would fain make an epic of it, and show how the Plains found at all points the Plateau guarded, how wits overcame numbers, and at every pass which the natives tried the great guns spoke and the tide rolled back. Yet I fear it would be an epic without a hero. There was no leader left when Laputa had gone. There were months of guerrilla fighting, and then months of reprisals, when chief after chief was hunted down and brought to trial. Then the amnesty came and a clean sheet, and white Africa drew breath again with certain grave reflections left in her head. On the whole I am not sorry that the history is no business of mine. Romance died with 'the heir of John,' and the crusade became a sorry mutiny. I can fancy how differently Laputa would have managed it all had he lived; how swift and sudden his plans would have been; how under him the fighting would not have been in the mountain glens, but far in the high-veld among the dorps and townships. With the Inkulu alive we warred against odds; with the Inkulu dead the balance sank heavily in our favour. I leave to others the marches and strategy of the thing, and hasten to clear up the obscure parts in my own fortunes.

Arcoll received my message from Umvelos' by Colin, or rather Wardlaw received it and sent it on to the post on the Berg where the leader had gone. Close on its heels came the message from Henriques by a Shangaan in his pay. It must have been sent off before the Portugoose got to the Rooirand, from which it would appear that he had his own men in the bush near the store, and that I was lucky to get off as I did.

Arcoll might have disregarded Henriques' news as a trap if it had come alone, but my corroboration impressed and perplexed him. He began to credit the Portugoose with treachery, but he had no inclination to act on his message, since it conflicted with his plans. He knew that Laputa must come into the Berg sooner or later, and he had resolved that his strategy must be to await him there. But there was the question of my life. He had every reason to believe that I was in the greatest danger, and he felt a certain responsibility for my fate. With the few men at his disposal he could not hope to hold up the great Kaffir army, but there was a chance that he might by a bold stand effect my rescue. Henriques had told him of the vow, and had told him that Laputa would ride in the centre of the force. A body of men well posted at Dupree's Drift might split the army at the crossing, and under cover of the fire I might swim the river and join my friends. Still relying on the vow, it might be possible for well-mounted men to evade capture. Accordingly he called for volunteers, and sent off one of his Kaffirs to warn me of his design. He led his men in person, and of his doings the reader already knows the tale. But though the crossing was flung into confusion, and the rear of the army was compelled to follow the northerly bank of the Letaba, there was no sign of me anywhere. Arcoll searched the river-banks, and crossed the drift to where the old Keeper was lying dead. He then concluded that I had been murdered early in the march, and his Kaffir, who might have given him news of me, was carried up the stream in the tide of the disorderly army. Therefore, he and his men rode back with all haste to the Berg by way of Main Drift, and reached Bruderstroom before Laputa had crossed the highway.

My information about Inanda's Kraal decided Arcoll's next move. Like me he remembered Beyers's performance, and resolved to repeat it. He had no hope of catching Laputa, but he thought that he might hold up the bulk of his force if he got guns on the ridge above the kraal. A message had already been sent for guns, and the first to arrive got to Bruderstroom about the hour when I was being taken by Machudi's men in the kloof. The ceremony of the purification prevented Laputa from keeping a good look-out, and the result was that a way was made for the guns on the north-western corner of the rampart of rock. It was the way which Beyers had taken, and indeed the enterprise was directed by one of Beyers's old commandants. All that day the work continued, while Laputa and I were travelling to Machudi's. Then came the evening when I staggered into camp and told my news. Arcoll, who alone knew how vital Laputa was to the success of the insurrection, immediately decided to suspend all other operations and devote himself to shepherding the leader away from his army. How the scheme succeeded and what befell Laputa the reader has already been told.

Aitken and Wardlaw, when I descended from the cliffs, took me straight to Blaauwildebeestefontein. I was like a man who is recovering from bad fever, cured, but weak and foolish, and it was a slow journey which I made to Umvelos', riding on Aitken's pony. At Umvelos' we found a picket who had captured the *schimmel* by the roadside. That wise beast, when I turned him loose at the entrance to the cave, had trotted quietly back the way he had come. At Umvelos' Aitken left me, and next day, with Wardlaw as companion, I rode up the glen of the Klein Labongo, and came in the afternoon to my old home. The store was empty, for Japp some days before had gone off post-haste to Pietersdorp; but there was Zeeta cleaning up the place as if war had never been heard of. I slept the night there, and in the morning found myself so much recovered that I was eager to get away. I wanted to see Arcoll about many things, but mainly about the treasure in the cave.

It was an easy journey to Bruderstroom through the meadows of the plateau. The farmers' commandoes had been recalled, but the ashes of their camp fires were still grey among the bracken. I fell in with a police patrol and was taken by them to a spot on the Upper Letaba, some miles west of the camp, where we found Arcoll at late breakfast. I had resolved to take him into my confidence, so I told him the full tale of my night's adventure. He was very severe with me, I remember, for my daft-like ride, but his severity relaxed before I had done with my story.

The telling brought back the scene to me, and I shivered at the picture of the cave with the morning breaking through the veil of water and Laputa in his death throes. Arcoll did not speak for some time.

'So he is dead,' he said at last, half-whispering to himself. 'Well, he was a king, and died like a king. Our job now is simple, for there is none of his breed left in Africa.'

Then I told him of the treasure.

'It belongs to you, Davie,' he said, 'and we must see that you get it. This is going to be a long war, but if we survive to the end you will be a rich man.'

'But in the meantime?' I asked. 'Supposing other Kaffirs hear of it, and come back and make a bridge over the gorge? They may be doing it now.'

'I'll put a guard on it,' he said, jumping up briskly. 'It's maybe not a soldier's job, but you've saved this country, Davie, and I'm going to make sure that you have your reward.'

After that I went with Arcoll to Inanda's Kraal. I am not going to tell the story of that performance, for it occupies no less than two chapters in Mr Upton's book. He makes one or two blunders, for he spells my name with an 'o,' and he says we walked out of the camp on our perilous mission 'with faces white and set as a Crusader's.' That is certainly not true, for in the first place nobody saw us go who could judge how we looked, and in the second place we were both smoking and feeling quite cheerful. At home they made a great fuss about it, and started a newspaper cry about the Victoria Cross, but the danger was not so terrible after all, and in any case it was nothing to what I had been through in the past week.

I take credit to myself for suggesting the idea. By this time we had the army in the kraal at our mercy. Laputa not having returned, they had no plans. It had been the original intention to start for the Olifants on the following day, so there was a scanty supply of food. Besides, there were the makings of a pretty quarrel between Umbooni and some of the north-country chiefs, and I verily believe that if we had held them tight there for a week they would have destroyed each other in faction fights. In any case, in a little they would have grown desperate and tried to rush the approaches on the north and south. Then we must either have used the guns on them, which would have meant a great slaughter, or let them go to do mischief elsewhere. Arcoll was a merciful man who had no love for butchery; besides, he was a statesman with an eye to the future of the country after the war. But it was his duty to isolate Laputa's army, and at all costs it must be prevented from joining any of the concentrations in the south.

Then I proposed to him to do as Rhodes did in the Matoppos,* and go and talk to them. By this time, I argued, the influence of Laputa must have sunk, and the fervour of the purification be half-forgotten. The army had little food and no leader. The rank and file had never been fanatical, and the chiefs and indunas must now be inclined to sober reflections. But once blood was shed the lust of blood would possess them. Our only chance was to strike when their minds were perplexed and undecided.

Arcoll did all the arranging. He had a message sent to the chiefs inviting them to an indaba,* and presently word was brought back that an indaba was called for the next day at noon. That same night we heard that Umbooni and about twenty of his men had managed to evade our ring of scouts and got clear away to the south. This was all to our advantage, as it removed from the coming indaba the most irreconcilable of the chiefs.

That indaba was a queer business. Arcoll and I left our escort at the foot of a ravine, and entered the kraal by the same road as I had left it. It was a very bright, hot winter's day, and try as I might, I could not bring myself to think of any danger. I believed that in this way most temerarious deeds are done; the doer has become insensible to danger, and his imagination is clouded with some engrossing purpose. The first sentries received us gloomily enough, and closed behind us as they had done when Machudi's men haled me thither. Then the job became eerie, for we had to walk across a green flat with thousands of eyes watching us. By-and-by we came to the merula tree opposite the kyas, and there we found a ring of chiefs, sitting with cocked rifles on their knees.

We were armed with pistols, and the first thing Arcoll did was to hand them to one of the chiefs.

'We come in peace,' he said. 'We give you our lives.'

Then the indaba began, Arcoll leading off. It was a fine speech he made, one of the finest I have ever listened to. He asked them what their grievances were; he told them how mighty was the power of the white man; he promised that what was unjust should be remedied, if only they would speak honestly and peacefully; he harped on their old legends and songs, claiming for the king of England the right of their old monarchs. It was a fine speech, and yet I saw that it did not convince them. They listened moodily, if attentively, and at the end there was a blank silence.

Arcoll turned to me. 'For God's sake, Davie,' he said, 'talk to them about Laputa. It's our only chance.'

I had never tried speaking before, and though I talked their tongue I had not Arcoll's gift of it. But I felt that a great cause was at stake, and I spoke up as best I could.

I began by saying that Inkulu had been my friend, and that at Umvelos' before the rising he had tried to save my life. At the mention of the name I saw eyes brighten. At last the audience was hanging on my words.

I told them of Henriques and his treachery. I told them frankly and fairly of the doings at Dupree's Drift. I made no secret of the part I played. 'I was fighting for my life,' I said. 'Any man of you who is a man would have done the like.'

Then I told them of my last ride, and the sight I saw at the foot of the Rooirand. I drew a picture of Henriques lying dead with a broken neck, and the Inkulu, wounded to death, creeping into the cave.

In moments of extremity I suppose every man becomes an orator. In that hour and place I discovered gifts I had never dreamed of. Arcoll told me afterwards that I had spoken like a man inspired, and by a fortunate chance had hit upon the only way to move my hearers. I told of that last scene in the cave, when Laputa had broken down the bridge, and had spoken his dying words—that he was the last king in Africa, and that without him the rising was at an end. Then I told of his leap into the river, and a great sigh went up from the ranks about me.

'You see me here,' I said, 'by the grace of God. I found a way up the fall and the cliffs which no man has ever travelled before or will travel again. Your king is dead. He was a great king, as I who stand here bear witness, and you will never more see his like. His last words were that the Rising was over. Respect that word, my brothers. We come to you not in war but in peace, to offer a free pardon, and the redress of your wrongs. If you fight you fight with the certainty of failure, and against the wish of the heir of John. I have come here at the risk of my life to tell you his commands. His spirit approves my mission. Think well before you defy the mandate of the Snake, and risk the vengeance of the Terrible Ones.'

After that I knew that we had won. The chiefs talked among themselves in low whispers, casting strange looks at me. Then the greatest of them advanced and laid his rifle at my feet.

'We believe the word of a brave man,' he said. 'We accept the mandate of the Snake.'

Arcoll now took command. He arranged for the disarmament bit by bit, companies of men being marched off from Inanda's Kraal to stations on the plateau where their arms were collected by our troops, and food provided for them. For the full history I refer the reader to Mr Upton's work. It took many days, and taxed all our resources, but by the end of a week we had the whole of Laputa's army in separate stations, under guard, disarmed, and awaiting repatriation.

Then Arcoll went south to the war which was to rage around the Swaziland and Zululand borders for many months, while to Aitken and myself was entrusted the work of settlement. We had inadequate troops at our command, and but for our prestige and the weight of Laputa's dead hand there might any moment have been a tragedy. The task took months, for many of the levies came from the far north, and the job of feeding troops on a long journey was difficult enough in the winter season when the energies of the country were occupied with the fighting in the south. Yet it was an experience for which I shall ever be grateful, for it turned me from a rash boy into a serious man. I knew then the meaning of the white man's duty.* He has to take all risks, recking nothing of his life or his fortunes, and well content to find his reward in the fulfilment of his task. That is the difference between white and black, the gift of responsibility, the power of being in a little way a king; and so long as we know this and practise it, we will rule not in Africa alone but wherever there are dark men who live only for the day and their own bellies. Moreover, the work made me pitiful and kindly. I learned much of the untold grievances of the natives, and saw something of their strange, twisted reasoning. Before we had got Laputa's army back to their kraals, with food enough to tide them over the spring sowing, Aitken and I had got sounder policy in our heads than you will find in the towns, where men sit in offices and see the world through a mist of papers.

By this time peace was at hand, and I went back to Inanda's Kraal to look for Colin's grave. It was not a difficult quest, for on the sward in front of the merula tree they had buried him. I found a mason in the Iron Kranz village, and from the excellent red stone of the neighbourhood was hewn a square slab with an inscription. It ran thus: 'Here lies buried the dog Colin, who was killed in defending D. Crawfurd, his master. To him it was mainly due that the Kaffir Rising failed.' I leave those who have read my tale to see the justice of the words.

# CHAPTER XXIII

## MY UNCLE'S GIFT IS MANY TIMES MULTIPLIED

WE got at the treasure by blowing open the turnstile. It was easy enough to trace the spot in the rock where it stood, but the most patient search did not reveal its secret. Accordingly we had recourse to dynamite, and soon laid bare the stone steps, and ascended to the gallery. The chasm was bridged with planks, and Arcoll and I crossed alone. The cave was as I had left it. The bloodstains on the floor had grown dark with time, but the ashes of the sacramental fire were still there to remind me of the drama I had borne a part in. When I looked at the way I had escaped my brain grew dizzy at the thought of it. I do not think that all the gold on earth would have driven me a second time to that awful escalade. As for Arcoll, he could not see its possibility at all.

'Only a madman could have done it,' he said, blinking his eyes at the green linn.* 'Indeed, Davie, I think for about four days you were as mad as they make. It was a fortunate thing, for your madness saved the country.'

With some labour we got the treasure down to the path, and took it under a strong guard to Pietersdorp. The Government were busy with the settling up after the war, and it took many weeks to have our business disposed of. At first things looked badly for me. The Attorney-General set up a claim to the whole as spoils of war, since, he argued, it was the war-chest of the enemy we had conquered. I do not know how the matter would have gone on legal grounds, though I was advised by my lawyers that the claim was a bad one. But the part I had played in the whole business, more especially in the visit to Inanda's Kraal, had made me a kind of popular hero, and the Government thought better of their first attitude. Besides, Arcoll had great influence, and the whole story of my doings, which was told privately by him to some of the members of the Government, disposed them to be generous. Accordingly they agreed to treat the contents of the cave as ordinary treasure trove, of which, by the law, one half went to the discoverer and one half to the Crown.

This was well enough so far as the gold was concerned, but another difficulty arose about the diamonds; for a large part of these had obviously been stolen by labourers from the mines, and the mining people laid claim to them as stolen goods. I was advised not to dispute this claim, and consequently we had a great sorting-out of the stones in the presence of the experts of the different mines. In the end it turned out that identification was not an easy matter, for the experts quarrelled furiously among themselves. A compromise was at last come to, and a division made; and then the diamond companies behaved very handsomely, voting me a substantial sum in recognition of my services in recovering their property. What with this and with my half share of the gold and my share of the unclaimed stones, I found that I had a very considerable fortune. The whole of my stones I sold to De Beers, for if I had placed them on the open market I should have upset the delicate equipoise of diamond values. When I came finally to cast up my accounts, I found that I had secured a fortune of a trifle over a quarter of a million pounds.

The wealth did not dazzle so much as it solemnized me. I had no impulse to spend any part of it in a riot of folly. It had come to me like fairy gold out of the void; it had been bought with men's blood, almost with my own. I wanted to get away to a quiet place and think, for of late my life had been too crowded with drama, and there comes a satiety of action as well as of idleness. Above all things I wanted to get home. They gave me a great send-off, and sang songs, and good fellows shook my hand till it ached. The papers were full of me, and there was a banquet and speeches. But I could not relish this glory as I ought, for I was like a boy thrown violently out of his bearings.

Not till I was in the train nearing Cape Town did I recover my equanimity. The burden of the past seemed to slip from me suddenly as on the morning when I had climbed the linn. I saw my life all lying before me; and already I had won success. I thought of my return to my own country, my first sight of the grey shores of Fife, my visit to Kirkcaple, my meeting with my mother. I was a rich man now who could choose his career, and my mother need never again want for comfort. My money seemed pleasant to me, for if men won theirs by brains or industry, I had won mine by sterner methods, for I had staked against it my life. I sat alone in the railway carriage and cried with pure thankfulness. These were comforting tears, for they brought me back to my old commonplace self.

My last memory of Africa is my meeting with Tam Dyke. I caught sight of him in the streets of Cape Town, and running after him, clapped him on the shoulder. He stared at me as if he had seen a ghost.

'Is it yourself, Davie?' he cried. 'I never looked to see you again in this world. I do nothing but read about you in the papers. What for did ye not send for me? Here have I been knocking about inside a ship and you have been getting famous. They tell me you're a millionaire, too.'

I had Tam to dinner at my hotel, and later, sitting smoking on the terrace and watching the flying-ants among the aloes, I told him the better part of the story I have here written down.

'Man, Davie,' he said at the end, 'you've had a tremendous time. Here are you not eighteen months away from home, and you're going back with a fortune. What will you do with it?'

I told him that I proposed, to begin with, to finish my education at Edinburgh College. At this he roared with laughter.

'That's a dull ending, anyway. It's me that should have the money, for I'm full of imagination. You were aye a prosaic body, Davie.'

'Maybe I am,' I said; 'but I am very sure of one thing. If I hadn't been a prosaic body, I wouldn't be sitting here to-night.'

Two years later Aitken found the diamond pipe, which he had always believed lay in the mountains. Some of the stones in the cave, being unlike any ordinary African diamonds, confirmed his suspicions and set him on the track. A Kaffir tribe to the north-east of the Rooirand had known of it, but they had never worked it, but only collected the overspill. The closing down of one of the chief existing mines had created a shortage of diamonds in the world's markets, and once again the position was the same as when Kimberley began. Accordingly he made a great fortune, and to-day the Aitken Proprietary Mine is one of the most famous in the country. But Aitken did more than mine diamonds, for he had not forgotten the lesson we had learned together in the work of resettlement. He laid down a big fund for the education and amelioration of the native races, and the first fruit of it was the establishment at Blaauwildebeestefontein itself of a great native training college. It was no factory for making missionaries and black teachers, but an institution for giving the Kaffirs the kind of training which fits them to be good citizens of the state. There you will find every kind of technical workshop, and the finest experimental farms, where the blacks are taught modern agriculture. They have proved themselves apt pupils, and to-day you will see in the glens of the Berg and in the plains Kaffir tillage which is as scientific as any in Africa. They have created a huge export trade in tobacco and fruit; the cotton promises well; and there is talk of a new fibre which will do wonders. Also along the river bottoms the india-rubber business is prospering.

There are playing-fields and baths and reading-rooms and libraries just as in a school at home. In front of the great hall of the college a statue stands, the figure of a black man shading his eyes with his hands and looking far over the plains to the Rooirand. On the pedestal it is lettered 'Prester John,' but the face is the face of Laputa. So the last of the kings of Africa does not lack his monument.

Of this institution Mr Wardlaw is the head. He writes to me weekly, for I am one of the governors, as well as an old friend, and from a recent letter I take this passage:—

'I often cast my mind back to the afternoon when you and I sat on the stoep of the schoolhouse, and talked of the Kaffirs and our future. I had about a dozen pupils then, and now I have nearly three thousand; and in place of a tin-roofed shanty and a yard, I have a whole countryside. You laughed at me for my keenness, Davie, but I've seen it justified. I was never a man of war like you, and so I had to bide at home while you and your like were straightening out the troubles. But when it was all over my job began, for I could do what you couldn't do—I was the physician to heal wounds. You mind how nervous I was when I heard the drums beat. I hear them every evening now, for we have made a rule that all the Kaffir farms on the Berg sound a kind of curfew. It reminds me of old times, and tells me that though it is peace nowadays we mean to keep all the manhood in them that they used to exercise in war. It would do your eyes good to see the garden we have made out of the Klein Labongo glen. The place is one big orchard with every kind of tropical fruit in it, and the irrigation dam is as full of fish as it will hold. Out at Umvelos' there is a tobacco-factory, and all round Sikitola's we have square miles of mealie and cotton fields. The loch on the Rooirand is stocked with Lochleven trout, and we have made a bridle-path up to it in a gully east of the one you climbed. You ask about Machudi's. The last time I was there the place was white with sheep, for we have got the edge of the plateau grazed down, and sheep can get the short bite there. We have cleaned up all the kraals, and the chiefs are members of our county council, and are as fond of hearing their own voices as an Aberdeen bailie. It's a queer transformation we have wrought, and when I sit and smoke my pipe in the evening, and look over the plains and then at the big black statue you and Aitken set up, I thank the Providence that has guided me so far. I hope and trust that, in the Bible words, "the wilderness and the solitary place are glad for us." At any rate it will not be my fault if they don't "blossom as the rose".* Come out and visit us soon, man, and see the work you had a hand in starting. . . .'

I am thinking seriously of taking Wardlaw's advice.

# APPENDIX

Buchan's *Prester John* appeared as the principal serial in Newnes boys' magazine *The Captain* from April to September 1910 (vol. xxiii, nos. 133–8) under the title 'The Black General', and something needs to be said about this, especially as comparison of the two versions shows more clearly the novel's strengths. (Fuller details can be found in my 'Buchan and "The Black General"', in David Dabydeen (ed.), *The Black Presence in English Literature* (Manchester University Press, 1985), 135–53.)

*The Captain* gave good value to its readers. Every monthly issue was fully illustrated, well printed, with many stories (mostly about public schools) and attractive articles in the how-to-do-it vein. There are at this time stories by P. G. Wodehouse and Percy F. Westerman. It is all exclusively male, though the editor (most unfortunately called 'The Old Fag') occasionally prints, at the back, a short letter from a girl, or takes occasion to advise his readers to stay away from girls who smoke. Each month's number is devoted to 'adventure', which means boys and men being 'manly' together: that is, from 'patriotic' or 'loyal' motives, vicious. The empire, rightly or wrongly, was seen as under threat: from Russia, especially in northern India, but also from secretly organized hordes of 'natives'. Such defensiveness is a familiar way of producing knee-jerk responses.

The magazine is hard-nosed imperialist. Around 1910 it had a long-running series about successful and admirable men, inviting emulation, under the title 'How I Began'. The May 1910 number (with Buchan's second instalment) opens with a long piece in lavish praise of Sir Hiram S. Maxim and his famous invention.

This was the gun that stopped the rush of Fuzziewuzzies at Omdurman, winning back the Soudan to civilisation . . . the war-correspondents . . . all agreed that it cut the Soudanese down like grain before a reaper, and that a perceptible wave of death could be seen passing over their ranks.

Illustrations elsewhere show native Africans being beaten by handy (and fully-clothed) whites—the natives being naked except for brief animal skins which give them the appearance of having tails.

There are, it must be agreed, incidental remarks in Buchan's *Prester John* to which objection may now be raised. Laputa's face is contrasted with 'the squat and preposterous Negro lineaments': a character, admittedly the least important in the book, refers to 'niggers' twice; and so on. Selective quotation (and misrepresentation) can multiply examples, though not many, and nothing in any way as exceptionable as a great deal in Haggard or Henty—or Conrad, come to that. But very serious objection has to be raised to the version of Buchan's story that appeared in *The Captain*. It is quite drastically altered. There are many changes, some of them major. They involve both deletion and rewriting. It is highly unlikely that John Buchan made the changes, on several counts. First, no evidence has appeared that he did. Secondly, we know from his correspondence that he would not countenance changes in a later reprint of this book. But above all, the alterations mark the destruction of a work of art into something made of cardboard, or worse.

There are over five hundred alterations, some as small as the cutting of a few words, some as large as the removal of half-a-dozen pages at a time. Large cuts include the religious details of Laputa's dedication, and the removal of most of the last three chapters of the novel. In all, the book is reduced by one-fifth. All the cuts can be seen to be working in one direction. The same is true of the rewriting.

We may begin with the title. Buchan's *Prester John* commands respect. The long history of the legend contained in those two words, and their association with matters of highest value—right rule, true religion, justice, and myth—are appealed to. The magazine's title is by contrast diminishing, and probably the words 'black general' are intended to be oxymoronic. In Buchan's book, Laputa is noble, ambivalent, learned, and of mythic stature: flawed, of course, but greatly flawed. In 'The Black General' he is shorn of almost all his tragic resonance and is little more than a peculiar black man, to be exterminated.

There is no space here to do more than summarize the changes and show the direction they point in. First, they systematically remove the detail of the hero's observation and reference. Everyone in the book is dehumanized in the serial, particularly the blacks, and especially Laputa. Robbed of his biblical and historical reference, not allowed his Miltonic, Bunyanesque, Scott-ish, Stevensonian setting, he becomes an ogre from a book of rather crude fairy-tales rather than a recognizable likeness of the great priest-king of ancient legend, Prester John. The insistent 'correction' of Buchan's African words and Scotticisms, not to mention his grammar and syntax (none being improvements) are simply irritating, though they suggest a general process to fit the magazine's readers which is depressing in several senses. More alarming is the alteration of Buchan's text to fit some suburban standard of taste, so that, to take two out of scores of examples, 'hell-for-leather' becomes 'at top speed', and 'the jog of that accursed horse' becomes 'my uncomfortable ride'. Worse is the shrinking of the hero's sense-impressions and responses to a flatter level of 'heroism'. His pain and weakness are carefully taken out. There are over thirty occasions where what is deleted in an incident, sometimes the only cut, is the hero's incapacity or hurt or despair or failure. It is the serial, not Buchan, who calls him 'a sturdy young Scot'. This is a serious loss, for with the pain goes not only humanity, but romance. Such greatness was not for *Captain* readers, evidently. Worst of all is the systematic and very obvious secularization of what had been biblically-based and even religious. The book allows full play to the great archetypal movements between death and rebirth, black and white, light and dark, king and priest, father and god, and more. Without this context, the adventure in the magazine shrivels to a prefects-study game, the religion only a crude militaristic 'christianity'. A whole five pages of text, covering all the religious significance of the dedication in the cave in

Chapter XI, have been removed: this desecration matches similar cuts throughout. The aspect of Laputa as priest-king has been removed entirely, as if the idea of such a black figure, a Prester John in truth, had to be kept from readers of a magazine called *The Captain*. With it goes, as also unacceptable, admiration for him, and any possibility of him as an unconscious father-figure. *Captain* readers are not to use their capacity for imaginative understanding, seeing that Laputa is, like Milton's Satan, a falling archangel. The argument that all such matters must be pruned because young minds cannot take in such dimensions is both foolish and dangerous.

# EXPLANATORY NOTES

*Map*: the sketch-map may have been drawn by Buchan. (The first edition has a relief-map like an aerial photograph which is hard to read.) It shows a mixture of existing and imaginary features, west of what is now the Kruger National Park, about three hundred and fifty kilometres north-east of Johannesburg. Much of *Prester John*'s action is set in the low veld to the east, radiating from the imaginary village of Umvelos. The transition to Blaauwildebeestefontein and the high veld to the north and west is marked by the massive Drakensberg mountains. Buchan has compressed the north–south dimensions. See pp. 31, 43, and David Ogilvie, '*Prester John*: David Crawford's Journeys', *John Buchan Journal*, 12 (Autumn 1992), 17–19.

3 *(Sir) Lionel Phillips*: a millionaire and life-long friend of Buchan. As a partner in the largest mining firm in the Rand, he had been elected chairman of the reform committee in Johannesburg and took part in the abortive Jameson raid, one of the key events which triggered the Boer War. For his part in this he was, with other British political prisoners, sentenced to death. The sentence was later commuted to imprisonment and an enormous fine. Among other books, he wrote *Transvaal Problems: some notes on current politics* (1905), a book not unrelated to Buchan's *African Colony* (1903). The friendship continued in England; two years before the writing of *Prester John*, Phillips had loaned the newly married Buchans his house, Tylney Hall in Hampshire, for the first part of their honeymoon. He was one of a significant number of Jewish friends whom Buchan greatly admired.

7 *grue*: shudder, shiver.

*Kirkcaple ... Portincross ... Caple*: Buchan lived the first twelve years of his life at Pathhead in Fife, a small town between Kirkcaldy and Dysart on the Firth of Forth, where his father was minister. Several Fife towns and villages fit Buchan's description here. The likeliest is the fishing village of Craill: Craill Bay 'is cradled by cliffs and divided by a burn' (Ogilvie, '*Prester John*', and see Janet Adam Smith, *John Buchan: A Biography* (1965)).

*burgh*: borough.

*podleys*: young coal-fish: a sort of cod.

*session-clerk*: records the doings of the church-session, the Presbyterian church meeting.

*provost*: mayor.

8 *fight with the roughs at the Dyve tan-work*: see Smith, *Biography*, 15: 'Occasionally there were fights, with his Kirkcaldy school-friends against the lads at the bleach-works or the sons of the local gentry.'

*cock-loft*: a room just under the roof.

*lads duly passed the plate*: the plate at the door in which the money of the offering would be placed. Here it means, very roughly, that they had been seen to have paid for their entrance, and would be assumed to be in the building.

*jowing*: ringing.

*elders had gone in*: that is, there was no one still outside to see them.

9 *Free Kirk*: Buchan's father had been a minister of the Free Kirk of Scotland—that is, the product of the Disruption of 1843 when many ministers left the 'Auld Kirk'. Communion (the Lord's Supper) would be infrequent, twice or four times a year.

*The Bible says*: according to Genesis, chapters 9 and 10, one of Noah's three sons, Ham, was the father of Canaan and thus was the ancestor of Arab nations, particularly those in north Africa. The account is confusing, but a key verse has been Genesis 9: 25, making such descendants 'servants of servants'.

*nigger: Prester John* is sometimes described as being full of words that are now more offensive than can be tolerated. In fact, one character, Tam (as here) says 'nigger' on two occasions (here, and on p. 27). For the occasional references to Jews, see the n. to p. 28. It is plain wrong to suggest that the novel is 'full of' such things.

10 *The glim was dowsed*: smuggler's slang; the light was put out.

*scrog*: bushy place.

11 *contracted*: Buchan as a young intellectual in Scotland in the early 1890s was on the fringes of an intellectual group which included Sir James Frazer, whose studies of ritual and magic across the world became famous in his *Golden Bough* (1890–1915). Buchan was influenced strongly by Frazer. See Christopher Harvie, *The Centre of Things* (1991), 166, 186.

13 *his minister's coat and his minister's hat*: the supremely civilized man in a pagan setting is a situation which haunts Buchan all his life. It can be seen from the earliest short stories right through to his last novel, *Sick Heart River* (1941). When that man is a Free Kirk minister, as in *Witch Wood* (1927), the matter is strong, and strongly treated, as the pagan powers seem increasingly to threaten him. Yet here, introduced and integrated with deceptive ease, the man contains both civilized and pagan in himself and is a minister to boot.

14 *'Wha called ye partan-face, my bonny lamb?'*: a partan is a crab, and the schoolboy insult is an accusation of bad-tempered ugliness. 'Lamb' (earlier versions have 'man'), increases the insult, as a 'bonny lamb' would be very white and inappropriately cuddly.

16 *links*: flat ground along a sea-shore.

18 *Furth! Fortune!*: 'Furth, fortune and fill the fetters' (that is, 'Out we go and bring in the prisoners'), the motto of the Murray and the Stewart of Athole clans.

*scholar*: what David, as a young man from the east coast of Scotland, doesn't become, makes a later and rather similar hero, Anthony Lammas, in *The Free Fishers* (1934).

20 *and buy Portincross House*: all of which he did, of course, though not quite in the way his uncle thought. Buchan as a small child at Pathhead, recovering from a bad accident to his head, spent a year in bed, and 'as soon as he had re-learnt to walk after his year abed' he had in 'the demesne of Dysart House, a place of sandy creeks and seaweed backed by a great forest of rhododendrons . . . his natural playground' (Smith, *Biography*, 15).

21 *Kaffir*: strictly one of a South African race belonging to the Bantu family. It originates in an Arabic word meaning 'infidel' (*Giaour*). In Buchan's day it was used with less pejorative loading, but it is now offensive to Africans.

*Zoutpansberg mountains*: the range referred to below, p. 43: 'North from Blaauwildebeestefontein the Berg runs for some twenty miles, and then makes a sharp turn eastward.'

*'Mpefu, Sikitola, Majinje, Magata*: Buchan's spellings generally represent what was current at the time. Such orthography has varied, mainly being 'corrected' from a form governed by the language of the recorder. Thus 'Machudi' (see n. to p. 150) is

now 'Magoeba'. In this list, however, "Mpefu' is recognizable as a chief of the Bavenda, and 'Magata' as Magato (properly Makhado), 'Mpefu's father. 'Majinje' seems to be a version of the famous Mujaji of the Lovedu tribe, strictly Mujaji II. Mujaji I was 'a light-coloured, good-looking woman and probably had some European blood in her veins', said to have been the original of Rider Haggard's *She* (Isaac Schapera, ed., *The Native Tribes of the Transvaal* (London: War Office, 1905), 50). Mojaji II was the last of the great 'Rain Queens' of the Transvaal; she was known to Rider Haggard and impressed General Smuts as being 'a woman who really was a queen' (Lawrence G. Green, *These Wonders to Behold* (Cape Town: H. B. Timmins, 1959), 34). All these chiefs had been placed by the Boers on native reservations in the general area in which *Prester John* is set. What Sikitola represents has not been discovered, though it may be a reference to Sintimulla, a chief in the area who fought alongside the Boers against 'Mpefu.

*fever*: probably malaria, a widespread and serious problem; then thought erroneously to cause Blackwater Fever.

23 *Laputa*: the name of the flying island in Book III of Swift's *Gulliver's Travels*, the inhabitants of which were addicted to visionary projects of complete impracticality. R. L. Stevenson uses the idea in a powerful passage in *The Ebb Tide* (1893), a novel which Buchan certainly knew well. A suicidal man swims, he hopes, to oblivion, in a tropical sea, towards the image of 'a very bright planet' on the water:

> that radiant speck, which he had soon magnified into a City of Laputa, along whose terraces there walked men and women of awful and benignant features, who viewed him with distant commiseration. These imaginary spectators consoled him; he told himself their talk, one to another; it was of himself and his sad destiny. (Tusitala edition, 115)

There is undoubtedly for Buchan a visionary quality in the name.

25 *Ethiopian*: the term has no direct link with the country of that name. It was used for a movement, prominent especially in America at the time, for Africans to have their own churches independent of any established institutions. At the time, Ethiopia was the only African country to have independent rule.

26 *takhaars*: long-haired Boers of the back-veld; a derogatory term for illiterate and poor farmers with uncouth manners and unkempt appearance.

28  *during the war*: the Boer War. One of the few remarks that gives an idea of the events in the novel in relation to that upheaval.

*vermin*: the remarks of Tam's friend, a peripheral attachment to an already peripheral figure, should not of course be taken as expressing the considered, life-long, views of the author of the novel, as, astonishingly, they have been. Aitken is expressing a common view in the South Africa of the time. Jewish success in the diamond industry caused great envy: Jewish traders who in horse and cart peddled goods around the country were despised by the Boer farmers; such itinerant Jews were considered too smart in business deals for the average simple uneducated farmer.

31  *Pilgrim's Progress*: Bunyan's story, after the Bible, was the central text of Buchan's father's household, and of Buchan's own, as it has been of very many Protestant Christian homes since its first appearance in 1678. Its importance for Buchan in all his writing is obvious; and see the opening pages of *Memory Hold-the-Door*, and William Buchan, *John Buchan: A Memoir* (1982) *passim*.

*Canaan*: Christian, while staying with Piety, Prudence, and Charity, is shown the distant Delectable Mountains, 'which were nearer the desired haven'. They call the country 'Immanuel's Land', not Canaan, though both names may be taken for the idea of the Promised Land. David's grip on the book is in other ways not secure: Christian is alone, and not with Hopeful. Since Buchan tells us in *Memory Hold-the-Door* that he could reproduce most of *Pilgrim's Progress* from memory (which other evidence would support), we can take the errors to be part of the characterization of David.

32  *fou*: full; that is, drunk.

33  *Sesuto*: or Sesotho; the language of the Southern Sotho (Basotho or Basutu) people north of the Orange River and west of the Drakensberg.

*Shangaans*: the Shangana-Tsonga people in northern and eastern Transvaal, part of Rhodesia and much of Mozambique.

34  *voorslag*: whip, literally 'first stroke'.

*sjambok*: a whip of dried rhinoceros or hippopotamus hide.

36  *brindled*: streaked.

*wildebeest ... hartebeest ... impala ... koodoo*: forms of antelope.

38   *Pietersdorp*: Pietersburg, the main town (now a city) in the northern Transvaal.

39   *spruit*: a small, deep, dry watercourse.

40   *red-water*: a disease of cattle which causes red colouration of urine.

41   *light naachtmaal*: a small tented wagon, such as was used by the scattered Dutch communities when they came together for several days at a location where a *predikant* (preacher, minister) could administer *Naachtmaal*, Holy Communion.

*'Kaffir queens'*: unknown; probably a local name in eastern Transvaal, just possibly for Helmet Shrikes, small birds with tufts like crowns, generally in flocks of seven and known as 'seven sisters'.

*taal*: language; Dutch patois spoken in South Africa.

*aasvogel*: vulture.

42   *toddy in the Scotch fashion*: whisky in hot, pre-sugared, water.

44   *kranzes*: cliffs.

45   *mountaineering*: John Buchan was an expert mountaineer and rock-climber. He was 'elected to the Alpine Club in 1906, on the strength of his writings about mountains . . . as well as his actual record in Scotland, the Alps and South Africa' (Smith, *Biography*, 153). More significantly for this novel, this long passage prepares the reader for the climactic, and extraordinary, escape from the cave in Ch. XXI.

*mamba*: see n. to p. 72 *Ndhlondhlo*.

47   *debouched*: flowed out.

48   *groan and yell*: Sir Walter Scott, *Marmion*, Introduction to Canto 11.

*kaross*: skin blanket.

*fifteen*: emended from the earlier version's 'twenty-five'. From his childhood, Buchan was a prodigious walker, to whom fifteen miles would not be remarkable, even under those conditions; twenty-five might be stretching the licence of romance a little.

49   *mopani*: well-known hardwood tree in south central Africa.

*jays and rollers*: jays are not recorded in that part of Africa; rollers are birds akin to kingfishers which fly like tumbler pigeons. The Lilacbreasted Roller is sometimes incorrectly called a blue jay.

51 *pipe*: cylindrical rock in which diamonds are found.

53 Monomotapa: the name given to successive kings of large tracts of southern Africa in the sixteenth century, as well as to their territories. Their legendary cities were a constant cause of exploration by Westerners.

*caciques*: West Indian chiefs or bosses.

*called Zimbabwe*: a unique stone-walled settlement, for over a century the cause of controversy about its date and origins. It was for long denied that Africans could have been the builders. The most recent evidence suggests that the ruins are indeed African and medieval. The literature is fairly extensive, and we cannot guess at the book which Wardlaw was reading.

*dorps*: villages, small country towns.

*Indian Mutiny*: Indian soldiers in the Bengal army of the British East India Company mutinied in 1857–8, leading to widespread rising against the British rule in India.

*Tchaka*: Tshaka, Chaka, or now usually Shaka; Zulu king and conqueror of the early nineteenth century, famous for the ruthless discipline of his newly equipped armies, which terrorized large areas, causing widespread depopulation. The pioneers of the Great Trek in the early 1830s moved into such emptied territories. A great leader and warrior, and a ruthless and much-feared tyrant, Shaka is said to have caused the death of more than a million people.

55 *whinstone*: hard rock.

*rummer*: large glass.

57 *hotching*: (Scots) fidgeting with eagerness.

58 *fossicking*: prospecting, working over.

61 *blackwater*: fever in which the urine is dark.

62 *stinkwood and essenwood*: see n. to p. 129.

*Kirkcaple cliffs*: as the African events build, a reminder of the opening of the novel, to prepare for the unexpected knowledge of Laputa that David shows in the following chapter.

*Cetewayo's impis*: in the 1870s, long-standing boundary disputes caused Cetewayo, king of Zululand, reviving Shaka's army system, to amass his impis on the border. A British force invaded Zululand in January 1879, but in what was known as the disaster of Isandlwana, it was humiliated. It then cost Britain many lives and five million pounds to break the Zulu power. (The Boers held aloof, a fact which was not forgotten.) Cetewayo, held a prisoner, claimed he had only fought to defend his country, and in 1882 he travelled to England and was kindly received by Queen Victoria, and reinstated. We are not necessarily intended to believe Japp: a parallel might be someone with a memory of Hitler's bombers over London in 1940, then claiming to be one of only two survivors of the blitz. See H. Rider Haggard, *Cetywayo and his White Neighbours* (1882).

63 *penitential Psalms*: psalms suitable for saying by penitents, i.e. numbers 6, 32, 38, 51, 102, 130, and 143.

66 *five pencilled words*: a characteristic Buchan feature in later adventure-stories, where everything depends on the interpretation of a few words. See *The Thirty-Nine Steps*, *Greenmantle*, *The Three Hostages*, and many others.

*our armoury*: essentially hunting-weapons of fairly large calibre, for going after big and dangerous animals.

67 *kraal*: hut or cluster of huts, here with the sense of such a place being the home of an indigenous tribe. The 'native' is saying that he has no home.

*aasvogels*: see n. to p. 41.

68 *amazing transformation*: another characteristic Buchan feature of the later novels. The master of such transformations—they are more than disguises—is Sandy Arbuthnot, e.g. in *Greenmantle*.

70 *years to decipher it*: again, a particular Buchan interest is the secret history of international events, with one character, not central to the action, the decipherer and informant—like the American spy Franklin P. Scudder in *The Thirty-Nine Steps*.

*both the Matabele wars*: Mzilikazi, or Moselekatse, was at first a brave warrior under the Zulu king Shaka (see n. to p. 53), but he broke away, and after tribal wars eventually founded the Matabele kingdom based on Bulawayo in what is now Rhodesia. 'The Lion of the North' clashed with whites when gold was discovered later in the century. In 1893 the Matabele under

Lobengula, continuing to fight the Mashona, were defeated by British forces, ending the first war. But in March 1896 a revolt led to the killing of many whites, and a protracted guerrilla war followed. Cecil Rhodes ended the conflict by walking unarmed into an assembly of five hundred Matabele warriors in the stronghold of Matopos and establishing peace.

71    *Prester John*: see Introduction, pp. xi–xii. The importance here is the extension of tribal power southward under the successors to 'Prester John'. Buchan, as is usual, here grounds his hidden version of international events in real historical fact.

72    *Ndhlondhlo*: the older spelling of the modern Zulu *ndlondlo*, an old mamba (and figuratively a person with a vicious temper). The black mamba, which can be over twelve feet long, is the deadliest snake in the world, greatly respected everywhere in South Africa.

77    *children of Ham*: see n. to p. 9.

      *commando*: a special raiding unit.

84    *cartel*: properly 'cartle' or kartel; the wooden bed in a South African ox-wagon.

      *stuff I talked*: David Crawfurd's 'playing the fool' allows us to see, by inversion, his callow rigidity and elementary racism.

87    *shebeen*: illicit liquor-shop.

88    *laager*: extemporized fortification.

93    *merula tree*: see n. to p. 141.

94    *token of gratitude*: like R. L. Stevenson, Buchan understands that the writing of this kind of adventure-story must include, at moments of suspense, reassurance that all came out well. Like Stevenson, Buchan also uses the occasion for a wry observation of the character of his hero, who is later enjoying, in his recognition of 'God's goodness towards me', his capacity for patronage from his elevated position at Portincross.

97    *Immanuel*: Isaiah 7: 14. The symbolic name given to the child who was announced to King Ahaz and the people of Judah as the sign that God would deliver them from their enemies. Matthew's gospel, 1: 23, applies it to Jesus as Messiah. In using this name, Buchan is making a double point about the significance of Laputa's ambitions. He will not only save his people politically, with the sense that the Old Testament carries at that point in Isaiah: he will also stand, blasphemously, as Christ.

Laputa is frequently seen in the story as corrupting, inverting, and paganizing the Christianity he has been professing.

98 *'true right'*: that is, the right-hand side of a stream as seen from above. (I am grateful to Richard Love and two coachloads of members of the Scottish Mountaineering Club for this information.)

100 *Samuel ordaining Saul*: 1 Samuel 10: 17–25. In the Old Testament story there is no specific, dramatic moment. The picture in the Sunday School book would no doubt include, correctly, an eager crowd; the old seer, Samuel; and the young man Saul, head and shoulders above the rest.

103 *en cabochon*: rounded on top and flat on the back, without facets.

*he prayed*: at the exact centre of the novel (see Introduction, p. xxv) is this strongly presented distortion of Christian preaching. The quotations are from Isaiah 25: 4–8, taken by Buchan probably from memory (the phrase in the penultimate verse should be 'spread over all nations'). The context, in that part of Isaiah, is prophetic utterance about both the overthrow of enemies and severe judgements on God's land and people. Throughout the Old Testament, including those chapters of Isaiah from which the passage comes, are phrases of violence appropriate to the uprising Laputa is organizing: 'in the city is left desolation, and the gate is smitten with destruction' (24: 12), 'the Lord shall punish the host of the high ones' (24: 21), and so on. Buchan has not used these. He has gone for a more oblique effect. There is appropriate reference to 'this mountain', and the sense that the wrongs of oppressed people will come right, especially in the revenge on 'strangers'. But much more effective is the large, and vague, suggestiveness, especially in the use of the opaque phrase 'the Terrible Ones'. Buchan locks in that large effect with the phrase about Laputa's relation to the God to whom he prayed: 'He prayed less as a suppliant than an ally.'

106 *ringkops*: the circlets into which Zulu and Swazi warriors wove their hair, with the aid of gum; they were indicators of seniority.

108 *some Latin writer*: Buchan, with his First in Greats from Brasenose, is unlikely to have been ignorant of the source, though he makes the schoolboy David Crawfurd suitably vague. Buchan has stayed ahead of modern classical scholars, however,

and the origins are not known. (As a means of causing death, it sounds more Oriental.)

110  *heart of darkness*: a phrase with biblical resonance, particularly echoing the book of Job, since 1902 associated with Conrad's tale of that name condemning colonial exploitation. (The analysis was prefigured in Stevenson's superb, and less portentously-titled, *The Ebb Tide* of 1894.) Here Buchan lightly touches on a phrase with several echoes.

*scapegoat*: Leviticus 16: 10.

*great Mr Peden*: The Rev. Alexander Peden, 'Peden the Prophet', described as the John the Baptist of the seventeenth-century Scottish Covenant, lived much of his eventful life as a fugitive, and was hanged in 1686.

111  *bourne*: boundary, goal, i.e. death. See *Hamlet*, III. i. 79, 'The undiscover'd country, from whose bourn|No traveller returns'.

112  *wacht-en-beetje*: (properly wag-'n-bietjie); plants with thorns that catch the clothing of the passer-by, as if causing delay.

114  *Sir Percival*: Malory, *The Quest of the Holy Grail*, III, *Sir Perceval*, 6.

117  *vlei*: low-lying ground where a shallow lake forms in the wet season.

121  *Reims*: riems, that is, leather thongs, the 'fresh rawhide ropes' of p. 117.

124  *their Ark of the Covenant*: in some of the oldest historical narratives of the Old Testament, incorporated, for example, in parts of Numbers or Deuteronomy, the ark, a coffer of acacia wood containing the tables of the law, brought victory if carried with the army, and defeat if lost.

126  *wolf*: probably hyena, in Afrikaans 'Aardwolf'.

*tambuki*: any of several species of tall grasses used for thatching African huts.

*rhebok and springbok and duikers*: antelopes.

129  *kopjes*: knolls or small hills standing alone.

*yellowwood, sneezewood, essenwood, stinkwood*: yellow-woods are the most magnificent of all South African forest tress, native to this part of South Africa. Sneezewood, a forest or scrub tree, the hard wood of which was found ideal for fencing or for fuel: it is now scarce. Essenwood, a large umbrageous evergreen, the

wood of which is used to make panelling and furniture. Stinkwood, a kind of large laurel, the heart of which fine wood smells
until dried, in demand for furniture. It is characteristic of the
young hero that he notes the topography so keenly.

130 *snowking*: sniffing about, hence prowling.

*Xenophon's Ten Thousand*: Xenophon, a Greek historian and
philosophical essayist, wrote his *Anabasis*, or 'up-country
march', 379–371 BC. It tells the story of the expedition of the
younger Cyrus against his brother, Artaxerxes II of Persia. It is
an account of remarkable endurance by a small army in unknown
and hostile country a thousand miles from home. After extreme
difficulties the soldiers arrived at Chrysopolis (Scutari) on the
Bosporus, opposite Byzantium (Istanbul) and famously greeted
that strait with the cry 'The sea, the sea!'

131 *mountain tops*: Shakespeare's *Romeo and Juliet*, III. v. 9.
'Walks' should properly be 'stands': the quotation may have
been conflated with Horatio's line in *Hamlet*, I. i. 164–5, 'the
morn . . . walks o'er the dew of yon high eastward hill'.

*threshold of freedom*: for the importance of this phrase, as found
in a French translation of *Prester John*, for the surrealist Belgian
painter Magritte, see my 'On the Magritte Trail', *John Buchan
Journal*, 13 (Autumn 1993).

133 *fanners*: sails of a windmill: properly small vanes to keep the
large sails in the direction of the wind.

134 *moss-cheepers*: meadow-pipits.

*klipspringer*: small antelope.

*good going on steep mountains*: this passage looks forward to
*The Thirty-Nine Steps*, ch. 6—where Richard Hannay longs,
incidentally, for a good Afrikander pony.

*Machudi*: see n. to p. 150. David Crawfurd's account is suitably
crass.

136 *knobkerries*: round-headed sticks used as clubs and missiles.

139 *Beyers*: C. F. Beyers was a Boer military leader famous for his
daring exploits with commando forces; later an anti-British
politician of some power. The complexities of situation at the
start of the First World War led him to become a fugitive.

*Wolkberg*: the 'Cloud Mountains' of the beginning of that
paragraph, a well-known feature of north-east Transvaal.

141 *kyas*: huts or houses.

*rondavels*: round huts with thatched roofs.

*merula*: marula or maroela, a large, common, local tree with fruit like a small plum.

150 *Machudi's glen*: Magoebaskloof, a beautiful mountain pass east of Pietersburg in the Letaba district. It was important to Buchan: see *Memory Hold-the-Door*, pp. 134–5.

*story of the Machudi war*: Magoeba (the Boer name for the chief of the Makgoba tribe) refused to move from the ancestral home in Magoebaskloof, to the new area allocated by the entering whites. After a protracted campaign, the tribe was eventually wiped out in 1895, with Swazi help. The Boer leader was not 'a Grobelaar' but Piet Joubert.

*some lines of Virgil*: probably from *Aeneid*, xi., *Timeo Danaos et dona ferentes*, that is, 'I fear Greeks bearing gifts.' A young narrator walking beside a charismatic man on horseback who startlingly quotes Virgil appositely is a situation repeated to great effect in *Witch Wood*, ch. 2.

151 *swept and garnished*: a perversion of the parable at Matthew 12: 44 and Luke 11: 25: it is the unclean spirit who finds the house swept and garnished, who then brings in 'seven other spirits more wicked than himself'.

160 *finger of Divine Providence*: David Crawfurd's Sunday School, and his father's preaching, have given him a kind of everyday Calvinism, without much theological depth, which can see small events as indicators of the special interest of God. See Introduction, pp. xxiii–xxiv.

*text from the Psalms*: Psalm 33: 17, 'A horse is a vain thing for safety.'

161 *more than Caesar and his fortunes*: in Plutarch's *Life of Caesar*, xxxviii. 3, Caesar, in a small boat without soldiers, daringly tries to persuade the boatman not to turn back in bad weather, telling him 'Thou carriest Caesar and Caesar's fortune in thy boat.'

164 *rampart, built of shining marble*: David's dream elevates the conflict to the level of epic, with echoes of Milton's *Paradise Lost*—'on the white wall were . . . horse, foot and artillery, the squadrons of our defence . . . what a general . . . how great a matter'. This lifts the narrative in preparation for the next three chapters, and particularly XX and XXI.

165 *Mr Alexander Upton*: Buchan's invention, though of course Buchan himself had been a South Africa correspondent of *The*

*Times* during his time there. By noting that the great events are not mentioned in the standard History, David Crawfurd—who, writing this as a Scots laird, no doubt normally took *The Times*'s point of view—is able to glance wryly at the tradition that romance tells a secret, and truer, history. Buchan was always able to make excellent fiction out of such a figure and such a secret; one thinks of Dickson McCunn in *Huntingtower* and *Castle Gay*.

166 *Laputa would be in a hurry*: John Buchan, military historian (who in four years' time would begin a definitive and immense history of the Great War, written as it occurred) was always particularly interested in what happened when one man alone, or a very small company of men, moved a phenomenal distance in a very short time. Since boyhood he had studied the Scottish campaigns of the Marquis of Montrose in the seventeenth century, campaigns in which such marches were a remarkable feature: he developed this knowledge into two books on him, the first published three years after *Prester John*, in 1913. Buchan's development of the form of such romantic audacities was to make his fictional lone hero end the ordeal seriously incapacitated, as Laputa does here, and as Richard Hannay, for example, does with his bout of malaria towards the end of the pursuit-in-the-hills section of *The Thirty-Nine Steps*.

169 *korhaan*: a South African bustard, i.e. a large wading bird.

170 *paauw*: another kind of bustard, now usually 'pou'.

*stembok*: antelope.

175 *thrawn*: (Scots); twisted.

180 *'Unarm, Eros ... the long day's task is done'*: Shakespeare, *Antony and Cleopatra*, IV. xiv. 35. Antony, betrayed by Cleopatra, defeated in battle, and then receiving a (false) message that Cleopatra was dead, addresses his armour-bearer in preparation for his own self-inflicted death. In the play, the moment is one of Antony's recognition of defeat on every side, and acceptance of the inevitability of death at his own hand.

182 *stater*: ancient Greek coin.

*Antoninus Pius*: second-century Roman emperor, whose clemency extended to Africa, and whose fame in Scotland rests on the building of a wall from the Forth to the Clyde, considerably north of the more famous one built by his predecessor Hadrian.

*cairngorms*: stones of brown or yellow quartz.

184   *'Ek sal'n plan maak'*: 'I shall make a plan.' This was originally
      the remark of a reprobate Boer farmer told by a preacher that he
      will burn in hell: 'Not so. . . . If I am so unfortunate as to get in
      there, I shall certainly get out again.' The preacher expostulated.
      The Boer replied, 'Wait and see: I shall make a plan.' See *The
      African Colony*, 120. Buchan was much taken with the remark
      and used it a number of times, e.g. in *Greenmantle* and *Mr
      Standfast*.

187   *like a Colossus*: David Crawfurd's notion is the popular one,
      that the great statue of Apollo was astride, instead of alongside,
      the harbour at Rhodes.

190   *'His goodness in the land of the living'*: Psalm 27: 3.

195   *Rhodes did in the Matoppos*: see n. to p. 70.

      *indaba*: important tribal conference.

197   *I knew then the meaning of the white man's duty*: see Introduc-
      tion, pp. xvii–xix.

199   *linn*: waterfall, deep glen.

203   *'the wilderness . . . blossom as the rose'*: Isaiah 35: 1.